STYX &
STONE

james w. ziskin

STYX & STONE

An
ELLIE STONE
MYSTERY

SEVENTH STREET BOOKS™
AN IMPRINT OF PROMETHEUS BOOKS
59 JOHN GLENN DRIVE • AMHERST, NY 14228
www.seventhstreetbooks.com

Published 2013 by Seventh Street Books™, an imprint of Prometheus Books

Cover design by Jacqueline Nasso Cooke
Cover image © Patrick Mac Sean/és/Corbis

Inquiries should be addressed to
Seventh Street Books
59 John Glenn Drive
Amherst, New York 14228–2119
VOICE: 716–691–0133
FAX: 716–691–0137
WWW.SEVENTHSTREET BOOKS.COM

17 16 15 14 13   5 4 3 2 1

Library of Congress Cataloging-in-Publication Data

Ziskin, James W., 1960-
    Styx & Stone : an Ellie Stone mystery / by James W. Ziskin.
        pages cm
    ISBN 978-1-61614-819-5 (pbk.)
    ISBN 978-1-61614-820-1 (ebook)
    1. Women journalists—Fiction. 2. Murder—Investigation—Fiction.
3. Columbia University—Fiction. 4. Nineteen sixties—Fiction. 5. New York
(N.Y.)—Fiction. 6. Mystery fiction. I. Title.

PS3626.I83S78 2013
813'.6—dc23

                                                                    2013022056

Printed in the United States of America

To Lakshmi

CHAPTER ONE

SUNDAY, JANUARY 24, 1960

About halfway between New Holland and Schenectady, a narrow road cuts through a fault in the wooded hills above the Mohawk: Wolf Hollow Gorge. Local lore has it that Iroquois Indians, poised on the lip of the ravine, ambushed a party of Algonquin invaders early one morning in 1669. The attackers poured down the walls of the dark glen in waves, whooping like demons, and slaughtered the Algonquins trapped below.

One mild Sunday evening in January, I found myself in Wolf Hollow, a willing prisoner in the backseat of a black Chrysler 300. I'm what people call a modern girl. The kind who works for a living in a man's world. I can hold my drink and I'm a good sport. I'm the kind who has her own place and sometimes invites a gentleman in for a nightcap. The finer the gentleman, the faster he slides from his end of the sofa to mine, the more roughly he gropes me. But his lips are soft, his tie is loose, and his arms have me pinned anyway.

Steve Herbert, barracuda lawyer with a square jaw and sharp, white teeth, had been pursuing me—the object of his baser desires—with devoted attention for some time. In the absence of a more suitable escort, I had recently been spending the odd evening with Steve, who was divorced, morally bankrupt, but good-looking and a fun time. I was too old for sock hops and earnest teenage boys, and my romantic options were otherwise few. Over his warm, heavy breathing, I became aware of an approaching noise outside the car.

I lifted my head to investigate, but Steve wrapped his big hands around my hips and pulled me back down on the seat. He planted the sting of gin on my lips, and his prehensile tongue drew me inside his mouth in an oral tug of war.

Then a light flashed in the window, and someone began tapping on the glass. I shrieked and elbowed Steve in the eye as he scrambled to right himself in the seat. The pint of Gilbey's fell to the floor and emptied at my feet. My heart thumping in my chest, I squinted into the light at the large shape outside the fogged-up window, shielding my eyes with one hand while I wiped the glass with the other.

"What the hell?" bellowed Steve as he caught sight of the figure outside the car.

Once the window was clear and I could see the dullard's grin, I knew we were in no danger.

"It's all right, Steve," I panted. "It's just Stan Pulaski."

"Who's he?"

"Deputy sheriff."

"Damn! The gin!"

"Don't worry," I said as I adjusted my brassiere and smoothed my hair—long, curly, and quite unruly in situations such as this. "He's not a real cop. It's Stan Pulaski."

I rolled down the window, and Stan stuck his melon head inside.

"Ellie? What are you doing in there?" He craned his neck to view Steve better. He pursed his lips then announced that the car smelled like a distillery.

"What can we do for you, officer?" asked Steve, barely concealing his annoyance.

"The sheriff wants us to shut down this lovers' lane, sir." Then he turned to me. "Where have you been, Ellie? Sheriff Olney's been looking all over the county for you."

Steve wasn't happy when I left him in the lurch for Stan Pulaski and his cruiser. Twenty minutes later, Stan roared into the parking lot of the Montgomery County Administration Building and pulled to a gentle stop before the door to let me out.

"You should steer clear of fellows like that, Ellie," he said. Stan was a little sweet on me. "There's no future there."

"I'm a big girl now, Stan," I said.

He nodded, then his eyes rather glazed over slowly. "Your hair sure is pretty," he said.

"Stan, tongue in mouth, please."

"Sorry," he said, taking up an official tone again. "Frank's waiting for you. You'd better hurry."

"Will you drop me home later? I lost my chauffeur."

He smiled. "Sure, Ellie. Anytime."

The outer office was empty except for Deputy Pat Halvey, who, bent at the waist, had thrust his head out the window and was looking at something across Route 40.

My voice surprised him and he jumped, whacking his crew-cut skull against the sash. The window, in turn, fell like a guillotine on his shoulders and pinned him to the sill.

"Darn it, Ellie," he said, rubbing his neck once I'd freed him. "Make some noise when you come into a room, will you?"

"Stan says Frank's looking for me."

"In there," he grumbled, throwing a thumb over his shoulder toward the sheriff's office.

Frank Olney sat wedged between the arms of the swivel chair behind his desk, flipping through some papers. The chubby forefinger of his right hand was stuffed into the ringed handle of a mug of coffee, which he held aloft as if he had forgotten to drink once he had raised it. He struggled to his feet, managing to lift himself from his chair without resorting to the use of a derrick, and waved me inside with his left hand.

"Sit down, Eleonora," he said, motioning to the aluminum chair in front of his desk.

I hate that name. It was a cruel joke of some kind, intended to make me seem interesting, but it sounds like something pulled out of a dusty, old carpetbag instead. My father said I was named for Eleonora Duse, the great Italian stage actress, and Eleonora of Toledo, wife of Cosimo I de' Medici. I remember standing before a Bronzino painting in the Uffizi when I was ten, my father proudly pointing out my namesake.

Eleonora was a beautiful, elegant lady with a fat little boy at her knee: her son Giovanni. Not far away, the same little boy, beaming from another Bronzino canvas, clutched a small, half-strangled bird in his chubby hand. I prefer to go by Ellie.

"Charlie Reese's been looking for you for two days," said the sheriff, retaking his seat. "Where do you disappear to?"

"I've been off since Thursday night," I protested. "And I'm always around."

He frowned. Frank was a prude who didn't quite approve. "Anyways, Charlie called me yesterday," he said, setting the coffee on the desk. "He needed to find you right away and thought maybe I could put out a goddamn APB on you." He pushed his coffee to one side, rearranged a paper, then fixed his eyes on mine. "I've got some bad news for you. Your old man called the paper Friday morning from New York to tell you your brother's grave was vandalized."

A rotten thing for someone to do, for sure, but hardly deserving a statewide manhunt. "I see."

"And they painted some swastikas on the stone."

Worse. No Jew, no matter how assimilated, no matter how secular, can escape the morbid awareness that, born at another time in another place, he could have been one of six million. It's a feeling of impotence in the face of a hatred you can do nothing to change. And while I had grown a thick skin about being Jewish in a Christian society, swastikas still stung me with waspish fury.

"Do they know who did it?" I asked.

The life drained from Frank's eyes, betraying the weight of another obligation to fulfill.

"What's this really about, Frank?"

The sheriff rocked nervously in his chair. "Charlie Reese says you got a wire from New York yesterday. Someone named Bernard Sanger. You know him?"

I shook my head.

Frank winced a bit, as if I were putting him out. "He said your father's in the hospital."

My father was an aggressive, dynamic man, impatient of the perceived failings of those around him. His frustration had always raised his hackles and his blood pressure, too. Had he finally blown his stack over some student's ignorance of the differences between a Petrarchan and Shakespearean sonnet? When I professed my indifference to those very distinctions one evening at dinner years before, he dismissed my argument with a wave of his hand.

"I know you relish the role of mock primitive, Ellie," he bristled. "But you're not as ignorant as you wish to make people believe."

My mother scolded us for baiting each other.

"What was it, a stroke?" I asked the sheriff, who shook his head. "Did Charlie give you any details?"

Frank drew a deep breath, swiveled in his chair a bit, then explained in his typically delicate fashion that someone had broken into my father's apartment and clubbed him on the head.

"The cleaning lady found him unconscious yesterday morning. This Sanger fellow says he's at Saint Vincent's Hospital." He paused. "Critical condition."

I stared dumbly at the sheriff for several seconds, struggling to reconcile his words with a reality I could accept. Finally Frank spoke.

"Can I get you some water, Ellie?"

My head was a muddle when I left the sheriff's office a few minutes later. How was I supposed to feel about my father? We weren't close, we certainly didn't speak often, and then only to make perfunctory inquiries into the other's health. We'd exchange lukewarm platitudes about the weather, the Giants, or the Yankees—yes, I follow sports, part of my one-of-the-boys charm—but there was a mountain of distrust and disquiet between us. He never asked me about my work, of which he had never approved, and he could barely disguise the churning resentment he bore me for the disappointment I had caused him on so many occasions. Newspaper scribbling did not conform to his idea of a noble and useful endeavor. The world needed journalists, to be sure, but Abraham Stone's surviving progeny—local reporter and hack photographer for a small upstate daily—had fallen short of the promise of the Stones who had rolled before.

When I landed in New Holland about six months after Mom had passed away, I welcomed the distraction it provided. I had tried to stick it out in New York, living at home with my grieving father after the terrible year of 1957, but it wasn't the moment to repair our relationship. He was adrift, and the only thing he knew for sure was that I displeased him. Finally, a college professor of mine steered me toward her old friend Charlie Reese and a job at the *New Holland Republic*. What harm was there in chancing it, she asked. For my part, I was happy to have found a job that didn't involve shorthand and fetching coffee. New Holland may not have been everything I had hoped for, but a girl can't be picky when it comes to careers. I considered myself lucky, but my father was ashamed of my choice. Our family's is a legacy of erudition and the arts, and I was not holding up my end. Although to his mind, my choice of career was the least of my offenses.

The chill in our relationship mellowed somewhat once I left home. Absence makes the heart grow fonder for some, but with us it was more out of sight, out of mind. Though our differences troubled me from time to time, the wound had calloused over and had become an ordinary bother, like arthritis or tennis elbow. Under the present circumstances, however, it merited my immediate attention; my father might expire at any moment, alone in a hospital bed two hundred miles away.

I called my editor, Charlie Reese, and told him my plans. He understood, said not to worry about work, and wished me well.

Before setting out for New York, I stopped at Fiorello's, the soda shop opposite my apartment on Lincoln Avenue. Over a coffee, I discussed the situation with the proprietor, Ron Fiorello, known to the locals as Fadge. He was a big man—six foot two and over three hundred pounds—a few years older than I was (twenty-three), and the closest thing I had to a friend in New Holland. We spent long hours sitting at the counter in his shop, talking late into the night. I enjoyed his wit and salty humor. He liked having a girl around.

I remembered the first time I realized we would get on. Having recently moved to New Holland, I had been frequenting the shop for a few weeks, enjoying the occasional cup of coffee over a newspaper, which I liked to read in a booth near the back. On that day, I arrived just before lunch, and Fadge greeted me at the door, a magazine tucked under his arm.

"Hi," he said. He looked distressed. "You're Ellie, right?"

"Yes," I said.

"Watch the store for a few minutes. I'll be right back."

He rushed to the back room and disappeared into the toilet, where he remained for nearly forty-five minutes. When he finally emerged, looking relieved and not the least bit embarrassed, he thanked me and asked me how I'd fared.

"Not a soul came in, so I read the dirty books," I said, motioning to the magazine rack against the wall.

"Didn't I see your picture in one of them?" he asked, so sweetly that I fell in love with him on the spot.

"That's terrible news about your dad, Ellie," he said, staring at me with his bulging brown eyes—he suffered from a thyroid condition. "Maybe it'll turn out all right, but just in case, don't let him leave you feeling guilty; that lasts forever."

Normally, I take the train to New York. You have to be sure to reserve a seat on the right-hand side of the car, though, or you'll have nothing to see but trees and embankments rushing by for four hours. That gives me motion sickness. On the right side of the car, you can stare lazily at the Hudson, broad and majestic, and admire the Catskills and Palisades, the flinty rocks and green hills, and wonder if you've just passed the tree where Rip Van Winkle slept for all those years. But there was no train to anywhere at this hour, so I got onto the Thruway at New Holland around ten o'clock, hoping my '51

Plymouth Belvedere would get me to New York. Charlie Reese had pulled some strings to get me the company car in early December. I suspected it was a lemon—old-fashioned and round and, yes, a shade of yellow—they had no other use for, but I was grateful to have it anyway. It meant I could cover high school basketball games without having to take taxis or beg rides on the team bus. The teenage boys always stared slack-jawed at my legs.

Four hours later, I was bouncing down the Henry Hudson Parkway, under the George Washington Bridge and past the piers, arriving at Saint Vincent's Hospital in the West Village around two thirty.

I had phoned the hospital before leaving New Holland to arrange a quick visit, since I would be arriving long after visiting hours had ended. They agreed to accommodate me. A short nurse with a pleasant smile identified herself as Mrs. Buehler. She showed me to my father's bed in the Intensive Care Unit. I never would have found him otherwise; the long, snaking tubes of a breathing apparatus obscured his bandaged head. His skin, normally a robust tan, was a waxen gray. Liver spots I had never noticed before spread over his forehead, cheeks, and hands. He looked like a corpse. I stood over the bed for a few minutes, unsure of what to do. Then the nurse spoke.

"Why don't you go home and get some sleep, Miss Stone?" she said. "He's stable, and you can speak to the doctor in the morning."

Feeling vaguely guilty for abandoning the vigil, I left the hospital and drove over to University Place and Tenth Street, where I parked my Plymouth. I grabbed my bag, walked across Tenth and down Fifth Avenue, and paused at the door of my father's apartment building. The neighborhood hadn't changed. I peered through the cold darkness at the most familiar landmark of my youth: Washington Arch. A grayish shadow in the night, it loomed an eerie portal. An icy breeze ruffled the collar of my coat, and I ducked inside 26 Fifth Avenue.

"Miss Eleonora?" called a voice from a chair across the lobby.

Rodney. He used to watch out for me like a mother hen, tie my shoes, and adjust my book strap when it was loose. And I used to tell him stories of my day as we rode the elevator to the fifteenth floor. He was a kind man who liked little children, perhaps because they treated him like a whole person, not a cripple with black skin. I crossed the polished marble floor, dropped my bag, and extended a gloved hand to the aging elevator operator. He pushed himself off the chair and stood lopsided but sturdy on his right leg, bent since birth. His tired face smiled sadly as he clasped my hand.

"I'm just sick about what happened to Professor Stone," he said, shaking his head. "Can't figure how someone got in here. I was on duty that night, and not a soul came through that door I didn't know."

"What time did my father come home that night?"

Rodney's face twisted in thought. "I remember seeing him come in, and I wasn't sleeping." This last observation seemed to be germane in fixing the approximate time. "Let's see, I came on at six, got off at two . . ."

"Never mind, Rodney," I said. "I'll talk to you again tomorrow. Try to remember when he came home."

"I know who'll remember," he said. "That young man who works with Professor Stone."

"Who's that? Someone named Sanger, perhaps?"

"I don't know his name, but he comes around here all the time. He'll know; he was with him."

"Could he be the one?" I asked, but Rodney shook his head.

"No, miss. They went upstairs together, then the young man buzzed the elevator about twenty minutes later. While I was bringing him down to the lobby, he said he forgot something upstairs. I called Professor Stone on the intercom right then and there from the elevator, and he answered. So, I handed the receiver to the young man, and they settled it between themselves."

"Do you know what he forgot?" I asked.

"No, miss. He must have mentioned it, but I wasn't really paying attention."

"So you didn't take him back upstairs to get it?"

Rodney shook his head again. "No, Professor Stone told him he'd give it to him on Monday."

"Did you tell the police about that guy?" I asked.

"About thirty times before they was through with me."

Rodney whisked me up to the fifteenth floor and left me alone in the long, still corridor. The walls hummed peacefully, almost inaudibly, as all these prewar New York residences do. Lugging my bag to the last apartment on the southeast corner, 1505, I fished two brass keys from my pocket and turned the lock, then the dead bolt. Inside, the apartment was dark. The smell of the house had changed; the last whiffs of my mother's perfumes had faded, and more masculine scents had settled in. The place was spanking clean, but the odor of old books and oriental rugs defies feather dusters and pine wax.

I flicked on the light, dropped my case next to the bench in the foyer, and stepped through the archway into the parlor. Everything looked different; it had been two years since I'd left. Flowers spewed from pots in every corner, on every end table. I recognized them as my mother's favorites, but couldn't remember what they were called. She had tried to teach me about flowers, but I was more interested in the boys who played baseball. Not a tomboy, but a fan. I suppose I still am. The wallpaper had been changed, and some new pieces of furniture anchored the grand old Kashmiri rug that my mother adored. Silk on silk, nine hundred knots per square inch—woven by children with very small hands, no doubt. One of the old paintings was missing: a Wyeth watercolor of a hillside, framed by a barn window. My mother had received it as a gift from the artist in the late forties. In its place was a portrait of my late mother beside a vase of orange tulips, painted by someone named Romich—most probably an artist she represented. Not my taste. On the mantelpiece in the parlor sat a simple gray vase. My mother's ashes were inside. I wondered how my father had managed the redecoration project, since the room didn't strike me as consistent with his dark and austere style.

My father had been found unconscious in his study on Saturday morning, struck on the back of the head by a heavy object, unknown at present. The police had scoured the room that very afternoon, but had taken nothing away. The fingerprint experts had left a dusty trail over most of the study, since, judging by the scattered books and papers, the intruder had touched nearly everything in his search for valuables.

Despite the late hour, I wanted to have a look at what had happened. I circled around my father's desk, swiveling his green leather chair with a distracted hand as I examined the room I had so rarely visited as a girl. The three windows behind the desk were dark, locked tight with the louvered shades drawn. The desk drawers had been pulled out, some dumped on the floor. I stepped over the mess and opened the shades to look outside. The airshaft: twenty feet of nothing, then a brick wall. No access and very little light. I had never understood how my father could work in that cave, but he liked the dark, insulated peace of the room.

I glanced at the ponderous book on his desk: a magnificent, 1861 Gustave Doré *Divine Comedy*. No surprise there; Dante was my father's life's work. He had more than fifty different versions in various languages. The papers strewn about on the floor had not been moved by the police. I knelt down and picked through a few of them. Students' dissertations, notes for lectures, decades of professional correspondence ... The contents of an academician's desk. His personal documents were scattered on the floor between a filing cabinet and the wet bar. I cracked an ice cube, dropped it into a tumbler, and poured Scotch over it. As one of the boys, I had learned how to drink whiskey, and hold it well. I had to hold my drink or be ready to defend my virtue.

The hi-fi, hidden inside a cherry wood cabinet, was untouched. A record sat on the turntable: Gounod's *Faust*. The encyclopedic collection of classical music records (78s and LPs) lining five long shelves of the chest above, had been ransacked. I say "classical" with a twinge of guilt, since my father insisted on pointing out the misnomer whenever he heard it. Classical, he declared, was a period of music dating roughly from the mid-1700s to about 1830. Mozart and Beethoven were classical composers, he maintained. Brahms and Tchaikovsky were Romantics.

One March evening fifteen years earlier, as we sped north up Sixth Avenue in a taxi, heading to the Ninety-Second Street Y to hear Lotte Lenya sing Weill, my brother Elijah referred to *The Three Penny Opera* as classical music.

"Kurt Weill is in no way classical music," corrected Dad. "You can say he wrote operas, music for the stage, or modern music. But you cannot say he wrote classical music any more than you can say he wrote West Texas Swing."

"But everyone calls it classical," Elijah said in his defense. "At a certain point, you've got to accept common usage. You don't speak Middle English, do you?"

"I don't need to accept incorrect usage," said Dad, and Elijah just shook his head and watched the streets whiz by.

"Daddy," I asked once I realized the argument was over. "Is Paul Whiteman classical music?"

He laughed. Elijah roared, and my mother patted my head.

"Not exactly, dear."

Back in my father's study, I surveyed the mess again. Most of the disks lay on the floor, including several that had been maliciously shattered and trampled. Among the items missing, I noted three small silver picture frames, a gold pen set that had belonged to my grandfather, and the strong box my father had kept in his desk. I swept a few pages of one of my father's manuscripts off the divan and plopped down to have a smoke while I nursed my drink. After shaking out the match, I realized the crystal ashtray, which had always sat on the low table before the couch, was gone, along with the silver Aladdin's lamp cigarette lighter. I placed the cool match on the table, and took my cigarette and Scotch into the parlor.

MONDAY, JANUARY 25, 1960

A brilliant January sun splashed through the south and east windows, warming my stiff bones: I had fallen asleep in one of the armchairs in the parlor. After a couple of false starts, I managed to brew myself a potent cup of sludge in my father's little Italian coffee machine.

Down the hall, past my father's study, three bedrooms squared off the northwest end of the apartment. My parents' room, an elegant, polished art-deco suite with bath and dressing room, was on the left. Elijah's room was directly opposite, and mine was between it and a second bathroom at the end of the hall. My bedroom smelled hollow and looked cold. The furniture was still there, shrouded by dust covers, just as I had left it two years before. If it hadn't been my own bedroom, I would have thought the child who had slept there was dead. But that was Elijah's room. I didn't even look inside.

I showered in my father's bathroom, put on my face, and dressed. Passing the study door on my way back to the kitchen, I heard a noise and froze in my tracks. I should have run for the front door, but, strangely, I couldn't help but look. My eyes came to rest on a woman, a Negro of about thirty. Dressed in a faded cotton wrap-around dress, tan hose, and black shoes, she glared at me, maybe from curiosity, maybe from suspicion. Then I noticed the man. He was across the room, toying with a paperweight on my father's desk, as if he was bored. I looked him over: solid, average height, light-brown skin, and clear-blue eyes. He gave me the creeps.

"What you doing here?" the woman demanded, her tones unmistakably Caribbean.

"I live here," I said tentatively, wondering why I wasn't running for the door. "I mean, my father lives here."

"Professor Stone's girl?" she asked. "Eleonora?"

I nodded. "Excuse my curiosity," I said, "but who are you?"

She laughed. "Oh, you're Professor Stone's girl all right!" (My father and I are said to have the same eyes.) I waited for an explanation. "My name is Nelda, your daddy's cleaning woman. It was me that found him," and suddenly her smile faded. "Terrible what happened to Professor Stone. Terrible."

"Who's he?" I asked, motioning to the man at the desk.

"That's Nelson, my brother. I'm afraid to come here alone after what happened."

Nelson was still standing there, paperweight in hand, grinning smugly at me.

"Tell me what happened," I said, turning to Nelda.

"I come in about this time Saturday," she began. "I opened the door and called to Professor Stone, 'cause I don't want to surprise him. Most days, he answers hello, but Saturday nothing. I called again, then I went to look. He was flat on the floor in the study, bleeding from the head! I thought he was dead. I screamed bloody loud. Then I called the police."

"Didn't you call an ambulance?" I asked.

Nelda's eyes darkened. "No, the police done that. What you mean by that, Miss Eleonora?"

I waved a hand and walked into the study and crossed the room. I approached my father's desk, and Nelson moved away, around the other side, and wandered to the door where he leaned against the jamb as if to block the exit. Nelda took up a position in front of me.

"Did you notice anything missing when you found him?" I asked.

"A couple of things. Silver things, gold, you know. I didn't look much, 'cause the police was in charge."

I thought a moment. "Are you the only person besides my father who has keys to this apartment?"

"I think so," she said. "Excepting you. Why're you asking such questions? Can't you see that a burglar come in here and bashed Professor Stone on the head? That's what the police said."

"I'm just wondering how the burglar got in," I said.

"Well, don't go suspecting me, Miss Eleonora. The professor is good to me, and I am always good to him."

Nelda told me she and Nelson had come to clean up the mess in the study, but I asked her to leave things alone for the time being. She cast a wary eye my way.

"We have not come to steal anything, Miss Eleonora," she said.

"No, I didn't think so. But I want to have a closer look at this mess before you put things back in order."

Nelda shook her head. "You going to be staying here, Miss Eleonora?" she asked.

"For a few days, anyway."

"Well, if you don't mind the mess, I won't clean it. Come on, Nelson," she called, and the man with the unsettling eyes followed her out.

"Your father's condition is critical," said Dr. Mortonson, calling my attention to a set of x-rays on a light box in his office. "He's suffered a depressed fracture of the skull behind the right ear. The resulting bleeding has created what we call an extradural hematoma. If you look closely at this shadowy area beneath the surface of the skull," he circled the area in question with his forefinger, "you'll see blood trapped between the meninges and the bone."

"What does that mean in practical terms?" I asked.

"The cerebellum was subjected to an increase in pressure, which, in turn, can cause brain damage, coma, or death."

"Can you relieve the pressure?"

"Of course." He yanked one of the x-rays from the light box and snapped another in its place. "These," he pointed to a pair of small, black circles on the film, "are the two holes we drilled to let the blood out. We discovered a clot and removed that, but there's still swelling from the general trauma. We're trying to reduce that by other means. If he regains consciousness, we'll be able to assess how much, if any, damage occurred."

"Which faculties are controlled by the cerebellum?" I asked.

"Motor functions, muscles, coordination. He may walk out of here like before, or maybe not at all."

"Paralysis?"

"Or death."

The man waiting for me in the visitors' lounge was a slightly built redhead in his late twenties, maybe thirty. Wearing a rumpled gray shirt, black tie, and brown jacket, he introduced himself as Detective-Sergeant Jimmo McKeever of the NYPD. I thought he looked more like a jockey than a cop.

"I'm sorry about your father," he said softly.

I asked him about the investigation.

"It looks like robbery. An intruder gained entry into the apartment, apparently through the front door, and surprised your father in his study."

"Are you sure my father was taken by surprise?"

McKeever started, as if I had ambushed him. "I believe so, Miss Stone. You see, the blow was struck from the back, which is consistent with, well, surprise."

His timidity was curious. I wondered if he was in the habit of speaking to girls. "Then you don't think my father might have known his attacker?"

The policeman wiped his lips with a handkerchief and laughed nervously. His eyes avoided mine. "Ah, I don't think so, but it's a possibility. What makes you think he knew the intruder?"

I shrugged. "Did you speak to Rodney the doorman?"

"Oh, yes," he said, gulping down some saliva. "Mr. Wilson was quite eager to cooperate. He told me about a young man who accompanied your father home that evening."

"You don't know who that man is, do you?"

He shrank into his jacket and shook his head. "No, miss, but he may be a colleague of your father's. I'm going to check on that."

"What else can you tell me about what might have happened?" I asked, amused by this funny little man, despite the circumstances that had brought us together.

"Well, we think we know what was taken. I have a list here," and he patted his pockets until he'd located the scrap of paper in question. "The cleaning lady helped us with this."

McKeever read off the list, mostly items I had noticed myself, plus a few knickknacks from the parlor. Nothing irreplaceable.

"Billfold?" I asked.

"Still in his pants' pocket. Nothing missing there."

"What about the bedroom? My father kept some of my mother's jewels in there. Mostly heirlooms, and quite expensive. He liked having them around."

"By all appearances, the intruder did not enter the bedroom."

I tapped a finger absently on my lip, thinking.

"What is it, Miss Stone?" asked McKeever.

"It's just strange," I said. "Why didn't the burglar search the bedroom? Most women keep their jewelry on a dresser or in a box. Jewels are lightweight, easy to conceal, and easy to unload."

"But your father lives alone. Your mother is . . ." McKeever stopped short, maybe out of reluctance to use the brutal word with me, or maybe he had just gotten my point.

"Yes, my mother is dead," I said. "But the burglar wouldn't have known that, unless he knew my father."

McKeever fidgeted, uncomfortable with any new scenario that didn't include a pat conclusion. "You say her jewels were expensive?"

"No Star of India," I said. "But they're the goods."

"Perhaps the intruder was scared off," he said. "Maybe he fled after hitting your father. To be honest, Miss Stone, the idea that this could have been the work of an acquaintance of your father's hadn't crossed my mind."

"I'm sure you're right," I said. "It's just those little details that bother me: How did the assailant get in, and why didn't he look for the real trove? And the billfold. Why overlook that?"

McKeever nodded, unconvinced. "You'd be surprised how many break-ins present similar inconsistencies. Take last week, for example. I investigated a burglary where only a bicycle and a jar of small change were taken. The thief ignored a drawer crammed with silver, some antique vases of some value, and an expensive hi-fi."

"What did you deduce from that?" I asked.

"That the burglar was probably a kid. He stole only the things he could carry and could use. My guess is that he rode off on the bicycle with the jar of change under his arm."

"Sounds like a logical conclusion," I said, and McKeever seemed relieved. "But how did your bicycle-thief burglar get inside in the first place?"

The detective's face flushed, and I could see I'd unnerved him again. "Well, through a window off the fire escape. We found it wide open."

I nodded. "But there was no open window at my father's place," I said. "And no forced entry."

By noon, I was on the Saw Mill River Parkway, rolling toward Irvington and the cemetery where my brother was buried. Elijah had skidded on the slick pavement of Route 9A after a June rain two and a half years earlier, and his motorcycle careened over the shoulder and plunged down a steep hill. He was dead on the scene, a quiet woodland in Westchester County. My parents decided that he should be laid to rest where he died, so he was buried in Irvington.

The caretaker was embarrassed by the desecration. He apologized a little too insistently, explaining that the vandals, probably local juvenile delinquents, had broken into the cemetery late at night and made no noise.

"It's such a big cemetery," he said, as we walked over the cold ground toward Elijah's grave. "I couldn't have heard them if they'd thrown a party."

"It's all right, Mr. Dibb," I said, touching the gaunt man's elbow. "I understand these things happen all the time."

"Oh, no, miss," he said, looking straight ahead and not at me. "We haven't had a desecration here since '52, and that was an act of personal vengeance."

"You mean no one has kicked over a headstone since then? It happens all the time where I live. Mostly troubled teenagers."

Mr. Dibb's concave chest swelled, his gray, stubbly chin thrust upward in self-satisfaction. "I keep an eye on things." Then, perhaps remembering the reason for my visit, his pride flagged, and his chest deflated. "Of course you can't be everywhere at once. Especially in a big place like this."

My brother's grave was indeed far from the caretaker's house. Secluded in a low-lying glen behind a hill, it was often sodden from settling rain and decaying leaves. Yet it was a beautiful place, somber to be sure, but serene and bucolic. A huge, black oak stood nearby, its trunk and branches twisted, as if by grief for the dead at its feet. Elijah's granite marker had been pushed over, cracked in half by a heavy blow, and smeared with three black swastikas in acrylic paint. I pulled my Leica from my oversized purse and shot a few frames to examine later on; I couldn't stand to look at the grave one more minute, and not because some idiot had scrawled a couple of swastikas on the stone. As Dibb walked me back to my Plymouth, I turned my head until the tears had dried from my cheeks. He wasn't looking at me anyway.

At 110th Street, a swath of flinty green slices through Harlem. Running north for thirteen blocks, Morningside Park cordons off Columbia University to the west from the flats of Harlem to the east. Columbia, or more precisely Barnard, was my alma mater, daytime home for four years of studies and many hours besides of visiting my father at the office: Hamilton Hall, where the Italian Department conjugated its verbs and deconstructed its texts. My father kept his office on the sixth floor, overlooking Hamilton's statue and the John Jay Building to the south. I studied history at Barnard and spent countless hours at Fayerweather Hall, but with my father's lukewarm support, I was submatriculated into the School of Journalism my junior and senior years. That put me in the Journalism Building most days, just opposite Hamilton Hall on the other side of South Field. I often met him at his office for lunch or to ride the subway home together in the evening.

The last time I had visited Morningside Heights was on a June day two and a half years earlier—just a week before Elijah died—when I took my degree. Now I was returning under less auspicious circumstances to ask my father's colleagues a few questions about a young man who had been seen with him the night of the attack.

The pall over the office was darker than I had expected, even for a Monday. When I introduced myself to the secretary, a handsome woman in her late thirties named Joan Little—according to the engraved Bakelite strip on her desk—I noticed her red eyes and raw nose.

"You're Professor Stone's daughter?" she asked, dabbing her eyes with a handkerchief. "What do the doctors say about your father?"

I explained the vague prognosis, that the doctors weren't sure if he would pull through, or how much brain damage might remain. Joan Little listened with a pained expression, embarrassing me with her *poor dear* gaze.

"It's been an awful few days," she said. "I saw your father on Friday. He was so upset about your brother's . . ." she balked at the word *grave*. "The horrible thing those vandals did."

"How did he react?"

Miss Little shook her head and swallowed some watery build-up in her throat. "He didn't say a word, but his temples were throbbing. He usually gets that way when he's furious, but Friday it was different; he was seething. That was raw sorrow, inconsolable loss, and fiery wrath. He was spitting mad." She buried her face in the handkerchief. Once she had composed herself, she continued: "Then Dr. Chalmers called Saturday afternoon to tell me about the assault on your father. Then Ruggero Ercolano." Again the tears in the handkerchief, this time a gusher.

I knew Victor Chalmers, the department chairman and a needle-nosed iceman, but Ercolano was new.

"Who's this Ercolano?" I asked. "And how did he know about my father?"

Miss Little looked up from her handkerchief and sniffled. "No, I didn't mean Dr. Ercolano called me about your father. I meant he's dead."

CHAPTER TWO

Ruggero Ercolano, thirty-three-year-old assistant professor, was discovered dead in his bathtub after midnight on Saturday by Professor Chalmers. Ercolano was turned on his side, half-submerged in the tub with an electric radio for company in the water.

"Oh, my," I said. "How did the radio get into the tub?"

Miss Little shrugged her shoulders. "The police think he placed it on a stool next to the tub, then upset it by accident."

"That's a terrible story," I said. "How was it Dr. Chalmers was in Ercolano's apartment after twelve on a Saturday night?"

"I didn't think to ask," she said. "But it is strange."

"Is he around?"

She shook her head. "He left about an hour ago. He was sending wires and making overseas calls all morning to Dr. Ercolano's family in Italy, and now he's gone to the funeral parlor to arrange transportation of the body." She paused, overcome by tears again. "Such a tragedy. But of course you have your own troubles just now. Is there anything we can do for you or Professor Stone?"

"As a matter of fact, yes," I said. "I'm looking for the young man who accompanied my father home the night of the attack."

"And you think he's here?"

"The doorman said he worked with my father. Maybe a student?"

"That must have been me," came a voice from over my shoulder. I turned to see a tall young man with curly dark hair and horn-rimmed glasses. "I'm Bernard Sanger," he said, extending a hand.

"I'm Ellie Stone."

"Nice to meet you finally," he said. "Your father and I were very close."

"Were?" I asked. "He was still alive when I saw him this morning."

"Of course," he stammered, withdrawing his hand before I'd shaken it. "I meant we were working closely together before this happened."

"What time did you leave him Friday?"

Sanger thought carefully for a moment, seemed to be organizing the order of events in his head, then answered: "Ten fifteen. The elevator operator should be able to corroborate that; he buzzed your father as I was leaving. I had forgotten something, you see."

"Yes, he told me," I said. "What was it, by the way?"

"His manuscript, *Daughters of Eve: Women in Dante*," he said. "We agreed he'd bring it to me today instead. Of course, as things turned out, he didn't."

"Why was he giving you the manuscript?"

"I was helping him edit it. If you look at the acknowledgments, you'll find my name figures prominently."

"Can't wait to check. Did you notice anyone in the hallway, stairs, or elevator?" I asked, steering him back to the subject.

"No, the building was quiet."

"Was my father expecting anyone? Did he seem preoccupied?"

"Not at all," said Sanger. "He told me he had some mail to read before turning in. That was all. He didn't mention anyone."

"Do you visit my father's apartment often?"

"At least once a week, and we often had dinner together."

Just then, Miss Little blew her nose again, and Sanger suggested we move to the lounge across the hall.

"No need to discuss this publicly," he said, glancing around.

The lounge was outfitted with modern, institutional furniture: some tables, several cushioned chairs, a couch, and a long pair of stockings, crossed and resting on the floor at a forty-five-degree angle. My eyes climbed the sleek legs, over the navy mohair skirt, slender waist, and silk blouse, through which one could discern the hint of a lace brassiere—just visible through the fabric, and intentionally so. At the top, a striking, fair-skinned beauty with black hair looked up from her book and smiled at us. She had big, green eyes.

"Let's talk somewhere else," said Sanger, and he tried to draw me out of the room by my elbow.

"Don't run off because of me, Bernie," said the young lady. Her offer put Sanger on the spot, so we pulled up two chairs.

"Where I come from, it's customary to make introductions," she said, sitting forward, the silk of her stockings brushing a soft whisper somewhere on her legs.

"Hildy Jaspers, Ellie Stone," said Sanger to get it over with. I took her hand.

"Not Professor Stone's daughter?" she asked.

I nodded.

"Hildy is a doctoral candidate here in the department," said Bernie, trying to wedge himself between Miss Jaspers and me. "But she's a modernist, so she doesn't have much occasion to work with your father."

"*Au contraire, Bernard,*" she cooed. Then to me: "I worked with Professor Stone last year on the curriculum committee, and he helped me prepare for my Latin exams."

"Hildy is writing a dissertation on Pirandello," said Sanger, as if to insult her. "The noted Italian dramatist . . ." he added for my benefit, positively succeeding in insulting me. "I'm writing on Dante, of course."

"I just love the theater, don't you?" she asked. "Experimental theater, especially."

Sanger stifled a snort. "Like your avant-garde troupe on the West Side?" Then to me: "They call it alternative theater, but the only thing alternative about it is the clothing."

Hildy blushed. "Really, Bernie," she said. "You're as outdated as your dusty, old Dante when it comes to art. And besides, there was only that one scene."

"It was *Our Town,*" said Bernie. "There's no nudity in Wilder."

"Is there any news of your father?" Hildy asked, ignoring him.

I mumbled something about too early to tell, and thanked her for her concern.

"If there's any way I can help, please let me know," she said, gathering her books to leave. "I think the world of your father. And I do hope he becomes chairman."

I'd bet he thought a lot of her, too, and often.

"Pretty, isn't she?" I asked to no effect. Bernie didn't hear me. His eyes were fixed on the gentle swing of Hildy's hips as she left the room, and she knew he was watching.

"Bernie," I said, shaking him by the elbow, "thump once for yes, twice for no."

"Huh?"

"I was asking about Miss Jaspers," I said.

"Hildy is a freethinking girl," he pronounced. "Her reputation is well established here in the department. She's quite emancipated, if you know what I mean. And attractive, in case you hadn't noticed."

"I had."

"The speculation runs thick about whom she's bedded. And every last one of the professors and graduate fellows saw her perform in that play."

"Including yourself?"

"I said every last one, didn't I?"

"You don't like her, do you?"

Sanger shook his head. "I wouldn't say that. There's a bite to our repartee, an edge on our acquaintance, but we enjoy the exchanges."

"Some might call it flirting. Do any of those rumors include my father?"

Bernie stiffened, then stumbled over an inadequate reply. I reminded him that my father was a healthy man, in good condition for his sixty-three years, and currently unattached.

"Have you heard any such rumors about Hildy Jaspers and my father?" I repeated.

"You know how nasty people can be," he said. "Just because he took pity on her and helped her with some Latin. But I don't believe it. I know what kind of man your father is, and he's not so frivolous."

The last thing I wanted to do was picture my father pitching woo to Hildy Jaspers, or anyone for that matter, but I wanted to understand his relationships within the department. It's hard to reconcile Eros with one's parents, especially if the object of desire is as potent as Hildy Jaspers. I shook the thoughts from my head.

"What about this Ercolano?" I asked. "Did people talk about him and Miss Jaspers?"

"Of course," said Sanger. "Ruggero, poor guy. I liked him, and he did well with the ladies. He was quite handsome."

"Terrible way to go," I said, thinking of Ercolano's last bath. "How do you suppose Chalmers happened to discover him after midnight?"

Sanger shrugged, then looked at me askance. "You sure ask a lot of questions."

"I'm a curious gal," I said.

"Well, if you're curious about Hildy, you might ask that man out there," and he pointed through the glass in the door. A thin man in his fifties, with salt-and-pepper hair cropped close to his scalp, was stooping to drink from the water fountain. Dressed in a dark-brown suit and tie, he appeared solemn and severe, hardly the type I'd picture with the spirited Miss Jaspers.

"Who is he?" I asked.

"Gualtieri Bruchner. Visiting professor from Padua. There's been some talk that he's the latest partner in Hildy's hedonistic pursuits."

"Think he'll talk to me?"

"He's an odd one. Reserved and formal, with the personality of a sardine: tight and oily."

"And he's Miss Jaspers's playmate?" I asked.

Again Sanger shrugged. He didn't understand it any better than I. "That's what some people say."

I excused myself from the lounge and approached the gray figure, whose rigid face, I discovered, was indeed handsome in an intense, severe way. I introduced myself, and he offered his hand almost as an afterthought.

"I am sorry to hear about your father, Miss Stone." His accent was stiff, though not especially heavy. "I do not know him well as I have only been in New York since June. But I hear only good said of him."

I doubted that; my father's temperament was contentious and antagonized many, myself first on the list. Some loved him, some hated him, and unanimity was not likely. "Thank you," I said. "Have you had the chance to work with him at all?"

"No. I work on modern topics, you see, and our intellectual paths do not cross often. However, I lunched with him last Friday. It was by chance, really; we met at the Faculty Club dining hall."

"What did you talk about? Since your intellectual paths don't cross often, I would imagine you'd have trouble making small talk."

Bruchner seemed taken aback. "Not at all. Although we specialize in different periods, we are not Welfs and Ghibellines. We share an interest in Letters. Your father told me about a book he was completing, and I discussed a paper I delivered recently at a conference on Marinetti and Futurism."

"Was that the one at the Harrisburg Sheraton?"

Bruchner looked confused.

"Sorry," I laughed. "I was mistaken. Do go on."

"He told me hoodlums had vandalized your brother's gravestone on Wednesday night," he said. His voice was a drone of dull tones, and I wondered how his students stayed awake. "The incident left him disturbed. His hands were shaking."

"I'm surprised he didn't have a stroke."

Bruchner stared into my eyes. "Although I tried to understand his rage, I could not; I have no children, you see."

Now it was my turn to stare at him. "Thank you for the kind words," I said. "I guess it's been a bad week all around."

"How do you mean?"

Was he kidding, or are academics truly as befuddled as people say? "Ruggero Ercolano," I prompted.

"Oh, yes, of course. Horrible, horrible."

I returned to the lounge where I'd left Bernie Sanger. We pulled a couple of chairs up to one of the tables and sat down. We weren't quite ready to cozy up together on the sofa across the room.

"What did you think?" he asked.

"Didn't I see him in a Charles Addams cartoon?"

"Pretty spooky. It's not that he's mean-spirited, he's just as cold as ice."

"Listen," I said. "I don't want to sound ignorant, but he said something I didn't understand. Something about Welfs and Bellinis. What's that?"

Bernie Sanger chuckled as only pompous intellectuals do. "Professor Bruchner meant Guelphs and Ghibellines," he said. "The Germanic influence must have been too much for him up there near the Austrian border. That's why he said 'Welf.' He also says 'vine' for wine." Bernie had a good belly laugh over that one.

"All right, then," I said, raising my voice to be heard over his cackle. "I'll bite. What are Guelphs and Ghibellines?"

Bernie swallowed the last of his laughter and explained: "The Guelphs and the Ghibellines were opposing political factions in late-medieval Italy. The Guelphs, named for a noble family in Germany: Welf, or Welfen in the plural, supported a political alliance between the pope and rulers from the line of the Welf family. In a nutshell, the Ghibellines were antipapalists and loyal to another Germanic line."

"Rather obscure reference, isn't it?"

"Not in Italian history," he said. "The struggle for political supremacy in medieval Italy was pervasive. Years ago your father wrote a very interesting article on the subject. I could let you have a copy if you'd like."

"No, thank you," I said, sorry I'd ever asked. "One more question, though. Hildy Jaspers said she hoped my father would become chairman, but he always hated the idea of administration. Had he changed his mind recently?"

Bernie shook his head. "No, there's been some scheming recently, by Ruggero in particular. Ercolano was pushing your father to stand for chairman; Chalmers's term is up at the end of the semester. But your father never agreed to be a candidate."

. The door opened and a stocky young man, dressed in a plaid shirt and black trousers with slicked-down black hair, entered. He nodded a polite hello to Bernie and me, then crossed the room, plopped himself down on the sofa, and opened a book.

"Ciao, Bernie," a voice called out from just behind me. A second young man had entered the room without my noticing and now stood above me. I looked up and started. He was a strikingly beautiful creature, like a Botticelli angel. Soft green eyes, gentle olive complexion, wavy brown hair, casual and loose, as if he'd just piloted a sailboat across a windy lake. He stood there, easy, engaging, instantly likeable, and smiled sweetly at me.

Now it was Bernie's turn to rouse me from my dream. I blushed crimson, unsure how long I'd been staring at the young man.

"Ellie Stone, this is Luigi Lucchesi," said Bernie, embarrassed for me if his obvious discomfort meant what I thought it did.

"How do you do," I said, holding out a hand. Luigi took it and pressed just enough to unsettle me further. Even his grip was beautiful.

"Please call me Gigi," he said. "Everyone does."

"Really?" I asked. "Gigi? Like Leslie Caron?"

Bernie chuckled. "Not exactly. It's just short for Luigi. Still, rather a silly name for a grown man."

Gigi smiled at the affront, seemingly taking no offense at all. Then he asked if I was Professor Stone's daughter.

"Yes. Are you a student of his?"

"Oh, no. I'm a visiting lecturer."

He looked awfully young to be a lecturer, but Bernie would have surely contradicted him if he hadn't been who he said he was.

"What's your field of study?"

"I specialize in history of science and art. This semester I'm teaching a course on Galileo's poetry."

"Galileo wrote poetry?" I asked. Again I had mortified Bernie. But Gigi didn't seem to mind.

"Some," he said. "But he's better known for other things."

As he spoke, I noticed his Italian accent was a dignified collection of precise vowels and guttural—not rolling—*R*s, what the Italians call *erre moscia*, or soft *R*. My father had described the phenomenon like this: "If you come from a wealthy family, it's a sign of class or affectation, depending on your political persuasion. If you come from a poor family, it's a speech defect, like a lisp." This was the first time I'd actually heard it. I was bowled over.

Gigi took his leave, his smiling eyes lingering on mine as he turned slowly toward the exit. Then he disappeared into the corridor, and I exhaled for the first time since I'd laid eyes on him.

"I'd bet dollars to doughnuts that Hildy Jaspers plays in his sandbox," said Bernie. "Not Professor Bruchner's."

My heart took a tumble.

"They seem very cozy with each other, but they try to keep everything on the QT."

I returned to Saint Vincent's at seven o'clock for visiting hours. My father's condition hadn't changed, and there was nothing for me to do but sit by the bed and watch the rise and fall of the respirator's bellows. The steady pumping of the apparatus was not new to me. I had seen it once before, at the Westchester hospital where my brother Elijah's body lay awaiting transportation to the funeral home after the accident. An old woman was tethered to the machine, which inflated her weak lungs with oxygen and sucked the CO_2 back out. The vision remains eerily clear in my mind, and I associate it with Elijah's corpse. At times his face blurs into hers: gaunt eyes and loose, colorless skin; a trickle of saliva escaping from the corner of her mouth; and thin gray hair, too weak to stick together, falling like dried grass on the foam pillow of a hospital gurney.

My mind drifted inexorably to thoughts of my older brother, his offbeat sense of humor, uncommon intelligence, and charm. A gangly kid, Elijah grew into a restless adolescent, rebellious in the often-strange world of Greenwich Village. There was the flirtation with a smoky crowd of beatniks on Bleecker Street and the time he ran off with a group of out-of-town toughs on motorcycles. He lived his adolescence as if it had been a challenge to my father's authority and cultural legacy.

In the meantime, Dad and I were enjoying a special affinity, as special as it ever got between us, grounded in the iconography of American childhood: sports. I loved the Yankees and the football Giants, perhaps to win his approval or just to be close to him by sharing his zeal. My father didn't seem to mind that I was a girl in love with boys' games; he just liked having an enthusiastic protégée.

My idols were called DiMaggio, Berra, Vic Raschi, Hank Bauer. For a time in the late forties, my favorite Yankee was Snuffy Stirnweiss. I liked the name. My father indulged me for a while, but when Snuffy was traded to the Browns and later to the Indians, he disparaged him as a middling player, whose only good years had come during the war when the best players were overseas. By the time Mickey Mantle came to epitomize Yankee pride and glory, I was too old and rational. Baseball is a childhood obsession; adolescence brings other fixations, and the spell of the game dissipates.

Ours was not a religious family, so Yankee Stadium was my temple. I preferred the upper deck in the infield while my father, more reflective and attuned to the history of the *House That Ruth Built*, liked the bleachers in dead center, where he could contemplate the monuments at any time. So while I enjoyed rare moments in my father's company, Elijah had always remained his favorite, and that despite his lack of direction and my father's constant disappointment. Whether it was my sex or my sins that he couldn't accept, I can't say. There was nothing I could do to warm his frozen affection for any length of time.

A nurse nudged my shoulder, rousing me from my thoughts, and told me it was time to go. Before leaving, I looked again at the harness of tubing affixed to his face, and I realized he hadn't moved since I'd arrived.

I stopped for a drink at a tavern across from McSorley's on East Seventh Street. As a woman, I wasn't allowed inside that establishment, but Jock Brady's welcomed me warmly. Two drunken gents at the bar stared at me for ten minutes before annexing the empty seats in the booth where I was sipping my Scotch. Good, sturdy proletarians, about forty, they probably worked for the city hauling trash or digging up streets. Their hands looked knobby and strong, with a little too much grime under their fingernails for my taste. They smiled gray, toothy grins at me. The one opposite me did all the talking.

"What's a pretty little thing like you doing here all by yourself?"

"I'm not so pretty," I said. Probably came across as flirting, which it wasn't, but I can't always control my sassy disposition.

The man introduced himself as Pat Duggan and his silent friend as Dennis. I inched toward the wall of the booth, but Dennis closed the gap I'd tried to create.

"A whiskey drinker, are you?" said Pat. "Dennis has a bottle of rye in his room."

"Leave her alone, boys," called the burly barkeep.

"We didn't mean no harm, Jock," said Pat. "Just trying to make her feel welcome."

"Get out of the booth," said the barkeep, my hero. "Don't go chasing my customers away, or I'll toss you out of here."

The two men reluctantly slid out of the booth, but continued to watch me with the singular focus of a border collie on a straying sheep. I downed my drink, intending to get out of that dingy place posthaste. But then the barkeep appeared above me and offered an apology.

"They don't mean no harm, miss," he said, wiping his hands on his apron. He was a big man of about fifty, tall, with a mammoth belly testing the resilience of the stitching in the seams of his white shirt. "We don't get many young ladies in here. At least not proper ones like you. Hope they didn't give you a fright."

"Not at all, Mr. Brady," I insisted.

Then, to prove a point to the bartender—or perhaps myself—I ordered another drink and moved to a stool at the bar, a few feet from the two leering Lotharios. They looked me over for the next few minutes until they grew tired of the exercise and turned their attention to the numbers they intended to play the next day. When I left an hour and two whiskies later, I felt I'd won the battle. Still, I had wasted my time and money on swill in a dank hole, with all apologies to the kind proprietor, Jock Brady. I thought of Gigi Lucchesi. I wouldn't find his type in such a place. I wondered where I might find him.

Out on the street, I walked briskly toward Cooper Union. Seventh Street was dodgy; the wet pavement steamed from a vented manhole, rubbish waited for the street cleaner, and a couple of men watched me from their roosts in doorways. I hailed a passing cab and went home to 26 Fifth Avenue.

The debris from the burglary still littered the floor of my father's study. Scotch in hand, I kicked off my heels and dropped into the leather chair behind his desk and surveyed the disorder. It was time to let Nelda clean it up.

I like to read. Books, magazines, newspapers, even crossword puzzles; the written word has always been my entertainment of choice. So, by second nature, I looked for something to skim while I relaxed in the low light with my drink. A loose manuscript page—154—was the only printed material on the desk besides the big book: the *Comedy*. The unfamiliar subject matter—something about Helen of Troy in the *Inferno*—separated from its sister pages lost my interest almost immediately. Nevertheless, I thought I should reunite the scattered leaves of my father's opus before Nelda threw them away.

Once on my hands and knees, however, I discovered something strange: the pages on the floor appeared to be older than the one on the desk. After I'd put them all together, my puzzlement grew. There were two pages marked 154: the one I'd found on the desk, and one that had been among the papers on the floor. Furthermore, the two 154s were quite different, one from the other, both in apparent age and content. The slightly yellowed page I'd found on the floor matched the others I'd picked up, with the exception of the very first pages of the reconstructed manuscript. The type was a little worn and the corners somewhat dog-eared. The older page 154 dealt with an early work of Dante Alighieri's, *La Vita Nuova*.

I took the manuscript back to the desk, where I considered it over my Scotch and a cigarette. Curious how the most abstruse text grabs your interest when it's in the wrong place.

The title page, as white as a combed-cotton bedsheet, announced: *Daughters of Eve: Women in the Works of Dante Alighieri*, with my father's name trailing below. The following page, equally as white, dedicated the work to my late mother. Next came the table of contents and other front matter, all as white as the title page. The text proper, however, began the long string of yellowed sheets, broken only by the extra page 154. I pored over the material surrounding pages 154, finding it obvious that the whiter one had nothing to do with the rest of the text. Neither, for that matter, had the title page or front matter.

Figuring the pages had been scattered during the burglary, I set out to find another manuscript. There were no typewritten or manuscript pages among the contents of my father's drawers, dumped on the floor during the burglary. Nothing in the bookcase or cherry wood shelving either. A row of filing cabinets next to the hi-fi produced other manuscripts: essays, book reviews, papers, and hardcover copies of two of my father's books, *Dante at the Edge of the City of Dis* and *Satan's Jailers: The Monsters and Fiends of the Inferno*, both published when I was a child. I remembered the sketches my father had made of the various beasts: Harpies; demons; Cerberus, three-headed sentry to hell . . . His talent for breathing life—or death—into the flat pages of a 650-year-old poem was never more impressive than in his drawings. Even today—especially today—magnified by twenty years, his demons try my faith with spindly fingers and horned crowns, dancing furiously in the shadows. Their memory still grabs my guts with an icy hand.

I flipped through the book, looking for my father's spooky drawings, but there were none. I wondered if he had saved them.

Resuming my search of the study, I found nothing that resembled, even remotely, the papers I'd found on the desk and floor. Not even in the wastebasket, where the only paper was an empty envelope from Carnegie Hall.

I poured myself another Scotch and sat down with the unmatched pages. It was understandable that two unbound manuscripts could be thrown together during a frenzied search. What I couldn't figure was what had become of the newer manuscript, *Daughters of Eve*. Though its absence puzzled me, I probably could have explained it to my own satisfaction had it not been for the other, equally mysterious omission:

Where was the title page of the older, yellowing manuscript? Bernie Sanger had seen *Daughters of Eve* on Friday night, or had he only spoken of it with my father? I scribbled a note in my pad to ask Sanger about both manuscripts.

Since the bed was not made up in my room, I turned back the fresh sheets Nelda had stretched onto my father's king-sized bed that morning. My parents had always slept in a huge bed—large enough to accommodate my father's ego, I used to think. In their bed, my mind wandered in a semiconscious state of near sleep, dragging me back through the years to the time when I had actually lived in the Fifth Avenue apartment. The city's late-night murmur—cars passing by fifteen floors below—lulled me to sleep; New York's bustle has never disturbed my rest. But that night, noises inside my own head cranked me through the wringer. I had heartburn—too much whiskey—and the noises in my head were dreams of my late brother.

I dreamt I could see him roaring down 9A, and suddenly I was with him on the back of the bike, wind rushing through our hair, Elijah urging the motorcycle on as we screamed with laughter. We leaned into each curve as one with the machine, side to side, our knees nearly scraping the wet pavement. The speed was raw, thrilling, and we owned the road, invulnerable and without a care.

Then the tire blew. In a split second, the front wheel jerked to the left, and Elijah yanked it back, struggling to regain control. He pulled too far too fast, and the wheel jack-knifed, sending us veering to the right. The handlebars twisted from his grip, and we skidded over the edge, tearing through a phalanx of brittle branches, cartwheeling down the embankment, and hurtling into the massive trunk of an oak before finally bouncing to rest on the wet forest ground. The front wheel, its punctured tire torn from the rim, continued to spin for nearly a minute, ticking gently as it slowed to a stop. I picked myself up, somehow unhurt in the twisted wreckage, and tried to rouse Elijah, who'd been tossed against a tree some twenty feet away. I shook his still body, and he looked up at me, his bloodied face tightening into a startled expression of disbelief as the realization dawned. He was about to die.

"No, it can't be," he whispered. "Why wasn't it you?"

It was absurd and unfair that he should say such a thing in my dream. Elijah would have given his life for me, but that's what guilt does, I suppose. And though I knew Elijah would never have asked that question, my grief and mourning were savaged by the awful suspicion that others might well have done.

The smoke from my cigarette curled its way to the ceiling, and I watched it flat on my back in my father's bed. Lying awake, I played tricks on myself to divert my thoughts from Elijah, but I failed except when I turned my attention to the burglary. In the dark, I wondered if the apartment was secure, if the service entrance in the kitchen was sealed as it had been when I was a child. Might someone else—besides Nelda and her snarling brother—have keys?

I got up and checked the kitchen. The service door was locked tight, sealed with putty and paint, with a 400-pound refrigerator in front of it. A team of husky cat burglars might have been able to breach the door and move the refrigerator, but a lone intruder, no way. I tugged at a couple of windows, finding them all secure, then fastened the chain and turned the bolt on the front door. Sure that all entries to the house were locked, yet barely more confident of my safety, I returned to bed where I tried to clear my thoughts and sleep.

I lay awake for hours more.

People often say that we experience tragedy as if in a blur, but that wasn't the case for me. I remember Elijah's sudden death, funeral, and burial with raw clarity. The abrupt telephone call to my ill mother, her ashen face as she stammered into the receiver, the confusion in my head and the knot in my chest as she held me to explain through her sobbing that my brother was gone. She could scarcely console me in her weakened state. It was she who needed solace, and, to my discredit, I was unable to provide her any. I don't know how my father reacted when he heard, but I only saw a silent block of marble for three days, and his hostility toward me only fossilized after the shock dissolved into acceptance and sorrow. His disappointment in me, heretofore buried deep beneath his denial, seeped to the surface, boiled over, and manifested itself in a variety of ways. Sometimes, when we were at the dinner table or reading in the parlor, I would look up to find him glaring absently at me, as if he didn't realize what he was doing. His darkened brow frowned, his lips curled in a half sneer, and his eyes, hollow and gray behind his glasses, looked to be shattered by a secret regret. Then, when he noticed me aware of his gaze, he said nothing and looked away. Other times, his rancor ran free, and he would rebuke me with a single word or a disapproving shake of his head. I was powerless to fight back, unable to right the wrongs he placed at my feet, so I waged my own subtle war of resistance.

But the night Elijah died, I wept alone in my room, raging against such unreal and staggering news. He couldn't be dead. He couldn't be gone. Not so suddenly, it wasn't possible. We had sat together on the subway that very morning, me on my way to Yorkville for lunch with a friend, him to a parking lot on Thirty-Fourth Street to collect his motorcycle. He jumped from his seat as the train came to a stop at Thirty-Third and Park and tapped me on the shoulder.

"See you tonight, El," he said, and I waved good-bye without looking up from my crossword.

The abrupt loss of his life ripped a gaping hole in my heart, and I couldn't believe there was any way of going on if it were true. This was the first death I'd ever experienced, and the ache was too thick and too vicious to accept. I closed my eyes to the world that night, insisting it was wrong, that Elijah would walk through the door as he had promised that morning on the train. When he didn't, when he was still lying cold in the mortuary the following morning, I gasped for breath in my bed, I shrieked in grief and horror, begging for it not to be so. And then the door burst open, and my father stood there, fulminating eyes burning mine.

"Your brother is dead," he whispered, nearly spitting. "Your mother is in grief. Control yourself!" and he was gone.

He hadn't even said my name, as if it displeased him so that he couldn't even pronounce it. I cried one last time, burying my face in my pillow, hoping it would smother both my sorrow and me. When it didn't, I rose quietly, wiped my eyes, and turned my grief to ice. I didn't cry again throughout the ordeal of the funeral and burial.

In comparison, my mother's death was an anticlimax, slow and expected. I felt relief when her misery ended. But the sting was not as acute; Elijah had blunted the pain. Her death followed too closely for me to have recovered. Hers was easier for me. I was cold; the cruel surprise of Elijah's death diminished Mom's, and only with the passing of time did I realize how much worse that was. It still haunts me how cavalier I was about her passing. My father surely took note and was sickened by me. It's funny that, while I've since come to grips with Elijah's passing, I have not yet put Mom's behind me.

CHAPTER THREE

TUESDAY, JANUARY 26, 1960

"Ellie, my dear, how are you?" The tall rail of a man in the doorway stretched a smile across his cheeks. Did he really believe people bought his practiced sincerity? Victor Chalmers, chairman of the Italian Department, was in his early fifties. A middling scholar—something like Snuffy Stirnweiss—Chalmers was better suited to administrative task-mastering than academic glory. In my limited dealings with him in the past, mostly at social functions, I had found him pedantic and hopelessly unaware of the scorn he inspired in others. At the graduation party my parents had arranged for Elijah, Victor Chalmers invited my brother to benefit from his insights into human nature. His advice, as insipid as it was condescending, was for him to respect his elders and mind their wisdom, for they knew better. I was standing nearby and overheard Elijah say that my father, who certainly qualified as a wise elder, had always told him to ignore fatuous counsel from blowhards. Yes, my brother was a wise guy, but, God, I admired him so. Chalmers blanched. His icy-blue eyes narrowed, and his jaw muscles flexed.

"You'll never be anything but a loser," he whispered so no one else would hear. Then he assumed his counterfeit smile, the same one he was brandishing now, and disappeared into the crowd of guests.

"I'm fine, Dr. Chalmers," I said, standing aside. "Won't you come in?"

"I can't stay long," he said, looking around the place from the foyer as he removed his hat and overcoat. "I just wanted to know if there was anything I could do for you or Abe."

"He's in good hands. As for me, nothing." I stared at him.

"Well," he said, folding his coat over the bench near the door, "I smell coffee. Would it be too great an imposition?"

"Not at all," I said, thinking what a great imposition it was.

"That's a good girl," he said.

I showed him to the parlor. He wanted something. When I returned from the kitchen with his coffee, Chalmers was nowhere in sight. I found him in my father's study, standing over the desk, contemplating the mess with a shaking head.

"A tragedy," he said, as I set the coffee on the low table before him. "New York is going to hell in a handbasket these days. My wife, Helen, was mugged just a month ago. New York used to be a civilized place."

I said nothing. Complaints of New York's decline probably began the day after Peter Minuet rooked the Indians out of their home.

"Hoodlums," said Chalmers, taking the cup of coffee I'd poured for him. "First your brother's grave, then this."

"Bad week for the department," I said, sitting across from him, pulling my skirt to cover my knees.

Chalmers rubbed his eyes. "Horrible. I spent yesterday making funeral arrangements for Ruggero, wiring his family in Italy. It's all too tragic. But what about you? You've got quite a mess to deal with, too."

"I haven't let the maid clean it up yet," I said. "I wanted to poke around before she moved anything."

"These records," he said, indicating the shattered disks on the floor. "Such a beautiful collection."

I looked down on the black shards, reading some of the titles from my sitting position: Mendelssohn's *Lieder ohne Worte*, some Mahler symphonies, a rare recording of Chopin preludes performed and signed by Arthur Rubinstein, and fragments of many others too sad to count.

"I love those *Lieder* by Mendelssohn," said Chalmers, looking with me. "A senseless waste." Then nodding to the pile of loose pages on my father's desk: "I see his manuscript was untouched."

"Have you read it?"

"Not yet, but Abe has discussed it with me. I was looking forward to seeing the galleys; they were supposed to be ready in two months."

"You're talking about *Daughters of Eve*?" I asked.

Chalmers nodded. "Was he working on another?"

"No," I said, snatching a handful of pages off the top of the pile. "But I'm having a hard time locating the manuscript."

"That's not it?"

I shook my head. "See for yourself," and handed it to him.

He turned past the front matter, then read a few lines of the text proper. "But this is his last book," he said, shuffling through the remaining pages to confirm his impression. "This was published six years ago. Where's *Daughters of Eve*?"

I shrugged. "I was hoping to find out today. Maybe Bernard Sanger has an idea."

Chalmers seemed troubled, more than I would have expected. He shook his head.

"I don't like the looks of this," he said, drawing on his cup of coffee and whistling it through his teeth, like an ass, as if aerating wine. "If it's been destroyed, the loss to scholarship will be tremendous."

"I've been thinking a lot about *Daughters of Eve*," I said. "Trying to figure out how it could have disappeared. These pages were scattered when I found them, but the pattern is unmistakable."

"What do you mean?"

"The title page, dedication, and acknowledgments are there, but the body of the text is gone."

"Yes," said the professor, following my lesson.

"At the same time, the title page is missing from the text I did find."

"Deduction?"

"Someone took *Daughters of Eve* and hoped to have this other manuscript pass for it. After all, the police would never imagine any difference."

"Why would a burglar steal a stack of manuscript pages? They have no intrinsic value, only scholarly."

The door buzzer sounded, and we both left the study to investigate.

There was a clicking at the front door: a key turning the lock. Chalmers grabbed an iron poker from the fireplace and shoved me behind him.

"It's just the cleaning lady," I said.

"How can you be sure? It could be a burglar."

"It's not a burglar; she rang the bell," I said, pushing past him.

The door swung open and Nelda appeared, her purse dangling from her right forearm as she struggled to control two large, brown grocery bags.

"Well, Miss Eleonora?" she called. "Ain't you going to help me?"

"You can put down the poker," I told Chalmers, who weighed it briefly in his hand, then leaned it up against the fireplace. I strode to the foyer and reached for one of the bags. As I did, the door to 1504 popped open.

"May I help you?"

A woman in her midforties stood before me and Nelda in a red silk peignoir. Chalmers joined us in the doorway and looked the lady up and down. I apologized for the disturbance, explaining I was her neighbor's daughter. She broke into a smile, then a laugh.

"Eleonora? Is that you, Ellie Jelly?"

I blushed. "Mrs. Farber, how are you?"

Angela Farber: the intriguing-woman-next-door of my youth. Elijah had had a major crush on her. I had forgotten about her and the endless rivers of *études*, *scherzi*, and preludes that flowed faintly from her piano through the thick walls that separated her flat from ours. She and her husband, Garth Farber, a bohemian painter of moderate success, had split when I was about twelve, and she had moved away, or run off. For some reason, she was back.

"Why, Ellie Jelly, you're as cute as ever," she cooed. "And here I am in my robe in front of strangers. I don't want to corrupt anyone," she said, eyeing Professor Chalmers, as she put the door between her racing silks and him.

Was she prematurely senile, drunk early, or flirting full-time?

"You poor dear," she said, turning her attention back to me. "How's your father?"

I gave her the same iffy prognosis I'd been repeating to all. "I'm going to the hospital for an update in a few minutes."

"It's just not safe these days," she said. "We pay all this rent, and still the riffraff gets in."

"Did you hear anything that night?" I asked.

She shook her head. "I remember him coming home around ten or so. I distinctly remember my lights dimming a little past ten, and that always happens when your father turns on all those little lights."

Mrs. Farber was referring to the picture lamps Mom had installed over the paintings in our house. The fixtures were imported from Germany and, for some reason, had always caused minor surges in the electricity whenever they were switched on.

"Then you didn't hear him come in," I asked as clarification. "You noticed the lights dim?"

"That's right," she said, blushing crimson. "I was expecting a gentleman friend, you see, and I was in a bubble bath. Sometimes I can hear his keys as he lets himself in, but not when I'm in the bath. That night the lights blinked when he turned his on, and they blinked brighter when he switched them off a while later. That was about ten fifteen."

I thanked her for her help and asked her to let me know if she remembered anything else.

"I sure will, Ellie," she said. "It's just terrible. He's such a nice man. I took care of his plants, you know, when he went away last August. It's just awful."

I nodded thanks.

"Come by sometime for a drink, Ellie Jelly. You are old enough to drink now, aren't you? We'll talk some more." She shut the door, and I became aware of Nelda and Victor Chalmers, who were watching over my shoulder.

"Well, Ellie Jelly," said Nelda with a smile, "you want to come have your oatmeal and milk?"

Attempting to curb my embarrassment, I ignored her and asked her to clean the apartment, with the exception of the study. I had changed my mind again; something about the mess bothered me.

"I'll go clean, Ellie Jelly," she mocked. "But stay away from that woman. She's got the devil in her head."

"What do you mean?" I asked.

"Where you think she went all those years she was gone? Your daddy told me she was in the crazy house. When the police sent her man away, he took her senses with him."

"Her husband went to jail? What for?"

Nelda shrugged. "Drugs, wasn't it? Ganja or dope. He was selling the stuff. They took him away from her, and she went mad."

"I didn't know," I said.

"Now you do," said Nelda. "While your daddy's sick I'll take care of you, Miss Ellie Jelly. And I begin with a warning: stay away from that crazy woman."

"I'll be going now," said Chalmers. "Another difficult day ahead: we've planned a memorial service for Ruggero at Saint Paul's Chapel this afternoon."

"What time?" I asked. "I'd like to come."

Chalmers seemed puzzled. "At four. But you never even met the man."

⁂

Janey Silverman was my best friend growing up. We had met at a scrap-metal drive in Washington Square during the war. I was six or seven. My mother and brother had hauled a set of pots and pans to the park in my old pram. Then she donated the pram, too, as it had a metal frame. Janey's mother had dragged her along to assist in the patriotic duty, and we played together in the old gazebo and chased each other around the fountain. Her mother yelled at her to be mindful of the buses rumbling under the arch, belching their fumes as they passed. Today, with motorized traffic prohibited, the park is safer for children shrieking with joy as they career off the landmarks like so many pinballs pinging off flippers and bumpers. Kids never seem to focus more than two feet in front of their noses, and will collide with anyone or anything not paying attention.

Janey and I became fast friends that summer, as armies clashed the world over. For the most part, we remained unaware of the war's progress, except when my father cheered a victory or bemoaned a defeat from his chair near the radio. The two of us followed the serials together, listened to the *Green Hornet* with my brother Elijah, *Amos 'n' Andy*, and *Fibber McGee*. In 1943, Janey joined the Brownies, and I ran home to beg my parents to sign me up. My father crushed that dream, insisting that no child of his would ever belong to a paramilitary organization.

Janey's father had an umbrella shop on Fourteenth Street, where, as teenagers, we would meet to change our clothes and paint our faces before jumping on the El for an errant evening cruising the lounges on the Upper East Side. We were barely sixteen, but the men didn't care. We had lots to drink, always offered by junior executives with plenty of cash but no scruples.

It was great fun for Janey and me, and we had a few close calls, like the time her mother smelled the cigarettes and alcohol on our breaths. Janey froze, but I was always quick with an alibi, and I explained it away as smokers on the subway and a new perfume we'd sampled at Stern's on Forty-Second Street. She bought it, and Janey and I learned to cover our tracks. Another time, we got ourselves invited to a mixer at a Columbia fraternity. Janey and I were a hit; alcohol was my personality in a bottle. We were basking in the attention of a couple of upper classmen, who seemed to have designs on us despite our age, when I spotted Elijah entering the crowded room. I whisked Janey off to the powder room and we slipped out a side door. My brother remained unaware of his wayward sister's mischief. There was more he never knew about, and more that even Janey never knew.

I phoned her from my father's apartment. Just three years earlier, right out of college, she had married an electrical engineer and moved to Sea Cliff, Long Island. She now had a one-year-old baby boy, who howled in the background as I spoke to her.

"I'm so happy for you, Janey," I said, but she snickered.

"You're the one with the life," she said. "You were always the popular one."

"Are you kidding? You were the pretty one that all the boys courted. Remember that Nelson from that Columbia fraternity?"

"He tried to rape me! Nearly did."

"I know. Good thing I was there to discourage him."

"Discourage him?" she laughed. "You told him I had the clap!"

"Sure, but it worked. He left you alone after that."

"And so did everyone else."

We laughed until her baby, Russell, began screaming again. Janey put the phone down and fetched him a pacifier. I could hear her speaking to someone—her husband, I think—and they bickered about the baby. Finally Janey came back on the line, and I felt I was putting her out.

"Do you ever hear from the old crowd?" she asked. "Bonnie or Jackie?"

"Afraid not," I said. "Bonnie's probably still in med school, and Jackie? Well, after what happened with Stitch . . ."

"Oh, right, I'd forgotten about that. Sorry, Ellie."

I didn't like the direction the conversation was taking. Old boyfriends and former friends were of little interest to me. The memory of Stitch was particularly painful, for I had lost a love and a friend to him.

We'd known each other casually through Jackie Rennart, a close friend from my days at Riverdale Country School. After high school, Jackie and Stitch had gone steady for about a year, then broken up on friendly terms. It was the summer after my junior year at Barnard, August 1956, when we ran into each other at the Warner Cinerama in Times Square. I found out later on that Stitch had planned the chance meeting carefully. I was suffering through a hellish blind date with the son of a friend of my aunt's. Stu Benson was as dull as an old safety razor, unless you considered his bizarre tics and antisocial habits interesting from a clinical point of view. His routine included the rhythmic constant pursing of his lips, the odd tracing of figure eights on the side of his face with his left forefinger; and the unabashed contemplation of my chest whenever food was unavailable.

Stitch had taken a seat behind us and tapped on my shoulder

halfway through *Cinerama Holiday*, just after Stu got up to fetch himself more popcorn.

"Ellie, I thought that was you," he said, and he was roundly shushed for his trouble. "It's me, Stitch Ferguson."

He whispered into my ear for a few minutes, drawing more censure from our neighbors, until I finally pulled him out into the corridor. As we left the auditorium, I looked back to my seat to see Stu returning with his bag of popcorn.

"Let's get out of here, Stitch," I said. "Do you know a place where I can get a drink of something?"

He did: his room in the Penn View Hotel near Herald Square. It was the beginning of a secretive affair that we carried on for nearly six months. I didn't feel right going public, given his past with my friend Jackie, and I was sure my parents would not approve. So I would meet him in his room, dreary though it was, and we camped out in the Murphy bed for drinks, meals, and sex; the rest of the room was too small and foul to make any use of. We had nowhere else to go for our trysting, which, in retrospect, was really just a lot of booze and balling. That's what Stitch used to call it: balling. Sometimes, we would spend an entire weekend in that bed, not even bothering to dress for two days. I didn't like the place; it was depressing, but I was crazy for Stitch. He was twenty-six, I was twenty, and he was tall and handsome in a prep school way, like a letterman from Princeton. Truth be told, he'd studied at Rutgers, but something about him really lit a spark in me. I couldn't resist him, and he got me to do things most girls would be ashamed of.

It ended suddenly one Friday evening. I called on him in his room, and he announced that he was getting married. To Jackie. They had started dating again about two months earlier. He had continued to meet me secretly in his room, all the while he was courting Jackie. I was floored, felt the wind knocked out of me. I ran from his place and wept in the subway, wandered around for hours, then got terribly drunk in a lounge in Murray Hill and was sick in a trash can on Madison Avenue.

They got married six months later. The last time I saw him, he apologized for the way things had played out. He hadn't intended for me to fall for him. He had just wanted some fun, and had heard I was a good time.

He taught me the hardest lesson in love I've ever had, and I have the scars to prove it.

"Listen, Janey," I said, "something's happened to my father. He was attacked in his apartment."

"Russell, leave the cat alone!" shrieked Janey from her end. "Kenny, can't you watch him for two minutes while I'm on the phone?"

She covered the receiver, and all I could hear was muffled exchanges. Then she came back on and apologized.

"Sorry, Ellie, what was that you said about your father?"

"Oh, just that I'm in town to visit him for a few days or so. Thought we might get together if you were free sometime."

"Of course! Call me next week, and we'll make a plan."

She hung up, and I knew I wouldn't call her again. I was on my selfish, intemperate path, not ready for adult responsibilities, while she had them crashing down about her.

⁓

The morning was brisk and sunny. I walked up Fifth Avenue, then over Thirteenth to Saint Vincent's, arriving at my father's bedside at ten thirty. The day nurse shrugged dolefully at me when I asked if there was any change in his condition. I took up the vigil, staring at the walls, examining the state of my manicure—disgraceful—and counting the tiles in the floor. After an hour, I broke down and fetched a copy of the *New York Times* from the newsstand near the elevator.

At twelve thirty, Dr. Mortonson made his rounds and asked me how my father was doing.

"He hasn't moved since I got here. That was at ten thirty," I said. "How long can he go on like this without a change?"

The doctor consulted a chart, pursing his lips as he read. "No change," he said. "I wish he were making some progress. This has me worried."

Great bedside manner. "Could you be more specific?" I asked.

"If there's no improvement soon, it could mean he's in for a pro-longed coma, perhaps even irreversible. Impossible to say at this point. We don't know the nature or extent of the damage, and until we do, it wouldn't be fair to make a prognosis."

Mortonson picked up his charm and plodded off to cheer some other patient's family. I left the hospital at three, planning to return after Ercolano's memorial service.

The pews creaked under the weight of Columbia's luminaries, from renowned scholars to administrative bigwigs, including Grayson Kirk, president of the university, who could scarcely avoid the service without loss of face. I arrived somewhere near the end of Chalmers's eulogy (*Alas, poor Ruggero, I knew him...*) and took up a position in the back of the nave. The dean of Columbia College made some brief laudatory remarks about a colleague he'd obviously never met. At the close of the service, Chalmers took to the pulpit again to offer some final words.

"We, the faculty and administration of this university, like to think of ourselves as a family. We have come together today to say goodbye to our colleague, our friend, and, yes, our brother. For Ruggero was part of our extended family. And, since his biological family could not be here today, I think it proper that we act as proxy and see the funereal ritual through to its conclusion. I invite you all, therefore, back to Hamilton Hall for a gathering to celebrate Ruggero's life. A buffet will be served." Then came the expected: "Ruggero would have wanted it this way."

I watched the mourners file out of the chapel. Joan Little dabbed her swollen eyes; Bernie Sanger walked on the balls of his feet, his eyes roaming the congregation, self-conscious as if he was being watched; Gualtieri Bruchner, appearing more charcoal than pale-gray this day, left the church with stony, impassive, dull eyes. Students and professors filed by on their way out. Chalmers headed up the aisle with his wife, Helen, on one arm, and an attractive girl of about twenty on the other.

Her hazel eyes, numbed by grief or boredom (it's hard to tell sometimes) caught mine, and I thought I knew her. Her pallid cheeks cracked the tiniest polite smile of recognition, she looked down as if embarrassed, and the three passed. I watched them recede, wondering if the girl could really be Ruth Chalmers, Victor's precocious young daughter. A shapely figure, dressed in black, swept past, leaving a perfumed breeze in her wake: Hildy Jaspers. Then the young man seated in front of me turned and smiled. It was Gigi Lucchesi. His beauty was as extraordinary and unexpected the second time around as it had been the first. He stepped into the aisle and waited to cede me the right of way. I nodded and started for the exit. That's when I noticed Hildy Jaspers stopped at the chapel door. She was gazing back in our direction, surely unaware of me. She smiled with her eyes. It wasn't the aching, self-conscious smile Ruth Chalmers had displayed moments earlier. Even without moving her lips, Hildy managed to flash a naughty, I-know-you-find-me-sexy grin, just with a sparkle of her eyes. I turned to see Gigi's stare fixed on her, and he was smiling. I made my way alone to Hamilton Hall.

Two long tables draped in white linen presented a banquet of modest proportions in the lounge where I'd met Hildy Jaspers and Gigi Lucchesi the day before. The centerpiece of the spread was an overcooked roast, sitting dry on a stainless steel platter. There were Italian macaroni casseroles, some with red sauce, some white, and one green. Heaps of lettuce, tomatoes, and croutons had been tossed in three glass salad bowls. There was poached salmon, bread, and wedges of Parmesan cheese. Someone's desk had been pressed into service as a full bar, complete with red and white wine and a variety of spirits.

Presiding over the drinks was a brawny bartender in a starched shirt—short sleeves—and black tie, one of those ruddy-faced Irishmen with an icy, inscrutable glare and jet-black hair pasted on his head. He looked lonely, so I took pity on him and ordered a double Dewar's on the rocks. He raised an eyebrow, but said nothing. It wasn't his place to comment on a customer's choice of drink, even if it was a small, brown-haired girl of twenty-three doing the boozing. I chatted with him—Sean McDunnough of Bensonhurst—and watched the people arrive.

It was a pitiful gathering. By the time I'd finished my second drink, I counted only eleven people, including the bartender and myself, all from the Italian Department. The faculty and administrators who had made appearances at Saint Paul's Chapel evidently felt relieved of any further obligations to the untenured Ruggero Ercolano.

The roll of the mourners included Chalmers, his wife and daughter, Hildy Jaspers, Gigi Lucchesi, Bernie Sanger, and a tall young man introduced to me as Roger Purdy.

I instantly pegged Purdy for a snot. He stood there slouching, his face screwed into a petulant scowl. He was sweating an oil slick, and I feared his highball glass would slide from his greasy hand and crash to the floor.

"Hello," he said, his voice oozing bother at having to speak to me. "Sorry about your father," he said.

"Do you know him well?" I asked.

"I'm sorry about your father," he repeated. "It wouldn't be proper to say anything more."

"My mother used to say if you can't say something nice about a person, don't say anything at all."

"Mine too," said Purdy, and he migrated to the other side of the room.

"What's his story?" I asked Bernie Sanger, who had just finished chatting with Ruth Chalmers.

"Hates your father," he said, chewing on the roast beef. "Hates me, hates everyone. Hated Ercolano."

"Why does he hate my father?"

Sanger shrugged, swallowed once, then again, clearing the remains of his last mouthful. "You won't believe why."

"Try me."

Sanger smiled. "Your dad gave him a B two years ago, the only B on his transcript. Roger is the worst grade-grubber I've ever seen. Terminal case," and he popped another forkful of food into his mouth.

"Would you say he hates my father more than he hates others?"

Sanger shrugged again. "Probably about the same. He's a miserable sort. Say, Ellie, what are you driving at?" He seemed amused. "You're not thinking that Roger Purdy attacked your father, are you?"

"He's not exactly Gorgeous George, but big enough to do the job," I said, watching him wipe his nose into a moist and crumpled handkerchief.

"I don't see it," said Sanger. "What would he stand to gain by robbing your father? He's the youngest son of Wilbur Purdy, of Purdy and Marchol Adding Machines."

"Really? We've got lots of those at the paper where I work."

"They've made millions on those things," said Sanger, eyeing the heir jealously. "So he has no motive for stealing odds and ends from your dad. It seems pretty clear to me that it was just a run-of-the-mill robbery."

"Not to me," I said, sipping my drink.

Sanger stopped chewing and gaped at me. "What do you mean?"

I looked at him pointedly. "You know, Bernie, I've been waiting for you to ask me about my father's manuscript."

"I beg your pardon."

"Hadn't you expected to get it from my father yesterday?"

"Of course, but I met you yesterday, and I already knew about the attack."

"Don't you want it now?"

"Of course I do," he huffed, putting down his plate to defend himself. "What are you driving at? What's *Daughters of Eve* have to do with this?"

"Did you work on it Friday night?" I asked, avoiding his question for the time being.

"No, we had dinner at a Spanish restaurant over on Perry Street, then I walked him back to his place to get the manuscript."

"Did you see the manuscript, or did you just assume it was there?"

I'd provoked him. Bernie was nervous or guilty or annoyed by my line of questioning. "Just say what you want to say. What's the big deal about the manuscript?"

I drained my glass. "Someone stole it Friday night."

CHAPTER FOUR

The bartender poured Bernie some wine from a fiasco of Chianti. He took the glass and digested the information I'd just fed him.

"Why?" he asked finally. "Why would anyone want to steal a scholarly text?"

"My father once told me a joke about a scholar who calculated the worth of a sheet of writing paper. For the sake of an argument, let's say half a cent."

Bernie nodded, indicating he was following me.

"Write a poem on that same piece of paper, and it loses all its value."

Bernie chuckled.

"The same can be said of scholarly work," I continued. "In a sense, it's worth less than the paper it's printed on."

"Then why would a burglar take it?"

"Because this wasn't just any burglar. I think my father made a formidable enemy of someone in academe."

"What?" Bernie spilled some wine on his white shirt. "Are you saying that someone from the Italian Department—this department— attacked your father and stole his manuscript?"

I shrugged.

"You're saying one of your father's colleagues tried to kill him? Just on the basis of a few missing pages?"

"Four hundred missing pages."

"That's absurd! Do the police share your suspicions?"

I shook my head.

"You can't run around saying things like that," he said in a tense whisper, grabbing me by the arm. "What if someone hears you? They'll think I agree with you. Chalmers would end my career before it gets started. As it is, I don't think he appreciated my talking to his daughter."

I felt a hand on my other arm—a softer grip and a better-looking interlocutor attached.

"Mr. Lucchesi," I said. "Nice to see you again."

"How's your father today, Miss Stone?" The pain in his eyes may have been an act, but in that moment I didn't care. I was just happy he had come to speak to me. Not that I could tell for sure what his motivation was; maybe he was indifferent and didn't want to show it, or maybe he was trying to impress me.

"No change," I said.

"Does Mr. Sanger make you thirsty?" asked Gigi, winking adorably at Bernie. "May I offer you a drink?"

"Now that's a gentleman, Bernie," I said.

"Geez, I would have asked," he said, waved a hand in the air, and walked away.

Then Hildy Jaspers appeared. She was a gin drinker. She confessed that her Achilles's heel was martinis.

"Let's make it a gin-tonic," Gigi said to the bartender. "She has to be careful not to get drunk in front of the profs."

Sean McDunnough mixed the drink, heavy on gin. He watched me as he poured, his red-iron face immobile except when he winked at me.

"So you're a chandelier swinger?" I asked Hildy.

"No," she said, sipping the drink the bartender had handed her, "I'm more likely to say something stupid." She paused. "Or take off all my clothes."

"Eleonora," called a strong voice from behind me. "I thought it was you."

"Professor Saettano," I said, holding out a hand. He had to switch his cane to the left hand to shake. Hildy and Gigi drifted away. Franco Saettano was the doyen of Columbia's Italian Department, a legendary Dante scholar, and the man who had hired my father in 1933. I knew him best of all the Columbia faculty. "How are you?"

He attempted a shrug, which came off more like a quiver. "I'm all right."

"I didn't see you at the service," I said.

Saettano drew some saliva off his lips with a quick swig of air. "I don't like such ceremonies," he said. "Reminds me of my mortality. And I hate listening to Victor Chalmers's oratories. He can't say hello without injecting a pedantic metaphor."

Unlike Bernie Sanger, Franco Saettano didn't have to worry about others overhearing his opinions on the department or its chairman.

"But how is Abraham?" he asked, his voice suddenly soft.

I didn't mind giving him the details; I knew he cared. He said he would try to visit my father in the coming days.

"I live in Riverside Drive," he said. "The Village is far for me."

Professor Saettano eased himself into a chair against the wall, taking the ponderous weight of eighty-six years off his tired legs, and we talked about Ruggero Ercolano.

"He was an able scholar," said Saettano. "Not brilliant, but qualified. A pleasant young man."

"I hear he liked the ladies."

"There was that, yes, but he was good. He'll spend some time among the lustful in purgatory before passing to paradise."

"What about my father?"

Saettano frowned. "Abraham has time still here on Earth. But his sins are of pride, not of the appetites." His eyes smiled gently.

"How are the arrogant punished in Dante?" I asked.

"Of course, there are many arrogant souls in the *Inferno* and *Purgatorio*," he said. "Some are seared by a fiery rain, while others are burdened with heavy stones around their necks. The punishment, you see, is rooted in a kind of divine irony: the horrors of each soul's damnation—or time passed in purgatory, as the case may be—are somehow fit for the sins of the lifetime. For the arrogant, who hold their heads so high in pride, the weighty stones force them to bow before God."

"Stones around their necks?" I asked. "Fitting for a prideful professor named Stone, wouldn't you say?"

Saettano smiled.

"Have you heard a rumor about my father challenging Chalmers for the department chair?"

"Of course," he said. "There was talk. Ruggero approached me to know how I would vote. I said Abraham would have my support if he wanted it. But in the end he decided to leave administration to Victor. For all his faults, he is nevertheless a good administrator."

"Don't you think it strange that Chalmers was the one who found Ercolano's body?"

The old man shrugged.

"After midnight on a Saturday?"

"That is unusual, yes," he said, bouncing his cane lightly on the linoleum floor. "But these things always have an explanation. The tragedy, of course, is that Victor did not arrive sooner."

"Well, the shepherd returns to his flock," said Chalmers, arriving before us. Saettano threw me a glance to make sure I'd caught the metaphor. "I was worried when I didn't see you at the service."

"Worried I was dead?" asked the old man.

The chairman's face dropped for a moment, his eyes flashing terror: Had he been humiliated? But just as quickly, his iceman face broke into a grin, as if he were suddenly in on the joke. Maybe.

"Poor Ruggero," he said, sipping a glass of Moscato.

"I didn't know him," I said. "How is it the radio fell into the bathtub?"

Chalmers shook his head. "Who knows? It's such a waste, dying so young and so pointlessly."

"Eleonora, here, was wondering," said Saettano in his strongest voice, "how it was that you were the one who found Ruggero in the tub."

Chalmers gulped—and it wasn't Moscato—then looked at me. He fidgeted, took a sip from his glass, and looked at me again. "I was in the neighborhood," he said, his eyes avoiding mine. "I often stopped by to see Ruggero. We were close friends as well as colleagues."

Chalmers cleared his throat and excused himself. He crossed the room and joined his wife, daughter, and a new arrival: a handsome young man with a mop of sandy hair. He looked vaguely familiar.

"Who's that with Chalmers?" I asked Saettano.

The old professor leaned on his cane, squinted through the smoke, then sat back. "His son, Billy."

God, how he'd changed, I thought, watching him from my seat. The last time I'd seen Billy Chalmers, he was in short pants running around Morningside Park ten years earlier. Now, about twenty-two, he had grown into a tall, angular kid, easy in his navy blue blazer, button-down shirt, and loafers. He looked like he belonged in a sculling clubhouse on the Schuylkill or trading chuckles at a fraternity mixer at Harvard. His vacant eyes suggested a lofty sense of superiority or perhaps a profound lack of interest.

His sister, Ruth, younger by about two years, was seated next to him. She was fair-skinned, with fine, light-brown hair and hazel eyes. Unlike her brother, she would never be mistaken for a prep. She was apparently a sensitive soul, too, as she seemed more upset than I would have expected.

I noticed Gualtieri Bruchner sitting in a corner by himself, plate balanced daintily on his knees as he broke apart some salmon with his fork. There were no knives. He was drinking water. Roger Purdy approached him in toadying fashion, no doubt to ask him which boot he wanted licked. Bruchner listened patiently, nodding from time to time and posturing as if about to speak, but I don't believe any words ever left his mouth.

Hildy Jaspers returned to join Saettano and me, bending from her standing position to speak to the venerable professor. He got a better view down her blouse than I did. A martini glass teetered in her right hand. She seemed oblivious to Bruchner across the room. Those rumors couldn't be true. Gigi Lucchesi was more her type than the austere professor.

"May I have a word, Miss Stone?" asked Hildy once she'd finished fawning over Saettano.

I nodded yes, and she drew me over to the bar. After ordering another martini, she led me out of the lounge and into the graduate offices down the hall.

"I need to talk to you," she said, leaning close to me. A ringlet of shiny black hair fell over her right eye, and she almost stumbled into me. "It's about Bernie. He's saying dreadful things about me."

"Why tell me?"

She drew back, frowned, then drank some of her gin. "I don't want you to have the wrong idea about me. And I don't want your father to know what Bernie's saying."

"He has other worries right now."

"Don't say that. I'm sure he'll be all right."

Chancing an explosion, I lit a cigarette near her eighty-proof breath. "What is it you don't want him to hear about you?" I asked.

She appropriated my cigarette and turned her back to me. "Bernie said I was seeing Professor Bruchner, among others." Blue smoke enveloped her in the semidark room. I lit myself another one.

"Are you?"

"God, no. He's quite spooky, don't you think? I mean, he's handsome in an intense, existential kind of way, but not my type. Besides, he's as old as Methuselah."

I circled around to look her in the eye as we spoke. "Why do you care if my father hears idle gossip?"

She didn't like me staring at her. "Your father is a well-respected scholar. I'll need his support and recommendation someday. I have my comprehensive exams coming up soon, and I don't need any more strikes against me. Being female is handicap enough. You know what I mean." She looked me up and down, then added: "Attractive female. It's even worse."

(Was that an insult or a compliment?) I told her I thought she had been playing that card to her best advantage. She shrugged indifferently.

"Did you see my father last Friday?" I asked.

Hildy inhaled a mouthful of smoke from the cigarette. "Of course. I ran into him in the office that afternoon."

I shook my head. "Sorry, I meant Friday night. Did you see Bernie Sanger or my father?"

She tapped her ash into a wastebasket next to a desk and shook her head. "I had a date."

"Why did you bring me in here?" I asked. "You don't really care what Bernie's saying, do you? It wouldn't be the first time he's said something."

"You're right about that," she said, stubbing out the cigarette. "He has a crush on me, you know. Ever since he saw me in that play last spring. Don't believe everything he tells you, Ellie. He's a good egg, but ruled by self-interest. And he doesn't want anyone near your father. He was very jealous when I helped your father redecorate his apartment."

"That was you?" I asked, a little alarmed. I didn't like the idea of Hildy Jaspers spending time with my father any more than Bernie did.

"Yes. Do you like the results? Your father was very appreciative."

By the time we returned to the gathering, the "throng" had begun to thin out. Bruchner, Purdy, and Bernie Sanger were gone, leaving Saettano at the mercy of the chairman. Helen Chalmers, eyes crossed somewhere between her nose and Joan Little (with whom she was talking), was struggling to stabilize her listing glass of sherry, some of which was now permanently part of her dress pattern. Ruth Chalmers sat alone near the buffet, staring miserably at a point on the floor. Billy Chalmers was nowhere in sight. Most important to my mind, however, was Gigi Lucchesi, who had vanished without a goodnight.

In company once again, Hildy disappeared from my side, and I wondered if she was afraid to be seen with me. I took another look across the room at Victor Chalmers. Saettano, slumping next to him, appeared to have fallen asleep, but there was another man talking in hushed tones with the chairman. I asked Joan Little who he was.

"That's Professor Petronella," she said. "Anthony Petronella. He was an assistant professor here until last year." Then she lowered her voice: "He was denied tenure, and Professor Ercolano took his place. I think he's teaching high school in the Bronx now."

⌇

A light snow was blowing through the evening air when I climbed out of the subway at Thirteenth Street and Seventh Avenue. I stopped at a gift shop and picked out the last wilted poinsettia left over from the holidays—it was the nearest thing to flowers that they had—before trudging over to Saint Vincent's. I wiped my heels on the bristle mat in the entrance and headed down a linoleum corridor to the bank of elevators. As I waited for a car to arrive, the row of phone booths to the left caught my eye. Of the seven booths, only one was occupied, and hunched over the receiver, speaking with great animation and intensity, was Gigi Lucchesi. The elevator door opened, and Gigi looked up. He signed off and squeezed through the folding door.

"Ellie," he said, joining me at the elevator. "I wanted to see your father, but they wouldn't let me in."

"They have strict rules about visitors."

"Yes, I suppose so."

We stepped inside the car.

"Have you read my father's book?" I asked as we rode the elevator.

"No," he blushed. "I'm a little more modern than Dante, and besides, he doesn't show his works-in-progress to anybody."

"What about Bernie?"

"To Bernie, of course, yes. I think he was helping to edit it. But why do you ask if I've read your father's book?"

"I just wondered if you could tell me what it was about."

Gigi shook his head no, then touched my shoulder to get my attention. He had my attention.

"I realize this is not a good time to ask you this," he began. "You don't have to say yes, but may I wait for you and accompany you home?"

"I was thinking of sticking around for a while," I said, actually considering putting off my visit to take him up on his offer. I tamped down the urge.

The elevator doors slid open. "I can wait for you in the lounge," he said.

"All right," I said. "I'll just be twenty minutes."

A nurse confiscated the poinsettia with a disapproving wag of her head. I took a seat on the aluminum chair beside the bed and watched my father inflate and deflate. I distracted myself from the dreary vigil by observing the various machines dispatch their duties. That bought me about fifteen minutes. A slender, red oxygen tank along the wall beside the bed sprouted a rubber hose. The hose stretched to a bellows mounted on an adjustable stand, and reemerged from the other side, running to my father's face, into his open mouth, and down his throat. That the setup was uncomfortable was obvious; kind of like swallowing a garden hose. The bellows, encased in a glass jar, acted as a surrogate diaphragm, regulating my father's respiration. Each breath seemed precarious to me, and I wondered how such a fragile mechanism could perform so reliably.

I asked the duty nurse for news of my father's condition, but she referred me to Dr. Mortonson, who wasn't there.

"As far as I know, there's nothing to report," she said.

I drew a sigh.

"Your father must be quite a fellow," she told me, as if to cheer me. "So many people wanting to visit."

I cocked my head. "Visitors? Do you know who they were?"

She shook her head. "A couple of men, two boys, and a young lady." She frowned in thought. "Or maybe they visited that other patient. I can't be sure."

"Strange. Did they all come together?"

"No, I would have remembered that. I'm positive there was a lady this afternoon, but I couldn't describe her for the life of me."

"Let's go," I said to Gigi, who was seated, relaxed, legs crossed, in the lounge, flipping through a worn copy of *Reader's Digest*. He looked up and smiled. What was I getting myself into?

It was dark and cold on Thirteenth Street. The wind was whistling across Manhattan from the Hudson, and Gigi took my arm, urging me toward Sixth Avenue. We pushed through the revolving door at 26 Fifth at about eight thirty.

"Evening, Miss Eleonora," said Rodney, eyeing Gigi with suspicion for several seconds before nodding an unfriendly hello.

"I been racking my brain," he said to me once we were in the elevator. "Trying to think of who came into the building that night, and I just can't figure who it could have been."

"Didn't Mrs. Farber have a visitor?" I asked. Gigi leaned a shoulder against the elevator wall and appeared to tune us out. Rodney glanced at him, pursed his lips, then turned back to me.

"No, miss. I know her gentleman, but he didn't stop in that night. Like I told you the other day, I came on duty at six, and nobody suspicious came in. And Mr. Walter—that's Mrs. Farber's gentleman—didn't come in at all, unless it was after two. I would've called up to tell her he was here. We don't allow visitors in without announcing them first."

The elevator eased to a stop on the fifteenth floor, and the door rolled open. Gigi waited for me to step outside first.

"What about the stairs?" I asked Rodney. "Could Mr. Walter have taken the stairs, maybe while you were in the elevator?"

"Not likely," he said. "Walk up fifteen floors? Besides, those doors are locked from the inside. You can't get in without a key, unless you're going down to the air raid shelter in the basement."

Gigi was still waiting for me to move, but I hadn't reconciled Mrs. Farber's story with Rodney's, and that bothered me.

"Mrs. Farber told me she was expecting company that night," I said.

"Probably just imagining things. She's been known to do some strange things."

The elevator buzzed, and Rodney had to go. I watched him as the doors slid closed. He looked at Gigi and frowned his disapproval without realizing it, and I felt the sting of reproof. I was used to it.

Gigi and I made our way down the hall to number 1505. Was I imagining things, or did he seem to know the way already? Before letting him inside, I glanced to my left: 1504, Angela Farber's place. I was about to buzz, when I felt Gigi's hand on my arm, pulling me away.

I shimmied out of my inhibitions when I dropped my coat to the floor in the foyer. My wool dress sparkled with static electricity in the dark, and Gigi kissed me full on the mouth. I left the lights out, finding no free hand to hit the switch, then Gigi proposed a drink.

"I don't usually drink spirits," he said. "Do you have some dessert wine? Moscato or port?"

"I think there's some sherry in the study," I said, somewhat breathless.

"And let's put on some music," he said.

Once in the study, Gigi made for the bar, while I looked for some appropriate music. I didn't want to ruin the mood by accidentally cueing up "Flight of the Bumblebee."

"Rachmaninoff," I thought, as Gigi fiddled with the sherry. "Where's the Rachmaninoff?"

If Rachmaninoff could knead me into a warm mass of putty in this man's hands—and I was sure he could—I was game. My father's burglar had scattered most of the records, but smashed only about twelve by my reckoning. In the low light, I sifted through the disks on the floor, ever more frenetic, as I searched in vain for the *R*s.

Tchaikovsky, Borodin, Chopin . . . Where was Rachmaninoff? Just one piano concerto, I thought, or better still, the Second Symphony. But in the jumble of records, the only *R* I could find was excerpts from Rossini's *William Tell*, or to be more precise, *Guglielmo Tell*.

"Why don't you play a record from the shelf?" asked Gigi.

And there, untouched by the burglar, wedged between Prokofiev and Ravel, was a row of LPs: the complete symphonies, "Vocalise," the four piano concertos, *Vespers* . . . Enough to keep me intoxicated all night long.

But once the music and sherry were flowing, once Gigi had removed my clothing, loving, gentle, deliciously naughty, I caught sight of a pair of my father's reading glasses on the desk. I froze. Folded casually on the blotter, they were catching the lamp's glow and mirroring it in both lenses, like a cat's eyes reflecting light off the retina. I looked away, tried to think of something else, of Gigi's warm breath on my skin, his lips brushing so nimbly over my neck, his hands stroking and caressing my thighs, his torso pinning me against the divan. But it was no good. I could only see the glasses glowing at me.

"Ellie, tell me what's wrong," he whispered.

"Let's get out of this room," I said, and slipped off the divan, out the door, and into my old room across the corridor.

CHAPTER FIVE

At midnight, there was a knocking at the door. I slipped into one of my father's paisley robes and padded out to the foyer to see who was there. Through the peephole, I made out three hunched figures in overcoats. When one of them turned, I recognized Victor Chalmers's needle nose.

"Who is it?" came a whisper from behind me: Gigi, clutching a sheet around his waist to conceal his nudity.

"Chalmers," I said, and he dropped the sheet.

"*Oddio!* Don't let him in!"

I shooed him away, telling him to wait in my bedroom. He took off on a run, and I watched him go, too distracted by the view to worry about the sheet he'd left behind.

"Rather late to be calling," I said to Chalmers after I'd opened the door. His wife, Helen, wrapped in a long fur, stood behind him, and son, Billy, the same patrician expression on his face as at the reception, slouched against the wall in the rear.

"May we come in?" said Chalmers finally. "I hate to intrude at this hour, but I must speak to you about Ercolano."

"It can't wait until tomorrow?"

The professor shook his head, then Mrs. Farber's door popped open a crack. It was one of those sudden noises, not loud but abrupt, and the four of us were startled. Angela Farber peered out tentatively.

"Walter?" she asked. "Oh, Ellie," she said, the disappointment obvious on her face. "I heard voices."

"I'm sorry," said Chalmers, staring at the woman in the doorway. "We must have been too loud."

Her eyes shifted from me to the three figures in the hallway, inspecting each in turn. Victor Chalmers was ever more embarrassed by the scrutiny, his wife stared coolly ahead, ignoring the woman, and Billy yawned.

"Good night, Ellie," said Mrs. Farber. "Good night," she said to the others. Chalmers nodded curtly, and she closed the door.

"Do you know her?" I asked him once we were all inside my father's apartment. Then I noticed the bedsheet and bent over to gather it up. It must have looked strange to my visitors, but they didn't ask.

"She does look familiar," said Chalmers. "But I can't remember where I've seen her, other than this morning when I stopped by. Maybe on a visit to your father. Of course," he said, touching his forehead. "She's been to a couple of lectures at the department. Taking an interest in Italian culture, it seems. Your father introduced us at a symposium. Let's see," he wondered, tapping his chin. "Was it Verga or *I promessi sposi*?"

He really was trying to remember.

"How did you get up here?" I asked, wondering if Mrs. Farber and Victor Chalmers weren't better acquainted than he admitted. "The elevator man is supposed to call."

My guests exchanged looks. "I must have asked for the wrong apartment. The man just let us up," said Chalmers, shrugging his shoulders.

"Who's on duty?" I asked, piling the sheet onto one of the sofas.

Again the shrug. "A middle-aged man. Stocky."

Raul, probably. I let it go for the time being, but I intended to find out.

"Would it be too great an imposition to beg a drink?" asked Chalmers, heading toward the study without waiting for an answer.

Billy, his mother, and I followed him down the hall, a few feet from the bedroom where Gigi was cowering naked. I knew he was still naked, because his clothes were on the floor behind my father's desk where he had shed them a couple of hours earlier. Chalmers made for the liquor cabinet as if mounting a frontal attack, helping himself to a tumbler of vodka and two ice cubes in a trice. I stood by my father's desk and toed a pair of men's briefs out of view. Chalmers had downed half the glass before remembering his manners.

"I'm sorry, Ellie. May I fix you something? You drink Scotch, don't you?"

Helen Chalmers sniffed.

"Nothing for me," I said, lighting a cigarette instead. Still no ashtray, so I used an empty paper clip box. "What about you, Mrs. Chalmers? Billy?"

The young man smiled. "No, thanks."

Helen Chalmers licked her lips without realizing, debating an answer, then asked for a sherry. Victor glared at his wife, but in company held his tongue. Wedging myself between Chalmers and the bar, I reasserted my rights as hostess and poured her a medium-sized glass. No sooner had Chalmers relinquished his claim to the liquor cabinet, than he appeared to have designs on my father's desk. I nearly knocked him over heading him off. His drink sloshed around in his glass, but nothing spilled. I took a seat, Gigi's underclothes safe once again.

Chalmers removed his coat, folded it gently on the arm of the leather sofa, then refilled his vodka. He sat down and invited his wife to do the same. Billy slumped into the adjacent chair.

"What's this all about?" I asked.

"Ruggero Ercolano was not alone the night he died," announced Chalmers *père*. "He was keeping company with a young woman."

"So? Why tell me?"

"Because you asked Franco Saettano, among others, how it was that I discovered Ruggero in the tub after midnight on a weekend." His tone was as accusatory as he dared, given the circumstances; he obviously needed something from me. "I want you to know the truth. He was not alone."

"Are you suggesting there was foul play?" I asked, rocking lightly in my father's chair.

Chalmers shook his head. "Of course not. Ruggero died stupidly, accidentally. But I'm worried about the implications of me being the one who found him. Thanks to you, Ellie, people are wondering what I was doing there."

"Well," I said, "what were you doing there?"

"You must understand, Ellie, that my reputation cannot suffer this scandal. I feel as much a victim as poor Ruggero. I was minding my own business, reading in bed. The phone rang, and someone told me Ruggero was dead in his bathtub, please rush over right away."

"Who phoned you?"

He bowed his head. "I can't say. I gave my word that I would never implicate her in this. She had nothing to do with Ruggero's death; it would be devastating, intensely embarrassing for her. It could ruin her life."

I stubbed out my cigarette. "You're not asking for my help; you want me to keep quiet."

Chalmers drew a sigh and stood to fix himself another drink. Billy just sat there on his chair, penny loafers and argyles crossed over each other at the ankle. I wondered why he and his mother had come.

"You might want to keep the bottle close, Professor Chalmers," I said as he poured, and just as wise as it sounds.

"It was Hildy Jaspers," he said in a low voice, ignoring my remark. "I don't know if you've heard the gossip about her at the department, but she's something of a good-time girl. That's her business, of course, and in these times I don't wish to pass judgment. But it has no bearing on Ruggero's death; that was an accident. She swore to me he was dead when she arrived."

I wondered what to believe. I had no ax to grind with Hildy Jaspers, even if she did seem awfully cozy with Gigi. Still, what she did on her own time was her business.

"Why did she call you?" I asked.

"She naturally turned to a person of authority, integrity, and discretion," he huffed. "Since I knew both her and Ruggero, she figured I was the one to call."

"What do you think, Billy?" I asked, baiting the father. "Does that seem logical to you?"

He shrugged. "Sure, I guess. She was in trouble, so she called him."

"Leave him out of this," said Chalmers. "Billy and Helen came along as a show of support. In the meantime, I would rather you not tell Miss Jaspers that I betrayed her confidence. She's a nice girl, after all. A little too giving of herself perhaps, but a nice girl."

I didn't like swearing to the promises of others. "In essence, Dr. Chalmers, you're asking me to put the whole thing to bed, just on your word."

"Look," he said, eyes steely gray, "I was in Bronxville Friday evening for dinner. Helen and Billy were with me. I only got the call from Miss Jaspers when I was ready to retire for the night."

"I'm not investigating you," I said. "Tell the police, not me."

"What about Miss Jaspers?" he asked. "Are you going to tell her I betrayed her confidence?"

"I can't say I won't ask her if it's true."

Chalmers slapped his glass down on the table. "Go ahead," he sneered. "Tell her you know she's just a randy little slut with the devil under her skirts!" Helen Chalmers choked on her sherry. Billy couldn't quite suppress a naughty smile. "You'll do it to get at me," continued Chalmers. "Because you've always hated me. You and your brother both." He paused for almost thirty seconds, then he picked up his drink. He continued in a softer tone: "So, go ahead and tell Miss Jaspers what you will. I'll stick to my original story if I must. *I* found Ruggero Ercolano in his bathtub."

"All right, then," I said, unwilling to retract my statement, especially if he was giving me the out. "Anything else?"

"Well, there's one more thing," he said. "I'm concerned about Bernard Sanger."

"Why so?"

"I don't trust him," said Chalmers.

"He conspired with Ercolano to make your father chairman," said Helen, and Chalmers threw another wicked look her way.

I remembered Hildy's caution on Bernie Sanger earlier that evening.

"He's a schemer, Ellie," said Chalmers. "Don't trust him."

"And a lecher," injected Helen Chalmers. "He asked Ruth for a date at the reception this evening. Imagine! He soiled Hildy Jaspers. Of course, she's just a tramp. But my Ruth? Never!"

"Don't fall off that high horse, Mrs. Chalmers," I said.

"Of all the nerve! Victor, aren't you going to say anything? I've a good mind to walk out of here right now."

"But then you wouldn't be able to finish your drink," I said, and Billy laughed.

Chalmers took a deep breath and rolled his eyes. "You are on a high horse, Helen," he said. Then to me: "But as for Sanger, I intend to say my piece in his reviews, and what I write will not bode well for his career in academe."

"What about my father?" I asked. "I understand Bernie's quite close to him."

"What of it?"

"I'm no expert, but as long as Bernie Sanger is my father's protégé, he'll get a fair shake."

"That won't be long," muttered Helen Chalmers.

I didn't answer her remark. Her husband, however, wasn't quite so magnanimous. He snatched the glass of sherry from her hand and dashed it into the wet bar sink. Then he turned to me.

"I must apologize for my wife, Ellie. Believe me, we're all hoping Abe makes a full and speedy recovery."

He stared at me for a long moment, then grabbed his coat, and nodded to his family. He'd said his piece. I showed them to the door, where I asked one more question:

"Where's Ruth?"

They paused in the hallway. "She's at home," said Chalmers. "Why do you ask?"

"I didn't have a chance to speak to her this afternoon. I've always liked Ruth."

Chalmers smiled and shook my hand. "Give her a call, Ellie. She'd love to see you. It would do her a world of good."

I waited in the hallway for a couple of minutes, listening to the elevator chain click its way down fifteen floors. Then, confident my visitors had left the building, I buzzed the elevator.

The door opened and Raul peered out. A gregarious, rotund man in his fifties, he had worked the elevator for ten years, always chattering, always smiling. My mother used to warn me never to tell him anything confidential because he was a terrific gossip.

"Those people who just left," I said, "How did they get up here?"

"I brought them," he said, perplexed by my question.

"Why didn't you call me?"

He smiled. "I didn't call you because they were going to 1504."

"Mrs. Farber? But they came to see me."

Raul shrugged his entire torso. "The gentleman asked for 1504. I thought they were going to Mrs. Farber's. I usually work days," he explained. "And I just had a knee operation." He pointed to his left leg. "So I haven't been around for the past three months. I don't know all the people who come at night. But us guys chat before coming on a shift, you know, to pass along messages."

"About Mrs. Farber," I prompted.

"Right. Well, you know that we announce all visitors. So, when I came on duty tonight, Rodney tells me Mrs. Farber is expecting her usual gentleman, and I'm supposed to let him up without calling."

"Mr. Walter?"

"That's the guy," said Raul. He shook his head. "Mrs. Farber called me about an hour ago to say she was expecting company. But since I never seen the guy before, when they asked for her apartment number I assumed they were OK. I thought it was a little strange for three of them to come. And from what Rodney said, I figured this Walter guy to be a little older, but that's not my business. Sorry for the mix-up, Miss Stone. And about your father, too."

"What about Mr. Walter?" I asked. "Did he show up?"

Raul shook his head. "She called me up about ten minutes ago asking if I seen him."

I returned to my father's apartment and found Gigi waiting in the foyer, wearing his shirt and nothing else.

"Where were you?" he asked.

"Just talking to the elevator man," I said. "Chalmers is gone."

"What did he want? Did he know I was here?"

I shook my head. "No. He wanted to talk to me about Ruggero Ercolano. To explain how he had happened to find the body at such an hour."

"And?" he said finally. "What was his explanation?"

"He said someone called him from Ercolano's apartment. A young lady. It seems Chalmers wants to protect this girl's reputation, so he didn't tell the police about her."

Gigi listened, attentive but not overly interested. "Did he tell you who she was?"

I shook my head.

He shrugged. "I guess we'll never know."

$$\partial\!\!\!\supset$$

I felt vaguely guilty about my night with Gigi. He was attractive and eager, and I had no qualms about what he wanted from me, but I couldn't shake the shadow of my father's regard, particularly in his own house. God knows I didn't want to care what he thought of me, but I was still subject to shame when I thought about how undignified the rut of intercourse would seem to him. (Why had I let that enter my mind?) And should I be enjoying so pleasant a pastime while my father hovered near death a few blocks away? The last few days had been a thorny journey for me. Returning home after so long, for the first time since my mother had died; sensing Elijah's presence and absence all about me; seeing my father so fragile, without a voice; and facing the prospect of the rest of my life as the last Stone standing. And then there was my shameful behavior with the shameless Mr. Lucchesi. He was a comfortable diversion, a blur in my head. I had lots to do but felt no drive to get on with it. I was like Ulysses in the thrall of a curly-haired siren. Or an incubus.

WEDNESDAY, JANUARY 27, 1960

The next morning, Wednesday, in the light of day, a palpable discomfiture hung in the air. After our intimacy, covered by the darkness of night, we had to face each other as the virtual strangers we were; we had little to say if we weren't flirting. I covered myself shyly with a robe before slipping into the bathroom to dress.

When I emerged a while later, I had composed myself, and the façade was up again. I smiled at my guest, waved for him to follow me to the kitchen, and asked him how to make a proper pot of Italian coffee, what they call *espresso* in coffeehouses like the Figaro on Bleecker. Once he'd finished his demonstration, as he rinsed out the machine, I took the coffee into my father's study where I planned to have one last look around before asking Nelda to clean up.

My father's collection comprised more than six hundred LPs and 78s, plus about a hundred reel-to-reel tapes. I examined the pile of disks on the floor, separating the shattered from the merely scattered. I matched the undamaged records to their jackets and stacked them on the corner of the desk. Of the broken ones, I collected the identifying labels in a separate pile that I planned to catalogue in case my father wanted to replace them. In case he'd still be around to want to replace them. Then I checked the titles against the orphaned dust jackets, all of which had been torn. It took only a few minutes to figure the damage: four LPs of Mendelssohn's (*Lieder*, *Italian Symphony*, and incidental music to *A Mid-summer Night's Dream*); two Mahlers (symphonies V and IX); Bruch (the violin concerto and *Kol Nidrei*); one Meyerbeer and Bloch (*Poèmes juifs*). Arthur Rubinstein, Gershwin's *Rhapsody in Blue* and *An American in Paris*; and Bruckner's Second Symphony. Thirteen disks by my reckoning, and an eclectic, anachronistic collection to boot. The destroyed records crossed generic boundaries and spanned centuries, in what appeared at first glance to be a random fashion. But what alerted me to a pattern was the destruction of more than one LP by a particular composer. Mendelssohn, Mahler, Bruch, and Gershwin each had been hit at least twice. The burglar hadn't destroyed all of their work, but they were certainly targets.

I circled the room, rethinking every detail with new intensity. The constant traffic through the apartment had disturbed nearly everything, making it impossible to reconstruct the state of the mess the morning after the burglary. Easing myself into the leather sofa, I sipped my coffee and thought hard. I stared at the torn dust covers on my father's desk, searching for an explanation, something to justify the burglar's apparent dislike of the music before me. It didn't take long, and I almost laughed at myself for not having seen it right away.

"What are you doing, Ellie?" asked Gigi from the study door.

"Thinking of changing the locks."

Gigi ducked out a few minutes before I left, asking me to buzz the elevator in five minutes.

"I'll take the stairs," he said.

I asked why.

He blushed. "A girl doesn't want everyone to know she's had a gentleman spend the night."

"You're no gentleman," I smiled.

"Five minutes, OK? I'll listen for the elevator to go up before I sneak out the front door."

I agreed, wondering if this was his routine or some spontaneous inspiration. God, he was beautiful. More than that, he was a kick. And I didn't know what I was doing with him.

CHAPTER SIX

Morning at Saint Vincent's: puffy-eyed attendants, slow starters even in summer, lean on their gurneys and flirt with the nurses. The residents and interns, wearing stethoscopes like badges, scurry up and down the corridors, attending to their urgent cases. The doctors shuffle in later, sipping their coffee, reading their charts, and mumbling directives to the nurses, all without the haste of their juniors. The patients just lie there.

I sensed something was wrong as soon as I reached my father's bed. His breathing was low, almost imperceptible. Yet despite the weakness, he seemed to be struggling for air beneath the breathing tube. I hit the call button and yelled for help. A few seconds later, a thin blonde nurse arrived.

"What is it?" she asked.

"Something's wrong," I said. "Look at him."

The nurse bent over the patient, checking his vital signs, while the respirator bellows continued to pump its usual rhythm. Still, it wasn't right. My eyes darted to the tube snaking from the oxygen tank to the bellows, following it along the floor to its juncture with the glass jar. I could hear air whistling through the respirator, so I knew the problem wasn't there. Maybe the bellows' exit tube—the one stuffed down my father's throat—was blocked or twisted. Starting from his mouth, I felt my way up the tube, and immediately found that it was lying on the floor. The nozzle of the glass jar was uncovered, oxygen hissing from its mouth into the room as the respirator tube lay harmlessly on the white-tiled floor below. The thumb-screw clamp on the nozzle was open wide. I snatched the tube off the floor and stuffed it onto the nozzle. My father's chest inflated immediately.

The nurse, noticing what I was doing, glided around the bed, slipping past the machinery like a nimble pixie. Without a word, she relieved me of the respirator tube, sliding the clamp back over the end of the hose and screwing it tight. When the apparatus was secure, she turned to me.

"What's going on here?" I demanded. "Isn't this the ICU? How about some intensive care?"

The nurse, whose name tag identified her as *R. Tielman*, smoothed her white frock and pursed her lips. "I don't know how this happened, miss, but I'm going to find out. I'll get a doctor," she said as she rushed down the corridor.

The confusion mounted. I became aware of a low, pulsing beat coming from the machine next to the bed. The rhythm bounced, dipped, then sped up and began to flutter wildly in short beeps. An intern arrived at a gallop, Nurse Tielman at his heels, and a second nurse bringing up the rear. The young doctor pushed past me and hunched over my father, checking his pupils, respiration, and pulse rate. He watched the blipping machine for a moment before turning calmly to Nurse Tielman.

"Riley, I need some epinephrine and digoxin. And get me a cardiac needle."

She took off on a run toward the pharmacy, and the doctor addressed the other nurse: "Phyllis, get a crash cart in here, now. And page Dr. Frankel. He should be in Cardiology."

Phyllis, too, disappeared, leaving me with the intern and my father, whose chest was rising and falling violently. He was struggling for his life. I felt powerless, useless, and in the way. Then the fluttering beeps ceased, and a steady, high-pitched tone shrieked from the EKG machine next to the bed. I stared at the paper-strip recorder. The stylus had stopped moving and was leaving a flat line in its wake on the scroll.

"What is it?" I demanded. "What is it? Tell me!"

The intern was massaging my father's chest, over the heart. He didn't turn to look at me. "You shouldn't be here for this," he said, the machine still howling like a siren. "His heart has stopped. Please wait in the lounge, miss. We'll send for you."

Stunned, I wandered out of the ICU and into the waiting room. I felt flushed, not faint, as I dropped into a chair. My eyes blurred, sweat beaded on my brow, and a nauseating watering filled my mouth. There was a ringing in my ears, an echo of the flat line alarm, and everything slowed to an unreal pause.

I deconstructed the events I'd just witnessed. How could the respirator tube have come undone? And when? Then, in horror, I recalled how I had dallied at my father's apartment, enjoying a few extra moments with Gigi before making my way to the hospital. Would five or ten minutes have made a difference? Might I have been there to hear the tube fall to the floor? How much difference might five or ten minutes of oxygen have made to my stricken father? Why was I such a wretch? He was going to die, damn it! And all because I'd wanted Gigi to show me how to make Italian coffee. I hadn't even paid attention to his lesson, captivated instead by the beauty of his face and not even watching his hands.

It seemed I'd been there for hours, though it was only forty-five minutes, when Nurse Tielman, the slim woman who had heard my cries an hour earlier, entered the waiting room. She touched my shoulder to get my attention.

"Your father's heart is beating again," she said. "He's critical, but stabilized for the moment. The doctor had to perform a tracheotomy to facilitate the ventilation. It looks worse than it is. It really is more comfortable for the patient in cases like this."

I breathed, and the ringing in my ears stopped. The world came back into sharp focus, and my heart was racing. I tried to speak, had to clear my throat before any words came out, then asked, "What happened in there?"

"There are three of us at this hour: Phyllis, Charleen, and me," she began. "Phyllis, the girl you saw in there, was treating an emergency on the other end of the ward. Char got a phone call about two hours ago. Really strange. A man mumbled something about her daughter, then hung up. Well, Charleen panicked and thought the guy had taken her daughter. She told Phyllis what had happened and ran home. She's going to catch hell for this."

"And?" I asked, sure I knew the punch line.

"And it turned out to be a prank," said Nurse Tielman with a shrug of her shoulders. "Her kid was in bed sleeping."

Feeling my legs beneath me again, though still flushed and agitated, I set out to find Charleen. The nurses' station was a circular fort that dominated the ICU from the middle of the ward. Inside the ring, as many as ten nurses could sit comfortably at one time. There was a stainless steel coffee percolator, a blood drive sign-up sheet, March of Dimes donation board, and a duty roster with fifteen names and phone numbers. I leaned over the counter and asked for Charleen.

"That's me," said the pretty Negro woman who looked up at me.

"My name is Ellie Stone," I said. "Abraham Stone's daughter."

The nurse blushed. "I'm so sorry, Miss Stone. I feel responsible for what happened, but that phone call . . ."

"I understand. But I was wondering if you could tell me about it."

"It was very spooky," she said. "I had just finished a round of the ward when the phone rang—this one right here," and she indicated the house phone on top of the counter, not the one on the nurses' side. "I picked it up," she continued, "and a man asked for me, then said something about my daughter. I couldn't exactly make it out."

"Did you recognize the voice?"

She shook her head. "It was rather faint, like he had a hand over the mouthpiece."

"Did he say he had her or that he was going to get her?"

"I don't know. It all happened so fast. He just asked for me, said something like 'I know,' or 'I can see your pretty little girl,' then he hung up. I was crazy with fear, Miss Stone."

"Is that her?" I asked, motioning to a curling black-and-white snapshot thumbtacked to a cork bulletin board inside the station. As I looked, I could make out the names on the duty roster next to the photograph.

She nodded. "She's in the seventh grade. Honors student."

"Very pretty. I understand your worry." I straightened up, surveyed the ward from my position then leaned forward again. "You said he asked for you. Did he know your name?"

"Yes. He asked for Nurse Lionel. That's me."

"He didn't say your first name?" She shook her head again. "Do you remember what time he called?"

"I didn't look at my watch, but I started my round at five thirty, and it usually takes me twenty or thirty minutes. I'd say he called at six. Maybe a few minutes before."

I looked at Nurse Lionel's left hand: no ring. "Why didn't you call home to see if your daughter was all right?" I asked.

She was embarrassed by my question and looked away. "Trudy and I—Trudy's my daughter—we live alone, just over in Jersey City. I'm not married."

"Don't you have a telephone?"

She shook her head.

"Do you remember anyone in particular hanging around the waiting room recently? Someone who might have seen the snapshot, maybe read your name tag?"

"There are lots of people trying to get in here," she said. "Our patients are quite ill, and their families and friends figure there may not be another chance to see them before they pass."

"But this is Intensive Care," I said. "Surely you don't let all of these patients have visitors."

"Of course not. But that doesn't keep them away. And between the permitted visitors and the people who wander around the hospital, there's plenty of traffic on this floor. It's a distraction for us, but we try to remember that these people are going through difficult times. We have to be firm but polite."

"Tell me," I said, retrieving a notepad and pencil from my purse, "do you remember any people wanting to see my father?"

"Well enough to give you a description? No. There was a man in his fifties with a young man—maybe his son; and there was another man, older, I think, who was very quiet; and there was a young man with glasses who's been here a few times. There may have been a woman, or a girl, I don't remember. Oh, and there was a very hand-some young man, too. They may have been for Mr. Gelb, whose bed was right next to your father's." She lowered her voice again: "He died last night."

I had some ideas of who might fit Nurse Lionel's descriptions, but what did that prove? In essence, it meant that my father's best and most loyal friends had made themselves suspects by showing their concern for him.

"May I ask a question, Miss Stone? Do you think one of your father's visitors made that phone call?"

I told her I did.

"But I don't know any of those people," she said. "And why would they want to hurt my Trudy?"

"This has nothing to do with you or your daughter," I said, jotting down a couple of numbers in my book. "Whoever called you was trying to get you off the ward for a few minutes."

"But why?"

I flipped my pad shut and slipped it back into my purse. "To murder my father."

Dr. Feldman, the doctor who'd saved my father's life, believed the respirator failure was an accident, that the tubes hadn't been secured properly. The oxygen pumping through the machine could easily have popped the tube off had the clamp been loose, he reasoned. I might have bought the good doctor's theory, had it not been for the mysterious phone call to Charleen Lionel. I figured the caller was my father's burglar. He had probably been hanging around the hospital for the past few days, looking for the opportunity to finish the job he had started in the study. Perhaps my father had seen him and would identify him as soon as he woke up. Or maybe my father never saw him, and the burglar hated him enough to risk a second attempt on his life.

I dialed the Sixth Precinct from the row of telephone booths Gigi Lucchesi had used the night before and asked for Sergeant McKeever.

Thirty minutes later, in the lounge outside the ICU, I was in conference with the quiet, redheaded detective.

"I've spoken with Dr. Mortonson and Dr. Feldman," he said, his eyes fixed somewhere over my right shoulder, "and they're convinced this is merely a case of a loose clamp letting go of an oxygen hose."

"Really?" I asked. "Don't you think a technician performs a couple of checks when he hooks up a patient to one of those machines? Loose clamps on oxygen tubes? That's like launching a Vanguard rocket and forgetting to close the door."

"Well, Miss Stone, that's one way of looking at it, but . . ."

"Did Mortonson tell you about the phone call to Nurse Lionel?" I asked.

McKeever nodded. "Yes, but I don't see how that's related. You see, the caller knew Mrs. Lionel by name and knew she had a daughter. I'd be more inclined to suspect some local pervert. Maybe a neighbor of hers."

"I've been coming here for just a couple of days," I said, "and you'd be surprised what I can tell you about Nurses Lionel, Riley Tielman, and Phyllis Corman."

McKeever cleared his throat and frowned nervously. "For instance?"

"For instance, Riley Tielman lives in Westchester County but occasionally spends the night on the Upper East Side."

"Did she tell you that?"

"No," I said, retrieving the pad from my purse once again. "Her home phone number is (914) UNderhill 5-2091. That's Westchester."

"And the Upper East Side?"

"On Wednesday and Thursday nights, she can be reached at ATwater 4-3591. That's somewhere in the east Seventies or Eighties."

"Well, if she didn't tell you these things, you must have asked someone else. But wouldn't the other nurses remember someone asking for Mrs. Lionel's number?"

"I didn't need to ask anyone. There's a duty roster tacked to the bulletin board in the nurses' station. It lists the names and phone numbers of the nurses who work the various shifts; in case one's sick, they call another on the list. The numbers are in plain view. I got them leaning over the counter as I spoke to Nurse Lionel. And I'd wager whoever disconnected the respirator got Nurse Lionel's name the same way."

"What about her daughter? How would a stranger know she had a daughter?"

"There's a photograph of a pretty little colored girl, also in plain view, near the duty roster. And in the three days I've been coming here, Charleen Lionel is the only colored nurse on the ward."

The police sergeant considered my presentation for a long moment.

"But who would want to kill your father?" he asked finally. "I don't see any motive other than robbery, and your father has nothing to steal here."

"Have you questioned any of his colleagues yet?" I asked.

McKeever looked down. "I didn't think it was necessary, seeing as this looked like a routine burglary."

"Did you know my brother's gravestone was vandalized last Wednesday?" I asked. "Two days before the attack on my father."

McKeever's eyes grew before me. "No, um, I didn't know that," he stammered. "Where did this happen?"

"In Westchester."

"And you believe the two crimes are connected?"

I shrugged. "It's possible. But there's another crime I'd like to ask you about."

Now he looked frightened.

"Sergeant, when a body turns up dead, do the police automatically send a Homicide detective?"

"Not necessarily," he said. "The preliminary fact-gathering may be done by the responding officer or a dispatched detective, but not Homicide unless things look fishy from the start."

"Could you find out for me who investigated the electrocution death of a man named Ruggero Ercolano? It happened last Saturday night."

McKeever seemed put out. "What's this all about, Miss Stone? Are you planning to solve every crime in New York during your stay?"

I had to smile. This diffident man had somehow found some sarcasm buried beneath his timidity.

"No," I said. "Just a case of vandalism on my brother's grave last Wednesday, a curious burglary in my father's house on Friday night, and . . . ," I drew it out for effect, "the *accidental* death of one of his colleagues twenty-four hours later."

The detective swallowed hard. "A colleague? This Ercolano guy?"

I nodded.

McKeever blushed, and I could tell he was stinging. He took a scrap of paper and a gnawed yellow pencil from his coat pocket. "OK, where did he live and how did he spell his name?"

After extracting guarantees that a police guard would stand watch over my father, at least until morning, I left the hospital and boarded an uptown train at Fourteenth Street and Seventh Avenue. It was almost three o'clock when I emerged from the subway on Ninety-Sixth and Broadway and headed west to Riverside Drive.

"Eleonora, come in and tell me what happened," said Saettano. "A heart attack, you say?"

"Something like that," I said.

Saettano helped me off with my black tweed coat and took my purse. I smoothed my hair and skirt in the foyer mirror, then he led me to his den, a quiet room with two armchairs, a sofa, and a magnificent view of the Hudson some ten stories below. He indicated a silver tray on the credenza against the wall.

"Please, help yourself, Eleonora," he said, motioning to the bar across the room. "I know you enjoy your drink."

I would have liked something, but not after that invitation. I moistened my lips with my tongue and declined politely.

Saettano took a seat on the more worn of the brown leather chairs. The late afternoon sun splashed over him, and he closed his eyes as if to absorb the warmth.

"The sun does my bones good," he said.

I sat in the chair next to his and squinted through the brilliant rays of the January afternoon. The old man laid his cane over his lap as if he intended to stay.

"Tell me, Eleonora."

"When I arrived at the hospital this morning," I said, "I found my father's ventilator disconnected. He couldn't breathe, and his heart stopped just after I reattached it."

Saettano mumbled something in Italian to himself. "Perhaps it was an accident?"

"The air tube had been pulled out of the ventilator. It was no accident."

"Who would do such a thing? It's monstrous."

"I don't know," I said. "But the burglary struck me as false from the start. I asked myself, why the random destruction of so many record albums? Why was the manuscript taken? How did the burglar get into the apartment? There was no sign of forced entry or struggle. And, if the thief had truly been after valuables, wouldn't he have taken my father's billfold or searched the bedroom? Any self-respecting burglar would have looked for jewelry, unless he knew there was no woman of the house."

Saettano listened patiently. I watched him watching me, his face effulgently orange in the sun, his eyes nearly transparent except for the whitish fog of cataracts. I continued:

"My father must have known the burglar. Or, rather, the burglar knew my father."

"How can you be sure?"

"I wasn't until this morning. It was just a vague doubt in the back of my mind. But then I sifted through the broken records, and the music finally clued me in. I separated the destroyed records from the ones merely thrown about the room. Let me run the names past you and see if you come to the same conclusion as I did."

Saettano nodded.

"Gustav Mahler," I began. "Felix Mendelssohn, Ernest Bloch, Max Bruch, Meyerbeer, Gershwin, Rubinstein, Bruckner . . ."

"No other records were destroyed? Just these?"

I nodded.

The old man turned to face the window. He tapped his forehead a few times with the bony fingers of his right hand. Then he cleared his throat to speak.

"*Dunque*," he said in Italian, his brow furrowed, "indeed, there appears to be a pattern. But one of those names spoils the pudding, as you say in English."

I knew what he said had something to do with the proverb about proof and the eating of the pudding, but to straighten it out would have distracted me from his point.

"All of the composers you named are Jewish," he announced. "Except one, or two, actually: Anton Bruckner and Max Bruch. And of course Mendelssohn practiced Christianity, but if what you're driving at is anti-Semitism, I suppose your burglar would consider him as Jewish as David Ben-Gurion."

Swayed by the preponderance of evidence, I had assumed that Bruckner, who'd lost a 78 and an LP in the pogrom, was a Jew. Now, my theory seemed flawed. Still, the others were all Jews, Mendelssohn's baptism notwithstanding.

"Your theory is an interesting one, Eleonora," said the old man. "After all, if you mistook Bruckner for a Jew, then perhaps a burglar as cultured as you could have made the same mistake. In the main, your instincts are on target. Bruch was not a Jew himself, but his *Kol Nidrei* and Bloch's *Poèmes juifs* are distinctly Jewish themes. Mahler was reviled by Nazi propagandists—and even Hitler himself—as a decadent Jewish composer. Rubinstein and Gershwin are easily recognizable as Jews by their famous names. And Meyerbeer, whose real name was Jakob Liebmann Beer, was obviously Jewish."

We both considered the idea in silence.

Saettano nodded finally and said: "Yes, I accept your conclusion, Eleonora, even if we must assume imperfection in the burglar's research. But what does it mean? How does this illuminate the crime?"

"I've been thinking about that," I said. "My mother's jewels and my father's cash were never part of the burglar's plan. And if greed wasn't the motivation, then violence was. My father knew his attacker, I'm sure of that now. Whoever attacked him knows he is Jewish and, obviously, hates him for it. This wasn't a real robbery. The burglar was after my father and his manuscript. The knickknacks he stole were a smokescreen to make it look like a robbery gone wrong. I think the burglary and the vandalism of my brother's grave were the work of one person."

"Then your father is still in danger. What can you do to protect him?"

"The police are watching him tonight, and I've already arranged for a guard for tomorrow."

Saettano nodded. "Good. Then what is your next move?"

"Actually, I'd like to pick your brain, if I may."

The old man smiled. "I don't see how I can help you, Eleonora."

"Tell me about Dante," I said.

At six, Professor Saettano and I sat down at either end of the eight-foot oak table in his dining room. Libby, the professor's companion, served the dinner and took a place next to him on the corner. I felt isolated on my far end. Saettano's diet permitted only lighter fare, so we began with a consommé and an Orvieto Classico; he was born in Umbria and had retained a nostalgia for its grapes.

"The *Commedia* is the perfect poem," announced my host, leaning to one side to see me around a centerpiece of dried flowers. "By perfect, I mean total, complete, circular. Dante Alighieri achieved a rare union: perfection of poetic form and theological doctrine. The very structure of the poem is part of its mystical mission." He sipped some soup, wiped his lips with the linen napkin tied around his neck, and strained to see me again. I tried to meet him halfway. "I'm sure you are familiar with the basic tenets of Christian dogma: from a condition of universal sin, we gain salvation or fall into eternal perdition. A kind of morality play with high stakes. Dante understood this, as the word *commedia*, or 'play,' indicates.

"In brief, the story is that of the poet who has lost the right way and finds himself in a dark wood. A slave to his fear, he is set upon by wild beasts: an allegorical crisis of faith. The spirit of the poet Virgil, summoned by a divine lady—Beatrice—comes to him and leads him on a journey of redemption through the horrors of hell and the sufferings of Mount Purgatory. Then Beatrice guides him through the empyrean of paradise to the very sight of God."

At Libby's urging, the professor interrupted his lecture to eat his cooling consommé. I watched her surreptitiously as we spooned our soup in silence. She was a short, vigorous woman of about sixty. I found her face to be stiff, at times stubborn, but never severe. Her gray hair, cut short for maximum ease of care, was pushed behind her ears. She wore a plain housedress and no jewelry.

"You're such a sloppy eater, Franco," she scolded softly, daubing his chin with her own napkin.

The old man said nothing, submitting meekly to his companion's authority. Then Libby cleared the bowls and disappeared into the kitchen.

"The *Commedia*," said Saettano, resuming his lesson, "is divided into three canticles: the *Inferno*, *Purgatorio*, and *Paradiso*, each counting thirty-three *canti*. The first *canto* of the *Inferno* is considered an introduction and makes the total perfect: one hundred *canti* in all. The rhyme scheme is *terza rima*, an intricate verse pattern in threes. Three is, of course, the number of canticles in the poem and of the Holy Trinity. Within this perfect structure, Dante built the perfect universe, from hell to the heavens."

Libby pushed through the door from the kitchen, bearing three steaming plates of spaghetti prepared with oil and garlic. Just another ascetic meal for the aging professor's delicate constitution: tasty, but not very substantial.

"What about punishment in the *Comedy*?" I asked.

"I was getting to that," he said, chewing a forkful of pasta Libby had chopped down to size for him. "As I told you yesterday at the reception for Ruggero, the *contrapasso* is a metaphysical *quid pro quo* of sin, judgment, and punishment. Souls condemned to hell are judged when they arrive. They are hurled into one of the nine circles of the abyss, and there they must suffer for all eternity, until judgment day. Each circle punishes a different category of sin, which is divided into three major types: sins of the leopard, sins of the lion, and sins of the wolf. These represent incontinence or lust, violence, and treachery."

"And violence is the most severe?" I asked.

"No!" he said, almost shouting. Then, remembering he was not in class, he took a friendlier tone. "Treachery is the most severe class of evil. Lust is an appetite, the lowest order in the rank of mortal sins. Violence falls in the middle. It is a physical offense. Treachery is a sin of the intellect. It includes all transgressions of reason and the mind, from treason to blasphemy."

"So, Judas Iscariot, say, would be in hot water in the *Inferno*?"

Saettano chuckled and looked to his consort, who shared his amusement. "You are confused by the ignorant stereotypes of hell, Eleonora," he said, not exactly flattering me. (First the remark about my drinking and now this.) "Dante's *Inferno* is not a furnace throughout. Contrary to popular imagery of hell, in Dante, its lowest circle is a frozen lake."

I blushed as I twirled the spaghetti around my fork.

"But you are right: Judas can be found in the very pit of hell, stuffed into one of Satan's three mouths. He is there with Brutus and Cassius, who betrayed Julius Caesar."

"What about the violent?" I asked.

"They are punished in a variety of ways. Some are cooked in a river of boiling blood. Others are burned by a fiery rain on an arid plain of the Inferno. The topography of hell is remarkably diverse."

"And the . . . incontinent?" (I was trying to be mature about it, but that word wasn't cooperating.)

"Again, it varies. There are many sins that fall into the category of incontinence. Lust, gluttony, avarice, and so on. Each punishment has its own penal logic. A famous episode from the *Inferno* tells of a pair of adulterous lovers, Paolo and Francesca, who are whipped about mercilessly by a thrashing wind."

I paused a moment to reflect on where I might land in hell: surely among the lustful. If so, I could count on running into a few people I have known. With all respect to the Florentine poet, I didn't buy a word of it.

Saettano was permitted two forkfuls of the final course of the meal: a grilled scallop of veal with a squeeze of lemon.

"You will not find me among the gluttons of hell," he said, chewing on his pittance. "I am assured eventual salvation, as I am already in purgatory here on Earth," and he smiled. I wasn't quite sure I got his joke, but I chuckled nevertheless.

We had coffee in the den. The sun had long since set, and the view from Saettano's window was the rippled reflection of a half moon in the Hudson and the illuminated skyline on the Jersey side. The room was dark except for the fire Libby had built in the fireplace. The red and yellow flames splashed light over us, and the old man seemed to draw the same strength from their heat as he had from the sun that afternoon. The three of us sat silently for several minutes before Saettano spoke.

"Why have you asked me these questions about the *Commedia*?" he said, turning his face from the fire's glow to look at me.

I shrugged. "Maybe it's my way of getting closer to my father. Dante is his life's work, and I know so little about it. I think I avoided it just because of him."

"Let us hope it is not too late," he said.

It was about nine when I put shoulder to glass and pushed through the revolving door of 26 Fifth Avenue. Rodney was sitting stiffly in his usual chair, but he was not alone. Across the lobby, sinking into one of the upholstered armchairs, Detective-Sergeant Jimmo McKeever looked like a half-folded convertible top. He rose from the chair, and the creased overcoat on his lap dropped to the floor. The little man bent over and furled it in like a sail.

"Please excuse the interruption, Miss Stone," he said, holding out a moist hand. "I was wondering if you had a few minutes. It's rather important."

"Of course. Please come up."

Rodney ferried us to the fifteenth floor, and I let McKeever into my father's apartment. His mood was troubled.

"Couple of things," he began. "I drove up to Westchester and checked out the cemetery."

"And?"

"I think it's unrelated to the attack on your father."

I stared him down, making obvious my disagreement. He sweated under my gaze then offered that there was no evidence to connect the two crimes, that there was little evidence period at the gravesite.

"I've also been looking into the Ercolano case," he said once we were seated in the study. "Did you know him?"

I shook my head. "I know some of my father's colleagues, but he was new to the department."

McKeever rubbed his pinkish eyes with the palms of his hands. "Detective Kinlaw from the Twentieth filled me in on the details of the case. Looks like a simple bathing accident, but who knows? He recommended that finding, pending the coroner's report. Everything was in order, everything according to Hoyle, so he wanted to drop the whole thing."

"And you?" I asked.

The cop drew a long sigh. "I think Ercolano was your burglar."

CHAPTER SEVEN

"I led a second search of Ercolano's apartment on Eighty-Seventh Street this afternoon," said McKeever as we sped up Tenth Avenue, then Amsterdam, in the backseat of a squad car. "We dusted for prints and asked the neighbors if they had heard or seen anything that night."

"Had they?"

McKeever looked out the window at the passing streets as we negotiated the trivium at Seventy-First. "A fuse blew, but nothing else that night. And it seems this Ercolano fellow was quite the ladies' man. The old widow next door says he had a parade of young lovelies filing in and out of his apartment at all hours. Thinks it's too bad what happened, but at least she won't have to listen to the bed banging against the wall every night."

He blushed and excused himself for his bad manners.

"Any descriptions of his regular visitors?"

"We've got some leads, no names yet."

The patrol car streaked past Eighty-Seventh Street without slowing down. I cranked my head around to watch the street sign recede.

"We're not going to Ercolano's place," said McKeever dryly. "I want you to have a look at something up at Columbia."

The campus was still in the cold January night. Having lived at home during my undergraduate years, I had never known the feeling of enclosure that clung to me now. Hamilton Hall was dark. McKeever nodded to the watchman waiting outside, who let us in and switched on the foyer light.

We rode the elevator to the sixth floor and the Italian Department, where McKeever led us to number 605: Ruggero Ercolano's office.

"Do you recognize any of this?" he asked, sliding open a desk drawer to reveal a potpourri of writing instruments, ink cartridges, and scattered papers.

I nudged a pair of gold pens in the drawer, turning them over to see better.

"I know these," I said. "My grandfather gave them to my father fifty years ago. He was a musician. And that strongbox in the back looks familiar. Have you opened it?"

McKeever nodded. "I'm pretty certain it belongs to your father. We found some money and silver things, but nothing with his name on it. We've dusted everything for prints, and we'll have the results tomorrow."

I sat down in the swivel chair behind Ercolano's desk and surveyed the scene, rocking lightly. The office was organized in a functionally efficient manner; not obsessive, just neat, logical piles of papers, books, and an Olympia typewriter. I glanced at the black telephone on his desk—extension 339—leafed through a library book on Byron, then looked up at the shelving against the wall. The spines of the books, lined up in straight rows, bore names like Manzoni, Verga, and Foscolo. Luminaries in the Italian canon, perhaps, but to my ignorant and Anglocentric mind, they were more obscure than Jude.

The other drawers of Ercolano's desk were empty except for some interoffice envelopes and a couple of writing pads.

"Anything in his papers?" I asked.

McKeever shrugged. "Memos, notes, some kind of book in progress. We're not finished going over it all yet, and it's all in Italian."

"What about his apartment? Does anything there match the articles stolen from my father's place?"

The detective shook his head. "But we can have another look."

"I'd like to browse through some files here first," I said. "The confidential personnel files in the locked cabinet behind Miss Little's desk."

McKeever gaped. "Well, all right. I don't see the harm."

We popped open the filing cabinet with little trouble—McKeever knew a few tricks—and dug in. The cop stood to one side as I pulled several files: Stone, Ercolano, Chalmers, Bruchner, Sanger, Purdy, Petronella, Jaspers, and Lucchesi.

Starting with my father's, I found a curriculum vitae; tax and payroll information; memos from the chancellor and president pertaining to awards, salary raises, and general administrative details. One interesting item chronicled Chalmers's attempt in 1952 to impose a loyalty oath among the department faculty. It was the height of the Red Scare, and Columbia's administration took a strong anti-Communist position. My father and Franco Saettano refused to sign, and Chalmers ended up as the only signatory.

I closed the folder and moved on to Ruggero Ercolano, a graduate of the *Università di Bologna*, with a PhD from Johns Hopkins. He was on a tenure track, due for review in the spring of 1962. The information was thin, and about all I could gather was his American Social Security number, visa, and vital statistics. There were some letters of recommendation written on his behalf, all laudatory—at least the ones in English were. I found a photostatic copy of the first page of his passport and visa stamp. A photograph of the late professor stared up at me from the grainy black copy, his jaw thrust upward and to the side in a pompous philosophical pose. Ercolano was born in 1926 in Parma and had been living in Bologna when his passport was issued.

Victor Chalmers, according to his CV, was born in 1907 in Baltimore, graduated Choate and Dartmouth before earning his doctorate in 1935 at the University of Chicago. He was hired by Cabrini College outside Philadelphia immediately thereafter, and came to Columbia in 1943 after a three-year stint at Georgetown. He was 4-F during the war. The file didn't say why.

Gualtieri Bruchner: visiting professor from the University of Padua. He was a specialist in twentieth-century Italian literary and cultural movements, from Futurism to Cubism to Neorealism. He came highly recommended, according to a letter from Professor Arturo Marescialli, an old acquaintance of my father's. Bruchner was born in

1908 at Merano in the Alto Adige region of northern Italy. He, for one, hadn't spent the war teaching grammar on the Main Line. A brief biographical sketch explained: A Jew, Bruchner was deported in January 1944 to Auschwitz. He was liberated from the camp on January 27, 1945 (fifteen years ago to the day) by the Red Army, then he spent another year in a displaced-persons camp in Germany before finally returning to Milan in June 1946. He pursued studies in classics and Italian literature at Turin from 1947 to 1953, rather late in life, but he gets a free pass in my book. Working full-time as an upholsterer in the FIAT automobile plant, Bruchner supported himself through six tough years while completing his degree. A virtual autodidact, the gray man had risen above prejudice, genocide, and the alienation of modern times to make something of himself. No wonder they had invited him to Columbia, even if for one year only.

Bernard B. Sanger, born 1934 in Coney Island, Brooklyn, had come to study Italian literature at Columbia after a stellar undergraduate career at City College. According to a letter attached to his original application for admission, he had wanted to study Dante at Columbia since reading my father's *Dante at the Edge of the City of Dis* for an undergraduate seminar on world literature classics. I found Bernie's letter pandering, but how can you gauge sincerity on a typewritten page? Under my father's tutelage, Bernie had distinguished himself among the other graduate students from the start, and, judging by the comments in his file, he was following the straight and narrow to a distinguished academic career.

Roger Purdy hailed from Greenwich, Connecticut, though I doubted he had spent much time there growing up. His CV told of seven years at Hotchkiss and four at Yale before coming to Columbia. His test scores were nearly perfect, and his outside references impeccable. I found a copy of an official transcript from May 1959, stapled to a stack of mimeographed letters. Circled in red ink on the transcript was a B for a course from the spring semester of 1959 titled *Divine Comedy*. My father's name appeared at the far right as the instructor. The attached correspondence began with a formal letter of protest from

Purdy, complaining to Chalmers of the unfair mark. There followed the chairman's response to Purdy and a brief note of inquiry to my father, who answered in a terse memo that Purdy had earned a B, no more, no less, and the grade would stand. The polemic continued with a letter from Purdy to the dean, the dean to Purdy, then to Chalmers, who in turn answered the dean. Purdy's father got into the act later, offering to make a generous donation of $2,000 to the university, ostensibly with no strings attached. My father was urged in subsequent letters to reconsider the grade. He did, offering to reduce it to a B-minus in light of an unattributed quotation he'd discovered in the course of his subsequent review of Mr. Purdy's final paper. The grade remained a B, and Chester Purdy withdrew his offer with no explanation.

Anthony Petronella served as assistant professor of Italian from September 1954 to May 1958, when he was denied tenure and asked to move on. A copy of Petronella's departmental review showed Professors Saettano and Stone opposed to Petronella's tenure. Chalmers had voted no as well, though he voiced no strong reasons. My father's argument against centered on Petronella's limited achievements within the narrow interests of his scholarship: eighteenth-century poets.

Hildy Jaspers, twenty-five years old, had graduated from Rosemont College on the Main Line outside Philadelphia. Her recommendations and academic honors painted a picture of a free-spirited intellectual, the brightest girl in class. On the personal side, however, a sister from Rosemont cautioned the department on Miss Jaspers's sometimes-wayward comportment, especially with members of the opposite sex. The faculty's evaluation of her application did not seem to consider the sister's alarm germane to Miss Jaspers's academic potential. Her grades at Columbia were excellent, though her dossier contained none of the high praise and promise of a Bernard Sanger, or the ugly grade war waged by Roger Purdy. In fact, there were no opinions anywhere in her file (besides the good sister's) on Hildy's human or personal side. I pictured the faculty meetings: four dour professors discussing the new crop of graduate students. Good work, yes, quite satisfactory, keen mind, excellent promise. But none was so bold as to be the first to volunteer an opinion on Miss Jaspers's shapely figure, coquettish behavior, or racy reputation.

Then came Luigi Lucchesi. I noted his birthday: June 21, 1933. A very young lecturer indeed. His file was nearly empty besides a CV, a few recommendations in Italian, and some reviews of his syllabus and teaching performance. All was satisfactory, except for a note by Victor Chalmers about Mr. Lucchesi's effect on some of the Barnard undergraduates. It seems his course on Galileo and the history of science was one of the most popular offerings in the fall of 1959 schedule.

As I replaced the files, I discovered another manila folder tabbed, *Minutes/Dept. Meetings.* Inside were typewritten sheets, one for each meeting, dating back about ten years. The department faculty met two times per semester, taking up business ranging from budgetary planning, to disciplinary action, to fellowship appointments. I consulted the minutes from the most recent meetings, which were dominated by the great Purdy grade scandal.

From December 14, 1959:

> *Professor Chalmers, citing Chester Purdy's proposed donation of $2,000, again urged Professor Stone to reconsider the change in grade, if only for the greater good of the university. Professor Stone refused, claiming academic integrity and independence, and demanded even-handed treatment for all students, not just sons of wealthy donors to the university.*

But there was also a mention of the Gigi Lucchesi issue:

> *Professor Stone raised new business, concerning a rumor he had heard about a Barnard undergraduate and lecturer Luigi Lucchesi. He wished to know why the incident had not been discussed officially in the last faculty meeting. Professor Chalmers insisted that it was a case of unrequited infatuation on the part of the girl, and that Mr. Lucchesi was blameless. Professor Stone was adamant that it be introduced into Mr. Lucchesi's record. Professor Chalmers offered to take up the issue at*

the next meeting to be held at the end of January 1960 after the holiday
break. Professor Ercolano was assigned to conduct an interview with
Mr. Lucchesi in preparation for the meeting.

From September 22, 1959:

After calling the meeting to order, Professor Chalmers introduced the
first agenda item: the continuing debate over Mr. Purdy's grade from
Professor Stone's Divine Comedy *course. Professor Stone refused to con-*
sider the question further, and the convened passed to new business.

Professor Saettano inquired about the status of Assistant Professor
Petronella's grievance against the department. Professor Chalmers
reported that the University Tenure Review Committee was studying
the matter, but that the chair of that committee had informed him pri-
vately that Professor Petronella's case was weak.

Re: the allocation of the $100 Ettore Romilda-Buondì fellow-
ship, nominations were submitted by each faculty member: Professor
Chalmers named Hildy Jaspers; Professor Saettano, his dissertation
student, Thomas Deane; Professor Stone submitted Bernard Sanger;
Professor Ercolano seconded Professor Chalmers's nomination; and
Professor Bruchner, as visiting faculty, had no vote. It was agreed that
the nominators would prepare written letters of support for their respec-
tive candidates, and that the departmental recommendation would be
decided at the next faculty meeting before being forwarded to the dean
for approval.

I flipped back to November 22, 1957:

Professor Chalmers called the meeting to order at 9:02 a.m. with Profes-
sors Saettano, Petronella, and Stone in attendance. Professor Chalmers
introduced the case of Miss Jaspers's Latin exam, which the depart-
ment had judged unsatisfactory at the February meeting. Professor
Stone repeated his insistence that Miss Jaspers retake the exam after
proper preparation. Professor Chalmers suggested that the department

*grant a pass on the condition that Miss Jaspers audit an undergraduate
Latin course. Professor Petronella seconded the motion. Professor Stone
voiced strong disagreement. Professor Saettano then proposed that
Miss Jaspers work with Professor Stone to prepare for a shorter Latin
exam, concentrating on the problem areas. The motion passed three to
one, with Professor Petronella dissenting. After the tally was recorded,
Professor Petronella changed his vote to create unanimity. The meeting
adjourned at 10:12 a.m.*

From February 6, 1958:

*Professors Chalmers, Saettano, and Stone were in attendance when
the meeting was called to order at 10:00 a.m. Professor Petronella did
not participate, as the sole item on the agenda was the discussion of his
tenure case. Professor Chalmers called for a preliminary, nonbinding
vote to be followed by discussion and a final, official vote. As the tally
was three against and none for, the convened forewent a second vote and
passed to the assignment of the final report. Professor Saettano asked
that he be excused from the duty of writing the official departmental
report. Professor Stone, citing his antagonistic dealings with the candidate, asked that he, too, be excused. Professor Chalmers nominated
himself and was approved unanimously to prepare the final report for
the University Committee on Tenure Review. Each of the attending
faculty was asked to submit a brief report to Professor Chalmers, out-
lining the major objections to the candidate's tenure. The meeting
adjourned at 10:12 a.m.*

Twelve minutes to give Anthony Petronella the thumbs-down.
When your senior colleagues blackball you unanimously in less time
than it takes to sing all the verses of "The Star-Spangled Banner," you
might get a little angry. It's an eviction, a rejection that transcends the
professional and comments, in essence, on your personal worth. The
rage must fester until you hate the elitist fools who gave you the air;
told the world you weren't good enough to play on their team. It must

be enough to make you gnaw on your hands and tear at your hair. Enough to kill?

But Petronella should not have known how the individual faculty members voted, as the process is supposed to be confidential.

"I think we should go if we want to have a look at Ercolano's place," said McKeever. "It's going on eleven thirty."

Jimmo McKeever was a funny little man. Normally, his timidity throbbed like a hammered thumb. But now he seemed different, more confident, as though an investigation was tonic for his nerves.

"Not the lap of luxury," said the detective, punching the light switch in Ercolano's apartment. "It's one bedroom, sitting room, and kitchen."

"And let's not forget the bathroom," I added, pulling off my coat and folding it over a chair near the door. "Is there anything I shouldn't touch?"

"No, we've been through here twice," said McKeever.

I strolled around the tidy flat, browsing through the late professor's belongings. The apartment was mostly empty; understandable given his short time at Columbia. The furnishings, a little worn but clean, had probably come with the apartment. A newish, twelve-inch Silvertone television set sat on an aluminum rolling cart against one wall, a bookcase filled with pulp mysteries and assorted American classics in paperback format leaned against the other. Probably part of the furnishings; not Ercolano's taste, I bet. Against a third wall, I saw a hi-fi on a cabinet. I knew where to find the radio.

The kitchen cupboards held odd pieces of unadorned tableware, adding up to perhaps three full settings. In the refrigerator, there were several bottles of some Italian wine called Gavi di Gavi, some veal wrapped in waxed paper, a jar of black olives, some Italian ham, a variety of vegetables, and varicolored condiments. Ercolano, it seemed, was a slave to appetites other than concupiscence.

The bedroom was as Spartan as a monk's cell: double bed and nightstand with lamp, copies of the *New Yorker* and the *Paris Review*, and a wind-up alarm clock.

I stepped into the bathroom, McKeever in tow, almost expecting to find Marat slumped over in the tub. The white tiles were clean beneath my feet, and I sensed the grit of scouring powder against the soles of my shoes. At arm's length from the bathtub and toilet was a magazine stand, filled with recent issues of news and cultural publications. The flat wooden top was bare. I nudged the stand with my foot, exposing an electrical outlet on the wall behind it.

"Is this where the radio was?" I asked, pointing to the magazine stand.

McKeever was staring at my legs. Then he remembered himself. "Yes, that's correct. You can see that it just reaches up to tub level. The radio could easily have fallen in."

"Provided something knocked it in," I said crouching, knees carefully tucked together, to gauge the level of the stand and the lip of the tub.

"What do you mean?"

"Well, Ercolano would have had to sweep the radio into the water," I said, standing up again. "If the magazine rack had been taller, he might have elbowed it accidentally, making it rock a little, and the radio could have fallen in that way. But given the height of this thing, an elbow might have knocked the radio off onto the floor, but not back into the tub."

"What exactly are you implying, Miss Stone?" McKeever had turned white.

I stood up, reached out to the rack, and jostled it. It stood squarely on its four balanced legs.

"This isn't a rickety old thing," I said. "It's sturdy, not likely to pitch a radio at the slightest bump."

"You're saying someone tossed it into the water, aren't you?" said the detective, his voice rising. "Do you see foul play in everything?"

"Whenever two and two don't add up to four."

"But why? There's no reason to doubt an accident here."

"Was the radio plugged into that outlet?" I asked, pointing behind the stand.

McKeever nodded. "Yes."

"I think not," I said. "A radio falling into water should blow a fuse, right?"

"That's right. We're reasonably certain of the time of death; several tenants said the lights went out at about ten thirty Saturday night. The super replaced the fuse five minutes later, and everyone went about their business. But what makes you think it wasn't plugged in here? That's where we found it."

"If the radio knocked out the fuse, it probably scorched the outlet where it was plugged in," I said. "Just out of curiosity, let's have a look around."

"All right," said McKeever, following me out into the corridor.

About five feet down the hall, behind an armchair, I discovered another outlet. I bent over to examine the electrical plate, whose white paint was smudged black around the prong slots.

"You found the radio plugged into the outlet in the bathroom?" I asked, standing up again.

McKeever nodded. "That's what the police report said. And the cord was only four, maybe five feet long."

I leaned around the corner to look back into the bathroom and estimated the magazine rack was about twelve feet from the outlet in the hallway.

McKeever glanced at me anxiously. "What is it?" he asked. "What are you thinking?"

"I think the radio was plugged into this outlet with an extension cord while Ercolano was in the bath," I said.

"What?"

"Then the murderer walked down the hall and tossed it into the tub."

"What? Murderer? What are you saying? The radio was plugged into the bathroom socket."

"Once the fuse blew, the murderer disconnected the extension cord and plugged the radio into the wall in the bathroom. Not too complicated."

"You see conspiracy in everything," said McKeever, shaking his head.

"I think I'm right. The black smudge on the hallway socket might be from an earlier short. Or maybe the blown fuse didn't scorch the bathroom outlet. Maybe. But then I have to ask myself: If Ercolano wanted to listen to music in the tub, why didn't he just turn up the hi-fi? It's just a couple of feet outside the bathroom door."

I crossed the room and took a seat on Ercolano's couch. McKeever remained standing, too shy to move my coat from the chair or to sit down next to me.

"You found nothing here belonging to my father?" I asked as I fished a cigarette from my purse.

McKeever dashed to my side to give me a light. He tossed his match into an aluminum ashtray on the end table next to the couch. If Ercolano had stolen the crystal ashtray from my father's study, he wasn't using it in his parlor.

"Do you know if Ercolano had a cleaning woman?" I asked.

"I'm not sure. His neighbors didn't mention it."

"It seems he was a neat fellow, to be sure," I said. "But this place is too clean for a single man without any help. I'd be interested to know who scrubs his floors and stocks his refrigerator."

McKeever patted his coat pockets, locating a scrap of paper after a few moments. He scribbled some notes and stuffed the paper back into the folds of his garment.

"Let's go talk to Mrs. Arnsberger," he said. "She's the widow next door who complained about the women."

"At this hour?"

"She said I could call anytime. Insomnia."

Tillie Arnsberger unlocked, unbarred, and unchained for nearly a minute before finally opening up her apartment door. Recognizing McKeever, she jumped to life, smoothing the cotton housedress over the long johns she had on underneath. Patting the curlers on her head as if putting her hair right, she invited us into the close, warm flat, shuffling across the worn carpet runner in an old pair of flattened men's bedroom slippers. The place smelled of mothballs.

"I don't like to judge," she said as she eased into an armchair, a cup of steaming tea in her hand. "But that man was a sinner."

"How so?" I asked.

"He was pleasant enough on the surface," she said, then leaned forward to whisper: "But he was a fornicator."

"Oh, my!" The word was unexpected, and I actually emitted a short gasp.

She nodded, sat back, and sipped her tea. "Women streaming in and out at all hours. Different women, mind you, some young and some not so young. And I could hear everything. Not that I was listening; it's just that these walls are no thicker than cigarette paper."

She reminded me of my own disapproving landlady in New Holland, Mrs. Giannetti, who kept track of my visitors and the empty bottles in my trash.

"Did you overhear anything besides lewd behavior?"

"His girlfriends were often jealous. They carped at him a lot."

"How many were there?"

"Couldn't say," she spat, shaking her head. "There were two regulars and lots of brief affairs. What kind of girl visits a man in his apartment? Really!"

Nice girls, sometimes, I thought. Other times not-so-nice girls. But I kept my thoughts to myself.

"Would you be able to recognize the two regulars?" I asked.

"I ought to. Used to bump into them in the morning when they crept out of here, hair all mussed and sleep in their eyes. The young one didn't like to look me in the eye in the morning. I suspect she was ashamed. The older one just smiled a dreamy smile and said hello on her way to the stairs. Probably doesn't have much reputation left to protect."

"Did Ercolano have a cleaning lady?" I asked.

Tillie shook her head, a smirk stretched across her wrinkled face. "No, but the older girlfriend used to scour that place at least once a week. I saw her on all fours in the open doorway, hair tied up in a red kerchief—a red-and-black kerchief—scrubbing his floors right out into the hallway."

McKeever and I exchanged glances. Ercolano seemed to have had some system.

"How old were these two women?" asked the detective.

"I wouldn't rightly call the younger one a woman," she said. "No more than twenty-one, twenty-three years old. About your age, dearie," she said to me. "A shame when a young girl loses her way and is spoilt like that."

"What about the older one?" I asked.

"Thirty-five, forty? I don't know. No debutante, but pretty enough and well preserved."

"You said they often quarreled," said McKeever. "Did you ever hear anything violent? Any fights?"

"Nope. The young one cried a lot, begging him, you know, to love her proper and all. The old one stood up for herself a little more. She mostly complained about the other women. In the end, though, he always had his way with both of them."

"Why do you suppose that is?" I asked.

"He was Italian. Need I say more?" I was sure she would. And she did: "That's all they think of: *amore!* Lust. After a while it poisons the soul." She shook her head in pity.

McKeever and I took another tour of Ercolano's rooms, leaving Mrs. Arnsberger to her post of chief snooper and morals warden. We poked through Ercolano's drawers, looking for something that might help trace the two women. There was nothing.

"What was he wearing that day?" I asked.

"Kinlaw told me he found a pair of trousers and a shirt on the bed. It looked like he took them off just before getting into the bath."

"Did he empty his pockets?"

"The guys from the Twentieth bagged everything. They found a wallet with cash, Italian passport, keys. The usual. This wasn't a robbery if that's what you're thinking."

I shook my head. "No, but I'd sure like to have a look at that stuff."

"I can get it," he said. "What do you think you'll find, anyway?"

"Who knows? You just have to look, that's all."

"Say, where does your nosiness come from?"

"I'm a reporter," I said, slightly exaggerating my modest role at a small, upstate daily. I wanted to impress him.

"If you were a man, you'd make a good detective."

I'm sure he thought he was complimenting me, but that identity—a girl wanting to do a man's job—had throttled me for too long. I wasn't trying to blaze any trails for women; I just wanted to be a reporter, one who didn't need to swat hands off her behind at every turn. For McKeever, I let it slide, though he noticed something was wrong.

"Don't you find it strange," he asked, trying to cover his gaffe—whatever it was—by changing the subject, "that there is no evidence a woman ever came here?"

"Not really," I said, still thinking of what he'd said. "The lady next door said his girlfriends were both jealous types. Maybe he didn't want to ruin a good thing by leaving someone's phone number lying around. Jealousy will make you rip up the floorboards to find that one hidden something that'll break your heart. It's that ache, that paradoxical desire to dig deeper and deeper until you finally uncover the thing that destroys your happiness. Compelling."

"You talk like you understand jealousy," he said.

"Not really. I understand broken hearts."

Downstairs, I stood in the lobby, staring out the door while McKeever pulled on his overcoat. The streetlamp on the corner of Eighty-Seventh and Amsterdam swayed in the cold breeze, tossing its light from side to side. A crumpled newspaper tumbled across the street and wedged itself beneath a mailbox in front of a cocktail bar: the Crystal Lounge.

"Have you checked his mail?" I asked, watching as the newspaper freed itself, pirouetted into the avenue, and was flattened by a speeding taxi.

McKeever's eyes grew.

"He must have a mailbox here," I said. "Have you checked it?"

The black mailboxes hung in a row on the vestibule wall to my left. An open slot in each door let you know if you had mail. Ercolano did.

The locks on most mailboxes are no great shakes. If someone wants your mail, he'll get it, Postal Service–approved lock or no. And so, we pried open the box with little trouble.

McKeever and I shuffled Ercolano's mail back and forth between us in the foyer. A phone bill, some throw-away mail addressed to *Occupant*, the latest issues of *TV Guide* and *Esquire*, a yellow postal return slip for an undelivered package, and a perfumed letter, addressed by a woman's hand.

While McKeever read the letter from the woman, I opened the phone bill, expecting a pack of hefty calls to Italy. Instead, I found a bill for $3.14. Local calls and little else.

"Take a look at this," said the cop, handing me the letter.

Carissimo mio,   *January 23, 1960*

How I miss you! Since our beautiful night together Wednesday and horrible argument Thursday morning, I have done nothing but think of you. I've waited for your call. This loneliness is unbearable! You are my drug, my love, my poison. It's no use; I can never stay angry with you for long. When you asked me to stay away from your place, I hated you. I swore never to let you near me again. But I've learned to accept you on your terms, because even though I never know when you'll call, I don't ever want to be sure that you won't. Come to me as soon as you receive this letter. I love you and miss you so.

Tua angela

I flipped the envelope looking for the return address but found none. The postmark was Saturday afternoon, mailed from Varick Street in the West Village.

"You know any Angelas?" asked McKeever.

"No," I said. "Well, actually, the woman who lives next door to my father is named Angela. Angela Farber. But it can't be her. Too much of a coincidence."

"What do you think? The younger one or the older one?"

"Older. Sounds like she has her own place."

McKeever nodded agreement.

"What about that?" I asked, motioning to the yellow paper in his hand. "Does Ercolano have a package waiting for him somewhere?"

"No," said the cop, handing it to me for my inspection. "It's from the Planetarium Branch on West Eighty-Third. A package he sent to Princeton, New Jersey, on Monday morning is still in New York: insufficient postage."

"Monday?" I asked. "Ercolano was dead on Saturday night."

McKeever gulped. "Well, maybe he mailed it Saturday. The post office is known to be slow."

I shook my head, staring at the little sheet of paper. "I doubt it. I'll bet Ercolano didn't mail this package."

"Why do you think that?"

"It doesn't add up," I said. "A letter with insufficient postage is one thing. But a package? When I send a package, I take it down to the post office and have it weighed. Then the clerk puts on the necessary postage."

McKeever nodded. "Yes, that's right. So, there should have been enough stamps on Ercolano's parcel."

"Unless he was in a rush and thought he had enough postage," I said. "But then it's got to be small enough to fit into a mailbox. Otherwise he would have had to go to the post office anyway. He would have weighed it. I'm curious to see this package. Do you think they'd let us have a look at the post office tomorrow?"

"No problem," he said. "I know a guy over at the Planetarium."

∂◡

The squad car was waiting outside Ercolano's building to take us home. McKeever dropped me off in the Village at twelve forty, promising to pick me up at nine o'clock the following morning to visit the Planetarium Branch.

"Good night, Jim," I said. I think I surprised him with the familiarity because he blushed.

"Good night," he answered, then paused. "Ellie."

Ben, another of the elevator operators, took me up to the fifteenth floor.

"Last night some people came up to my father's apartment," I said. "You always ring to say who's coming, don't you?"

"Yes, miss."

"Always?" I asked. "What about Mrs. Farber's gentleman?"

Ben frowned. "I don't mind nobody's business but my own. And I don't talk about who visits who in this place. Excuse me for saying so, Miss Stone."

"I'm asking because the three people who visited me last night weren't announced by Raul. When I asked him why, he said he had thought one of them was Mrs. Farber's gentleman friend, so he let them in, no questions asked."

"That's right. Some tenants tell us to let certain people in at any time, no need to call up."

"Have you seen Mr. Walter since my father was attacked?"

He shook his head. "No, miss. But I'm not on duty all the time. Why don't you just ask Mrs. Farber about it? It's really not my place."

The elevator lurched to a stop on the fifteenth floor, and Ben pulled the door open. He was no Raul when it came to jabbering about the tenants.

"Good night, miss," he said firmly.

I fumbled for my keys in front of my father's door and dropped them onto the thick brush doormat. As I bent down to pick them up, the clicking of a latch startled me.

"Oh, Ellie, it's you."

"Hello, Mrs. Farber," I said, jingling the keys in my hands. "You're up late tonight."

"I can't sleep these days," she said, letting the door open more fully.

"Would you like to talk about it?" I asked.

CHAPTER EIGHT

A ngela Farber led me to her parlor, a warm, womb-like cloister with salmon-colored walls and some white Chinese silk rugs. Chiffon drapes hung in front of drawn curtains, lending a soft, shrouded intimacy to the room. A mezza-coda Steinway anchored the far wall, some Schumann romances on the music stand.

She was wearing a black-and-gold kimono that reached the floor. She'd drawn her black hair back in a simple braid, and I suddenly thought of my brother. I could see how she would have inspired lusty fantasies in the heart of a young boy.

"A drink, Elijah?" she asked, wheeling to look at me, right arm cocked as if to ask a question. Then she shook her head and laughed. "Sorry, I mean Ellie!"

I stated my preference and took a seat on the sofa, while she poured me some Scotch over ice.

"Why the trouble sleeping?" I asked once she'd handed me the tumbler. "Worried about intruders?"

She sat on the other end of the couch and sipped some sherry.

"It isn't that," she said. "I'm lonely. I spend all my days cooped up in here. And my nights, too."

"What about your friend?" I asked. "Your gentleman caller. Don't you see him anymore?"

"He doesn't call," she said. "I haven't seen him in three weeks. Only spoke to him once or twice in all that time."

"I thought you were expecting him the night my father was attacked."

She shrugged. "I was expecting him, but he stood me up. He called to cancel at the last minute."

"Have you tried to contact him?"

"I've phoned, written. I even went to his apartment building, but he wasn't in."

"Why don't you try to get out a little?" I said. "The next thing you know, he'll start to wonder why you don't call. You'll be busy, shopping, going to shows, meeting new people, and he'll pull a muscle trying to kick himself in the seat of the pants for ever having let you get away."

She smiled. "You're sweet, Ellie. You got a fella?"

I downed another mouthful of Scotch and shook my head, thinking of Gigi Lucchesi. "I haven't met Mr. Right yet."

"Then play the field, Ellie. And don't waste your time with the working stiffs. Go for the rich guys. I did that for a few years after my husband, Garth, went away," she said, the naughty blush of nostalgia glowing behind her glassy eyes. "I was living in Miami Beach, having a grand old time. I had lots of boyfriends."

What about the crazy house Nelda had mentioned? And why was Angela Farber telling me this anyhow?

"I used to haunt all the hot clubs in Miami Beach: the Fontaine-bleau, Sans Souci, the Latin Quarter . . . Rich men with shady connections. And always married. But I didn't care. For the first time in my life I was wanted, really wanted by someone. Sure, they were louses, after one thing, but they showed me a good time getting there. One fellow, Tony, took me to Cuba. My, the Tropicana was something else, and the backstreet clubs. They put on some pretty racy shows, I can tell you. But that was before those damned Communists took over." Her enthusiasm waned, and she assumed a matter-of-fact demeanor to finish her tale. "But that's how it is, you know. Once a gentleman finds out you're divorced, his designs on you change, at least when you're my age. Used goods. A good time, but not for marrying, you know."

I gulped. Jesus, was I going to end up like Angela Farber?

"Sorry," she said. "Maybe we should change the subject."

"That's all right," I said, examining the amber-colored mixture of Scotch and melting ice in my glass. "Maybe you can help me figure something out. You said you hadn't seen your gentleman friend in three weeks."

"That's right," she said.

"What about last night?"

"What about it? You saw me last night in the hallway. I was alone."

"But weren't you expecting him?"

"I was expecting to see him Friday, when he called to break our date, but it's been three weeks since I've seen him. I called Raul last night, but only because I thought Walter might show up. Tuesday used to be one of our regular nights."

"You didn't know that man in the hallway last night? Professor Chalmers?"

She leaned toward me, and her kimono opened to expose part of a milky-white breast. I tried to look away. "I've seen him at lectures at your father's Italian Department, but I've never exchanged a word with him. I doubt he knows my name, and he's certainly not my Walter."

I nodded, putting the elevator incident to rest. "Why the sudden interest in Italian?" I asked.

She shrugged. "My mother was Italian, from Naples. I used to speak a little Italian. Dialect, you know, at home. Not the fancy way your father speaks it. And he's not even Italian!"

"He always wanted me to learn it," I said. "I spent a summer in Italy with him a long time ago, but I'm not very good at it. What about you?"

"Well, one day last September, I was feeling nostalgic for the sound of the language, so I asked your father if they had any social events that might interest me. He knew I liked poetry, music, and the arts, so he suggested a few lectures. That's where I saw that Professor Chalmers."

"Do you still attend lectures?"

She shook her head. "Dry stuff, most of it. They take all the beauty out of the poetry, those professors, reducing it to some abstract intellectual exercise. In the end, they don't really care for the poetry. I find most academics boring. No offense, Ellie."

"None taken," I smiled.

"So, I gave it up. I found a more enjoyable pastime."

"What's he like?" I asked. "Your Walter, I mean."

A devilish smile stretched across Angela Farber's face, pulling at the character lines around her blue eyes.

"He's fiercely handsome," she said. "He's not muscular, but he's very virile. That comes from the Latin word for *man*. He taught me that part about Latin. He teaches me so much: books, art . . . We complement each other, you know. He teaches me about art and literature, and I teach him about music." She paused a moment. "At least, we used to."

Then she turned suddenly sad, her mien darkening and her eyes glazing over. It was as if she'd suddenly forgotten I was there. She just held her glass absently, and I could see her grip loosening. I gently pulled the glass from her hand and placed it on the table before her. She sat back on the cushion and drew a heavy sigh, still no more aware of my presence.

I put my own drink down and rose to leave. I'd never seen anyone check out so quickly.

"Good night, Mrs. Farber," I said, but she didn't answer.

⁂

The phone was ringing as I let myself into my father's apartment. I dropped my coat onto the bench in the foyer and crossed the parlor to answer.

"Hello, Ellie," said a playful voice from the other end. "Do you want to come over?"

I tried to compose myself before answering. "I don't even know where you live (inhale), (exhale) Gigi."

"253 Charles," he whispered into the receiver. "Apartment 5-S. Or shall I come to your place?"

I thought a moment. I wanted to get away from my father's house, away from Angela Farber's miserable love life, and my own future.

"I'll come there," I said and put the receiver back into its cradle.

Before leaving to give in to my weakness for Gigi Lucchesi's virile beauty—damn it, *virile* was the word Angela Farber had used—I summoned enough presence of mind to phone Saint Vincent's ICU. Nurse Riley Tielman answered.

"Is there any news on my father's condition?" I asked after identifying myself.

"None, Miss Stone. Your father's resting comfortably, but there's no change."

"What about the police? Have they posted a man there?"

"Yes. An officer has been sitting next to his bed since this afternoon. He's a big, strapping, young cop. Good looking, too," and she giggled.

"Just remember why he's there," I said. "And don't let him leave my father alone, not even for a minute. If he has to eat or use the men's room, I want someone to sit by the bed till he gets back."

"Yes, Miss Stone."

"I'll see you first thing tomorrow morning. And that handsome young cop of yours better have his eyes on my father, not you!"

She giggled again. "Oh, Miss Stone. You must understand how it is when a handsome man crooks his finger . . ."

⌇

Manhattan's geometry is fairly uniform. Miles and miles of rectangular blocks, drawn by the parallel streets and their perpendicular avenues, line up north to south and east to west, spanning different neighborhoods and crossing ethnic boundaries. The symmetrical routine might become tiresome if it didn't constitute the ribs of the world's greatest city. There is, however, a section of Manhattan where the grid has been shaken out of line. A map shows the streets like uprooted strata of a tectonic plate, stood on end by some geological spasm. East of Seventh Avenue, from Fourteenth to Canal Street, Manhattan is unnavigable to the stranger. Jones, Barrow, Christopher, Charles, Tenth, Perry, Eleventh, and Bank Streets slope one way; Bleecker, Greenwich, and West Fourth another. It's one of the rare sections of Manhattan with triangular blocks, some no larger than wedges of cheese. This charming neighborhood is the West Village. I enjoyed walking its streets as much as any in New York, but on this cold January night, I hiked up my collar, pulled my gloves on tight, and slipped a pint of Scotch into my coat pocket; I doubted Gigi kept a stocked bar and I'd rather be prepared than dry. Once outside, I made a beeline for Charles Street and Gigi Lucchesi, walking like a jittery horse with blinders.

"Hey, you again?" came a voice from behind me on the stairs. "I told you to stay away from here."

I reeled around to see a middle-aged man in a T-shirt in a doorway on the fourth floor landing.

"Excuse me?" I said.

Then the door opened, and Gigi grabbed my arm. "It's OK, Mike," he said to the man. "She's a friend."

"What was that about?" I asked once we were inside.

"That's just the super," he said. "I had a persistent admirer a while back. She caused some trouble, broke a window. Don't worry about him. Come in and relax."

Gigi's apartment was a medium-sized, cozy studio on the top floor of a five-flight walk-up. The two windows on the west side of his room looked out on the side of another building, but to the south you saw a streetlamp, a handsome brick Federalist row house across Charles, and a good swath of night sky.

I turned my attention to Gigi, putting the super, Angela Farber, and Nurse Tielman's handsome cop out of mind. In his own surroundings, Gigi was casual. Instead of the collared shirts and navy cashmere pullovers I'd seen him wear at the department, he now had on a loose-fitting cotton turtleneck and denim jeans. He may have just finished beating a rug, for all I knew, but he was the most gorgeous man I'd ever seen.

"Let me pour you a drink," he said.

"I'll have this," I said, placing my bottle on the table. Then I noticed he already had an unopened fifth of White Label in his hand, and I felt like a boor. This wonderful man, who did not drink spirits, had made a point of stocking my favorite! Backing into the bathroom, I said, "I'll just be minute."

Gigi rolled over and extended an arm across the rumpled sheets. He opened his eyes.

"What are you doing, Ellie?" he asked.

"Thinking about something," I answered from a caned chair across the room.

"What do you have to think about? Come back to bed. Come back to me."

I obeyed and slipped into bed beside him. His skin was warm and smooth, and he smelled like a man, deliciously musky without the stale perspiration. He wrapped an arm around my stomach and laid his head against my cheek. I stroked his soft hair from his temple to his neck, caressing my Ganymede with the tips of my fingers. We whispered for hours more in the dark. He told me about his home, his life, and his dreams.

"Don't you miss Italy?" I asked.

"Yes and no," he said. "I like it here; I'd like to stay at least another year."

"Why's that?"

"Because I'll be too old for military service by then."

"Is the army so bad?"

"It's eighteen months for nothing, Ellie. Italy is a peaceful country now. I don't want to waste my time." He paused. "I'd rather spend it with you."

THURSDAY, JANUARY 28, 1960

I woke before Gigi the following morning, Thursday, worried I was falling hard for someone who would just toy with me before moving on to another as beautiful as he. I rose quietly from the bed.

For several minutes, I watched him from across the room as he slept. In his slumber, he looked like an angel, a far cry from the devil I'd spent the night with. His beauty was just too much. Feeling like a voyeur, I pulled my Leica from my purse, focused on the rumpled-haired idol sleeping before me, and clicked off a shot. Then another and another, zooming in on his innocent face, the delicate arc of his closed eyelids, and the pout of his soft lips. A golden light spilled through the south window, cut the bed in half, bathing his face and bare chest in the sun's rays, and I regretted having no Kodachrome with me. Still, armed only with black and white, I knew these photographs would be beautiful.

Once I'd finished the roll, I stowed my camera in my purse and drew a sigh of relief; he'd slept through it all. I had my stolen memento. Now, dressed only in the bulky turtleneck he'd worn the night before, I glided about the kitchen alcove on soft, bare feet, trying to remember the coffee-brewing lesson he'd given me the day before. I wanted to beckon him to consciousness with the sweetest of reveilles.

"Oh, you're up," I said, catching him gazing at me in the bright morning sun. "You like it?" I asked, twisting and stretching over my shoulder to get a glimpse of myself. I laughed. "It's all right, I suppose. Gives me something to sit on."

"I like it," he said. "I'd like to see more of it."

Sipping my coffee, I asked, "May I use your toothbrush?"

Saint Vincent's is barely five minutes from Gigi's door. I arrived at the ICU a little after eight o'clock and found Sean McDunnough waiting for me.

"Thank you for helping me out this way," I said.

"No need for thanks," he said. "You're paying me."

I explained the routine. He was to watch over my father until a regular nurse or I replaced him. I had arranged for one of the night nurses to sit beside the bed from midnight to six o'clock. McDunnough could go eat, rest, do whatever, so long as he was back by the appointed hour. I reviewed the names of the nurses, the attending doctors, and the medication they were giving to my father. McDunnough listened without a word, as if taking instructions from the nervous hostess of a cocktail party.

I left Saint Vincent's at eight thirty and made my way quickly back to my father's apartment at 26 Fifth Avenue. Rodney held the elevator for me, and I skipped across the lobby to climb in. A heavy-set colored woman, dressed in a thick overcoat, was untying the scarf she'd wrapped around her head. At her side stood a pretty little girl of about seven, wavy brown hair hanging to her shoulders, with bangs grazing her eyelids. She stared up at me earnestly, nose pink from the morning cold, unaware that her woolen hat, which she clutched by the chin-strap, was dragging on the floor.

"Good morning, Miss Ellie," said Rodney. I returned the greeting, silently wondering what time he'd come on his shift. Oh, God, what if he'd started at midnight and was about to punch out? He'd know I'd been out all night.

"Who's this?" I asked him, motioning to the little girl, hoping to divert attention away from me.

"That's Miss Susan Farrell," said Rodney, beaming at the child. He used to look at me that way. "She's just been out to the park for a stroll with Mrs. Thomas here. Pick up your hat, sweetie," he chided gently. "You're dragging it in the dirt."

"Your hair's in your eyes, Susan," I said, reaching out to brush the fringe away. It fell back into place.

"She's always pushing her hair out of her face," said Rodney. "Ain't that so, Mrs. Thomas?"

Mrs. Thomas grunted.

"Here, I have an idea," I said, fishing in my purse. "What if I gave you this barrette, Susan?"

I held out a simple tortoiseshell barrette with a spring clip for her inspection. Her eyes grew large, and she reached out to touch it.

"I remember when I first wore a barrette," I said. "I felt terribly sophisticated and pretty. My father told me I was the prettiest girl in New York. May I clip it on?"

I brushed Susan's bangs to the right and affixed them with a smart click of the barrette. Susan froze, as if afraid the clip would fall off if she moved her head too abruptly. She craned her eyes upward to see, her head still motionless. Then a huge grin spread over her face, and she thanked me in a sweet voice.

"That's Miss Ellie, Susan," said Rodney. "She used to run in the park like you do." Then he looked at me. "Now she's all grown up."

The elevator reached the twelfth floor and came to rest. The doors rolled open, and Mrs. Thomas took Susan's hand and led her out. Once on the landing, Susan turned her body and head as one to look back at me. She smiled again and waved good-bye. I felt a rush of awareness, a sudden recognition that had eluded me throughout my brief interlude in the elevator: I was looking at myself. The little girl had the same hair, the same blue eyes, the same runny nose I had worn as a child. I stood transfixed, transported for one short moment, looking back in time into a mirror at my mislaid innocence. How singularly mesmerizing to stand before a shadow of one's self and stare blankly for the wonder of it, without intellectualizing or drawing any wisdom or insight from the exercise.

Then I heard a door open down the hall, and a great commotion ensued. There was a rustling and a jingling, panting and then a bark. I couldn't see the dog, but he sounded big and sloppy. Mrs. Thomas shrieked at the animal to stay away from her, while Susan thrilled at the greeting. I stepped out of the elevator to see a great golden retriever slobbering over the little girl.

"Milo! Milo!"

The reunion was of the sweetest, with energetic lapping and squeals of joy, both canine and human. Then Susan spoke again:

"Milo, look what I've got! It's a barrette!"

"Mind that dog stays away from me!" said Mrs. Thomas.

"I'm giving this to you, Milo," Susan said, presenting the barrette for his inspection, and she clipped it onto the poor dog's head.

Instantly, Milo froze in place, exactly as Susan had done when I'd put it in her hair. His big, black eyes grew large, and he looked a bit uneasy and self-conscious.

"You're the prettiest dog in New York, Milo," she said.

Then Susan grabbed his collar and pulled him down the hall toward home, the dog still none too pleased to have been tagged with the barrette.

I stepped back into the lift and smiled at Rodney, who still didn't seem to approve of my grown-up behavior. But in that moment, I didn't care. Moments later, once the elevator had deposited me on the fifteenth floor, I whisked down the corridor, light in my step and quite pleased with myself. When I reached my father's door, I fished for my keys, then became aware of a sudden malaise. I turned my head eerily slowly, unlike little Susan's stiff about-face, and considered the door to my left: Mrs. Farber's. I had just seen my past, dragging her woolen hat on the floor of the elevator, and I wondered if my future was waiting behind this door, pickled and bitter, used up and left to decay slowly. I closed my eyes and swore to myself; it was too early to have a drink.

I showered, changed, and waited for the locksmith to arrive. By 9:45 he had installed a new deadbolt on the front door and given me three sets of keys. McKeever was waiting for me downstairs, and we were on our way uptown at 9:50.

"We got the lab results back this morning," said the cop as we crossed Fourteenth Street. "The place was covered with Ercolano's prints, as you might imagine, and two other unidentified sets, probably belonging to women."

"I thought you could trace anyone with a good thumbprint," I prodded.

"Only if we have their prints on file," he said. "Of course, we could check the samples against the prints of the victim's acquaintances, but . . ."

"But we don't know who they are."

McKeever nodded.

He tapped on the cage to get the attention of the patrolman in front. "Hand me that bag," he said to the driver as we sped past Twenty-Third Street. The patrolman stuffed a parcel through the slot in the enclosure. Then to me: "These are Ercolano's personal effects, everything that was in the pockets of his clothes. I ran up to the Twentieth last night after I dropped you off and picked them up."

A crumpled brown paper bag; somehow I had thought the NYPD handled evidence more carefully. I reached in and fished out a full book of matches, *Crystal Lounge* emblazoned across the top: the bar opposite his apartment. I put the matches aside and retrieved a flattened wallet.

"Can you tell if he kept it in his right or left pants pocket by the curve in the leather?" I asked.

McKeever blanched then, realizing I was kidding him, smiled.

I unfolded the wallet and found a brand-new New York State driver's license, issued to Ruggero Ercolano of the Eighty-Seventh Street address. A five-dollar bill and three ones were creased neatly into the billfold. I found a recently issued American Social Security card tucked into one of the small pockets, and nothing else. No phone numbers, reminders, receipts, nothing. Again from the bag I pulled his passport and thumbed through the pages, finding nothing more interesting than the pompous photo and an entry stamp from Idlewild on July 19, 1957. Deeper still in the sack was a set of latchkeys: two silver and a small mailbox key. The last item in the bag was a gold tie clip with the engraved initials *RGE*. I flipped open the passport to check Ercolano's full name: Ruggero Giovanni Ercolano. I hunched over the slim gold bar for a closer look. Very few scratches.

"Either this is almost new," I said, showing it to McKeever, "or Ercolano hated it and never wore it."

"What makes you think that?" he asked.

"This gold finish scratches easily. Maybe it was a gift. Any way of tracing the buyer?"

McKeever laughed. "Shall I start there?" he asked, pointing to a jewelry shop on the corner of Thirty-Fourth and Sixth. "There are hundreds of jewelers in Manhattan, more in the other four boroughs, and that's assuming the clip was bought in New York."

"It was bought in New York, all right," I said. "In a little place on Fifty-Seventh and Fifth Avenue. Tiffany's. This is their signature tie clip. All the smartly dressed preps have been wearing them since I was in school."

"How can you tell it's from Tiffany's?" he asked, dubious of my eye.

"It says 'Tiffany & Co.' right there, flatfoot," I said, shoving the clip under his nose.

McKeever took the tie clip in his hand, turned it over and over. "Hmm, missed that," he said, then slipped it into his breast pocket. "I'll check it out," he said.

"Nothing else?" I asked, tossing the effects back into the bag.

"He was a simple man," said McKeever dryly. I was beginning to like him more all the time.

The squad car pulled to a stop in front of the Planetarium Branch of the post office, and we climbed out. Never a parking problem when riding with the police.

Joe Fenster, McKeever's man at the post office, showed us to the caged repository, deep behind the service windows where the postal clerks ripped and sold geometric patterns of stamps. Great wooden cubbyholes held packages and letters of various sizes, all too large or too important to be left in someone's mailbox. Each piece of mail was numbered, and McKeever and I had a crumpled yellow slip with one of those numbers written on it. Unlit, soggy cigar squeezed between his fat lips, Fenster led us through the rows of boxes, detailing the Planetarium's operations and traffic figures as if he owned the place. Finally he stopped, plucked the wet cigar from his mouth, and jerked a thumb over his shoulder:

"There she is," he said. "I don't even gotta look."

She was. I wanted to contradict him, just to watch him swallow his smug grin and cigar, but I thought he might not let us have the package: twelve-by-nine and about three inches deep, wrapped in brown kraft paper.

"Princeton University Press," said McKeever, reading from the address. "Any idea what it is?"

"Let's open it," said Fenster, as if pawing through people's mail really licked his stamps. "What is it?"

"It's my father's manuscript," I said. They both looked at me. "And I guarantee page 154 is missing."

McKeever nodded, and Fenster pinched my behind.

Outside, McKeever opened the squad car door for me, and I climbed in.

"That Joe Fenster's a character," he chuckled as the car pulled away from the curb. "I've known him since PS 62 in Queens. What'd you think of him?"

"His sister should have put him down when she gave birth to him." McKeever gaped at me.

"He's a pervert, Jim," I said by way of explanation. "Pinched me good and hard. I'll have a bruise on my bottom tomorrow to prove it."

The squad car took us uptown to the Columbia campus. McKeever stepped out and circled to my side to open my door. For a few seconds I was alone in the car with the patrolman driver. He looked at me through the rearview mirror and smiled.

"Frankly, miss," he began, "if I wasn't on duty, I'd pinch you too. And believe me, you'd know you was pinched." He winked in the mirror just as McKeever opened my door.

McKeever and I trudged through the sunny cold, toting the manuscript box, until we arrived at Hamilton Hall.

"Is Professor Chalmers in?" McKeever asked Miss Little, producing his badge.

"Dr. Chalmers just went into a meeting with Professor Bruchner," she said, waving a hand nervously in front of her face.

"Can you please announce us?"

Joan Little excused herself, with a polite smile for my benefit, and crossed the room to knock on a door marked *Conference*, opposite the lounge where I had met Hildy Jaspers and Gigi Lucchesi three days before. She slipped inside, only to emerge a few moments later.

"You may go in," she said.

Victor Chalmers and Gualtieri Bruchner were seated opposite each other in the conference room. Chalmers seemed unnerved by the interruption, while Bruchner just looked past us, as if the disturbance were an unavoidable delay.

"Sergeant McKeever, is it?" asked Chalmers, jumping to his feet to shake the policeman's hand, then mine. "Hello, Ellie. How's Abe today?"

I shrugged. "Someone cut off his oxygen yesterday. He suffered heart failure and nearly died."

After a sufficient display of outrage over the renewed attack, Chalmers got into the spirit of the detective's visit. Bruchner remained impassive.

"How may I help you, Sergeant?" asked Chalmers.

"I wonder if you could take a look at this," he said, holding out the brown-papered parcel.

"Of course. What is it?" he asked.

"We were hoping you could tell us," I said.

He flipped open the top and shuffled some pages. His eyes darkened.

"Do you recognize it, Professor?" asked McKeever.

Chalmers nodded, turned a few more pages, then looked at me. "This is Abe's manuscript," he said. "This is *Daughters of Eve*."

The title page in the box bore a different name: *Saints and Whores: Dante's Women*, by Ruggero Ercolano.

"Plagiarist!" whispered Chalmers, closing the lid on the box.

I found it telling that an academic would see the intellectual transgression before the physical.

"My God!" he said, suddenly. "This means that Ruggero . . ."

"Are you prepared, sir, to swear a deposition that the manuscript in your hand is indeed the work of Abraham Stone?" asked McKeever in his most official tone. "Will you swear to it under oath?"

"Without hesitation," declared Chalmers, chin jutting high in righteous indignation. "Abraham Stone consulted me often on this manuscript. We shared ideas and discussed alternative approaches and conclusions. This is his work, all right. I never would have believed Ruggero capable of such treachery."

"What was Ercolano's field of study?" I asked, interrupting Chalmers's censure of his late colleague.

"Why, nineteenth century, of course."

"And, for the benefit of Sergeant McKeever, who was absent from class that day, when did Dante write the *Divine Comedy*?"

Chalmers frowned. "He completed it around 1321, shortly before his death."

"Would you say it's common for nineteenth-century scholars to publish seminal works on medieval poets?" I asked, feeling like a DA on cross-examination.

He gulped. "Why, no, not at all. In fact, I'd say it's fairly rare."

"And is it standard practice for scholars of Italian birth to write their books in English? Flawless English?"

"No," he shook his head violently. "Now I'm confused."

McKeever's head dropped, and he asked me: "Why must you spoil every solution I come up with?"

"What's this about, Ellie?" asked Chalmers. "Did Ruggero steal Abe's book or didn't he?"

I laughed. "He'd have to have been an idiot to think he could get away with it."

"But you found the manuscript in his apartment."

"No, it was returned by the post office. Take a look at the address."

Chalmers glanced down at the parcel in his hands. He gave a start.

"Princeton University Press? Your father has a contract with Princeton for this very book!"

"It seems unlikely that Ercolano was so naive. It's like stealing the Mona Lisa and trying to fence it at the Louvre two days later."

"Then what does it mean, Ellie?" asked Chalmers, desperate for answers to this horrible breach of academic code. "How did the manuscript come to be in Ruggero's possession? Who would have done such a thing?"

I looked to McKeever, who just shook his head in dismay for what I was about to say.

"I would guess it was the same person who tossed the radio into Ercolano's tub."

CHAPTER NINE

McKeever and I went through Ercolano's office again, looking for something we might have missed. I scoured his notebooks and lesson planner, finding nothing unusual. Victor Chalmers watched from the doorway, wringing his hands. Behind him stood Gualtieri Bruchner.

The drawers yielded the same articles as the night before: *niente*. The detective and I chatted for a moment, ignoring the curious chairman a few feet away. Then Bruchner intruded meekly, begging to ask a question.

"What is it?" asked McKeever.

"I was wondering," he began with his *Mitteleurope* accent, "if you had noticed that key, Sergeant."

McKeever and I looked to where Bruchner was pointing, the floorboards beside the wall that separated Ercolano's office from my father's. We were quite startled to see a brass key and cardboard tab lying in plain view.

"Was that here last night?" McKeever asked, holding the key carefully by the cardboard clip. He handed it to me.

I shook my head as I examined it. "I'm sure it wasn't. And isn't there a cleaning lady who comes through here at night?"

Chalmers nodded.

"What do you think it opens?" asked McKeever.

"That's one of our key clips," said Chalmers. "It has a number, 33; Joan will be able to tell you which door it opens."

McKeever took the key to the secretary, who was surprised to find it missing. She rose from her desk, crossed the room to a bookcase, and reached up to retrieve a key from the top shelf. She then used that key to open a box mounted on the wall next to the bookcase.

"Well, I'll be . . ." she said, holding key 33 up to an empty slot in the box.

"What does that open?" asked McKeever, looking over her shoulder.

Miss Little wheeled around, flushed, and threw a glance to Chalmers. "It's the key to Professor Stone's apartment."

"What?"

"Yes, he kept a key here," she said, blinking furiously. "You know how he sometimes forgets his keys. Well, he thought it would be a good idea to keep one here in case he needed it."

"That's outrageous!" said Chalmers. "Anyone could have taken that key."

"No, Dr. Chalmers," said Joan. "I'm the only person who knew he kept his key there, and no one has a key to this box but myself."

"We all just watched you take the key down from the top shelf," said Chalmers. "Surely others have seen you do the same."

"But I'm the only person allowed access to this key box," she protested. "No one should have opened it."

McKeever and I exchanged wry smiles. "This is New York, ma'am," he said.

"Well, this makes it look pretty bad for Ruggero, doesn't it?" said Chalmers. "He must have seen where Joan hides the key. That's how he got into your father's place to steal the manuscript."

"Or anyone else in this place," said the cop. "Can you account for your whereabouts on the nights of January twentieth and twenty-second?"

Chalmers was floored. "You suspect me of desecrating Elijah Stone's grave? And assaulting my colleague in his home?" Chalmers glared at the detective, then me, his face hot, eyes bulging. "I was in Boston on the twentieth," he said, "and in Bronxville on the twenty-second. There are witnesses to attest to that. Instead of casting doubt on me, you should investigate what Ruggero Ercolano was doing with Abe Stone's manuscript."

Chalmers excused himself and left in a huff.

"What do you think?" I asked McKeever.

"Let's just say that if I put the blame on Ercolano, no one will question it. Case closed."

"Could you do that with a clear conscience?"

He shrugged sheepishly. "I've got a docket full of pendings down on Tenth Street. There's a little old lady who was knocked off in her apartment on Bleecker. The captain dumped that on me yesterday. I got a homo rape/murder for a month now in Sheridan Square; I can't tell you where my day starts and where it ends. My wife and kid don't know me anymore."

I nodded. "OK, don't worry about it. An old man gets clubbed in the head, and a corpse takes the blame. It'll look good in the report; might even get you a promotion."

"It isn't like that."

I knew I was being unfair to him, but I was angry.

"I'll do what I can to help you," he said, awkward and ashamed. "I'll have someone look into the tie clip at Tiffany's this afternoon. And we'll check the prints on the key against Ercolano's."

"Sure," I said, not looking at him.

"It doesn't surprise me," said Roger Purdy in the lounge. "Ercolano was a mediocre scholar, after all. I'm sure he saw glory in that manuscript." He chuckled with contempt. "Only an intellectual destitute would sink so low as to plagiarize."

"You seem to be an expert," I said.

Purdy twitched. "What do you mean by that?"

"You talk as if you know plagiarism when you see it. That's all."

Purdy glared at me, not sure how to take my explanation. Then he decamped, almost stepping on his tail as he shoved past Bernie Sanger at the door with a straight-arm reminiscent of the Heisman Trophy.

"What's he so steamed about?" Bernie asked, joining me in the lounge.

"He doesn't like me very much."

"Do you have a moment, Professor Bruchner?" I asked, peering into office 602.

"I suppose . . ." he said, looking up from his reading. "Come in."

"I won't take much of your time," I said. "Just a couple of questions."
Bruchner nodded.

"You said you had lunch with my father last Friday, and that he told you about his book."

"That's correct."

"Did he mention Ruggero Ercolano in connection with the book? Perhaps he had shown it to him."

"Not that I recall," said Bruchner, his gray face looking more and more like granite. "He told me Princeton University Press was planning to publish it in the autumn. Then we exchanged ideas on the content of the book. He did not mention Professor Ercolano."

"Did you say you'd read it?" I asked.

Bruchner shook his head determinedly. "No, I did not say that."

I poked around the department until noon, and then retired to my father's office. There, I stumbled across a portfolio of magnificent charcoal drawings, the ones he had sketched when I was young. The first in the series was three beasts: a leopard, a lion, and a wolf. Then there was a wild-eyed, broad-backed giant of a man, white hair and beard whipping in a fierce wind. His ashen arms bulged with sinewy muscles, and his rugged hands gripped a great wooden spar, which he wielded to push his bark through the rough waters. Dad had drawn him rearing up, at the apex of his backstroke: the infernal gondolier about to plunge his pole into the heaving river's pitch. In the bottom right-hand corner, it read, *The Ferryman, Charon, on the River Acheron. A. Stone, Feb. 24, 1940.*

I pulled up a chair and spread the large pages out on my father's desk. His talent impressed me even more now that I was an adult.

With nothing but a pencil and his fantasy, he had scratched onto paper fearsome and unholy beasts. The lines of each drawing were like scars rasped across the page; wounds that had healed on paper. His art filled me with a silent awe.

There followed pages and pages of beasts, demons, netherworld landscapes, and tortured souls. Some were drawn in rich detail, some left unfinished, others were almost minimalist in their austerity, but all eloquent enough to move me. One drawing in particular, *Beatrice Beholding God, Canto XXXIII, Paradiso*, was virtually a blank page. But the soft lines, so deftly placed, so hushed, so delicate, presented the faint image of an angelic face, in rapture in the brilliant light of God's glory. It was beautiful. I wondered if I could create a similar effect in a photograph by overexposing it. Then I laughed at myself and my mechanical artifice.

I replaced the sketches carefully in their case and tied the portfolio together. Just then, Bernie Sanger tapped on the open door. He stood in the hallway, refusing to come in.

"Got to run to the library," he said. "I just stopped by to tell you Chalmers is looking for you. Wants to take you to lunch."

The Faculty Club is not exactly the stodgy, genteel fraternity one might think. In essence, it's no more than a cafeteria. Besides the waiters, the only difference between it and the student dining halls is the napery; the students get paper, the faculty get linen. The food, though doled out onto the plate in fancier patterns, smelled no better than what I remembered from my undergraduate days.

The colored man who checked our coats greeted Chalmers by name, and the professor shunned him as if he had a virus.

"Bucking for a tip," he whispered to me.

We sat at a table for two not too far from a window that looked over the common. A handful of students were crossing the green. They seemed so carefree and unburdened, and I thought of my college days with nostalgia; ours was a complete family then. I watched for a moment while Chalmers bickered with the waiter over our table.

"I usually sit over there," he said.

"I'm sorry, sir," said the waiter. "But the chancellor and his guests are at your table today. Would you like me to ask them to move?"

Wrestling with the waiter's sarcasm, Chalmers twisted in his seat to see the party at his table.

"Well, they've already started," he said finally. "I suppose we'll have to eat here."

The waiter disappeared, and Chalmers smiled at me.

"So, Ellie, tell me more about your father."

"The same. But I've hired a guard."

"A guard? What for? I thought it was clear Ruggero hit your father on the head and stole *Daughters of Eve*. Ruggero is dead; he can't harm Abe now. Isn't that what the police think?"

"They're willing to accept that scenario if nothing else develops."

"I can see you still don't believe it. Why not?"

"Because yesterday someone disconnected the tubes on my father's respirator."

"Yes, of course," he said. "I'd forgotten."

"That's the most compelling reason. But I can't dismiss the absurd attempt someone made to discredit Ercolano with my father's manuscript."

Chalmers shook his head violently. "But how can you be sure he didn't mail it? A preponderance of evidence indicates that he did. And while he was not a medievalist, he worked a great deal on poetry. Maybe he wanted people to think he was a scholar of great versatility. Is there any evidence to suggest he didn't mail that manuscript?"

"The package was too big to fit in any mailbox I've ever seen. Would you agree?" Chalmers nodded grudgingly. "Therefore, he would have had to drop it off at a post office. In such a case, he would have had it weighed and used the proper postage. The book never would have come back if Ercolano had mailed it."

"Maybe he put the stamps on and dropped it off. I saw stamps on the package, not a metered ticket."

"You're right," I said. "Whoever dropped off that package knew there was not enough postage to get it to Princeton."

"But why?"

"To discredit Ercolano. Look, you knew Princeton University Press was publishing my father's book, and Bruchner told me he knew it too. This was no state secret. So how could Ruggero Ercolano be foolish enough to paste his name across the title page and try to pass it off as his own? With the very people who knew better than anyone that Abraham Stone had written it, his publishers?"

"You tell me," said Chalmers, confused.

"Because he didn't. The person who mailed it didn't want Princeton to get it either. He wanted it to come back and, if push came to shove, he wanted the police to find it. Let's face it; the police don't know anything about academic publishing. Whoever mailed that manuscript counted on the police taking it for a simple case of plagiarism. You know that nineteenth-century scholars don't just tear off books on Dante, whether they like poetry or not. But the police? The police would think it was a case of an Italian professor filching a book on an Italian poet. Motive and opportunity, end of story."

Chalmers nodded. "You may have a point there."

"Victor!" A portly, ruddy-faced, middle-aged man in a gray suit slapped Chalmers on the back. "Victor, who's that at your table?" He said, cocking his head toward the chancellor. Then he roared with laughter.

"Hello, Brad," said Chalmers, rising from his seat to shake the man's hand. They chatted for a few minutes about a recent vote in the faculty senate, confirming a nominee to the board of trustees. Finally, Chalmers remembered himself and introduced us.

"Bradley Harrower, professor of English, Eleonora Stone, distinguished Barnard alumna."

"No relation to Abe Stone," said Harrower, his statement really a question.

"His daughter," I said, taking the hand he'd offered.

Harrower's red face grew serious. "It's a tragedy what happened to Abe. We're all pulling for him, you know."

"Brad and your father are old nemeses on the rules committee in the senate," said Chalmers. "Brad, here, thinks your old man is too rigid and old fashioned in his thinking."

"Torquemada was progressive compared to my father," I said. "But I suppose the world needs old rugs like him as much as new ones."

"Well put, Ellie," said Chalmers, patting me on the shoulder. "Please excuse us, Brad, we have some delicate business to discuss."

"Abe's manuscript?" asked Harrower, aping a wince, as if the subject were so distasteful.

"What about it?" asked Chalmers.

Harrower wiped the expression off his face, replacing it with equally affected horror at his faux pas.

"Why, that Ercolano stole it," he said. "I heard it from Rob Bryant in History. He said he'd heard it from a graduate student or a lecturer. Is it true?"

Chalmers frowned. "My God, word travels like wildfire."

"But is it true?"

"We're not sure, Ellie and I."

"Excuse me," I interrupted. "I know with certainty that Ruggero Ercolano did not take my father's manuscript. In fairness to your deceased colleague, Professor Harrower, you should debunk that ugly smear whenever you hear it. It's a lie."

"Well, if he didn't steal your father's book, who did?"

"Someone who got access to the keys in the Italian Department."

"You mean a faculty member? Or a graduate student?" asked Harrower, his incredulity passing to itchy curiosity. "My God, Victor, what's going on in your house?"

When we were alone again, Chalmers begged me not to announce my suspicions in front of gossips like Brad Harrower.

"Once this mess has been cleared up, I don't care who knows the truth," he said. "But for the time being, Ellie, please grant me this one favor: don't fan the fire with conjecture."

"I'm sorry if I embarrassed you, Dr. Chalmers," I said. "But someone should stand up for Ruggero Ercolano."

"Absolutely," he said. "But it's not yet opportune, don't you see? Someone from the department leaked the rumor about Ruggero stealing *Daughters of Eve*. I can't do anything about that now. But to deny the rumor right now will only invite questions of just who was responsible for stealing the manuscript. It's unfair, I know, to hear Ruggero slandered, his reputation maligned, but for the time being it's the only way to proceed."

"You're understandably concerned for your own reputation," I said.

"Because I'm innocent, damn it! I've told you and the police that I was out of town when Elijah's grave was vandalized. I liked Elijah, even if he didn't like me. And I was at dinner with friends on Friday, so I couldn't have seen your father, let alone club him on the head."

"You were in Bronxville that night, correct?" He nodded. "With Mrs. Chalmers and Billy?" Another nod. "Where was Ruth?"

Chalmers choked. "What?"

"Ruth," I prompted. "Where was she that night?"

Now he laughed. "You can't possibly suspect Ruth. Oh, Ellie, that's absurd."

"I'm just asking. Why didn't she go to Boston or Bronxville with you?"

The smiles disappeared. "Look here, Ellie," he began. "I don't quite see how Ruth's business is your affair, but out of respect for your father, I'll answer. Ruth was with friends those nights. That's all she told me; she's a big girl, and I trust her."

"Any idea who her friends are?"

"Why don't you ask her yourself?"

When Chalmers got up to sign for our lunches, a busboy began clearing the table. Reaching around my shoulder to pick up my glass, he dipped his head slightly and whispered in my ear.

"Are you the daughter of that Professor Stone?" he asked. "The one who was attacked in his home?"

I pulled away to see him. No more than seventeen or eighteen, dressed in a baggy white shirt and pants, he continued clearing, as if I hadn't moved.

"Yes, I am," I said.

"Ditch the prof after lunch and meet me out back on the loading dock," he mumbled. "I got to tell you what happened here last Friday."

I stared at him. He scooped Chalmers's salad dish into his cart, still pretending I wasn't there.

"I can't talk to you here," he mumbled, his lips barely moving. "Meet me out back in ten minutes."

The kid finished clearing our dishes and pushed on to another table. I watched him make his way through the dining room, then Chalmers returned.

"Are you coming back to the department?" he asked.

"No," I said. "I've got to meet someone at the library."

Chalmers's eyes frosted over. "Mr. Sanger? Miss Jaspers, perhaps?"

I shook my head. "An old classmate," I said.

"Be careful of those two," he admonished. "They're schemers, working toward their own ends. One or both may have leaked the story about your father's manuscript."

While we'd been inside the Faculty Club, the day had turned gray and wet. The beautiful sunshine that had illuminated my model that morning was gone, replaced by a misty rain, not frozen, but raw enough to turn your bones blue. The loading dock at the back of the Faculty Club dining hall was empty. I leaned against a cement post at the base of the dock.

"I saw your old man last Friday."

The busboy.

I pushed off the post and turned to see him in the doorway of the loading dock, shivering in shirtsleeves as he pulled a Salem from his breast pocket.

"He came in with one guy, then he noticed another man. That's when the trouble started."

I knew Bruchner had been there, but I wondered who the third man could have been. "Tell me what happened."

"It was a bad scene," said the kid, huddling over his match to protect the flame. Then he lifted his head, cigarette fuming in the drizzle. "I thought he was gonna have a stroke."

I took a step closer, just a few feet below the kid, and rested an elbow on the dock. He didn't look at me as he smoked.

"I didn't think an old guy could cuss like that."

"Who?" I asked.

"Your old man," said the kid, looking at me now. "And he was like Sugar Ray, swinging at that other guy. Took three of us to hold him off. Scratched my arm, right there," he said, holding out the underside of his forearm for proof.

"Who did he go after?" I asked, wondering if I should apologize for his wound. "The man he was eating with?"

"No, your old man came in with the younger guy. They were eating and talking, nothing special. Then the other guy—the older one—showed up by himself. He sat down on the other side of the cafeteria, and your dad started fuming."

That was strange. I thought my father had eaten lunch with Bruchner, but this sounded quite different. Bruchner's story didn't match the busboy's.

"Why was he fuming?" I asked.

"Hell if I know. He just kept staring daggers at him from across the room. I was working his table, so I was keeping an eye on him. Jerry, the waiter I work for, makes me watch the tables like a hawk, like we'll get more tips if we do. But that ain't happening. No offense, but these profs are cheap motherfuckers."

The kid laughed, took a puff on his Salem, and blew the smoke high in the air. "I was filling up his water glass while he was talking to the younger guy about it, but they were speaking Italian. You Italian?"

I shook my head. "What happened next?"

"Your old man got up and started charging across the room. The other guy tried to stop him, and asked me to help. So we set off after him, caught him just as he got to the table. He jostled it a little, and the guy eating alone got a lapful of hot soup." He laughed. "Your old man was pointing at him, saying, 'Show me your tattoo, show it to me if you've got the guts.' I thought it was strange. Then he started to yell something in a foreign language, but not Italian. I don't know no Italian, but there's a couple of guys in the kitchen from Italy. They're always jabbering in Italian, and your old man didn't sound like that. One of the guys said it was German or something. Your old man speak German, too?"

I nodded. "Did he show him the tattoo?"

"Yeah. Pulled his sleeve up and showed him a bunch of numbers on his left wrist. That's when your dad jumped at him, reaching for his throat, and snagged the guy's shirt at the collar, right here," he said, pointing to his left collarbone. "Tore the shirt right open. The guy near fell out of his chair, trying to get away. 'The other one!' your father was yelling, 'I want to see the other one!' Then he hollered some more in German."

"I don't suppose my father got to see the other tattoo," I said.

"Naw," he drew on his cigarette. "But I did. I wasn't the only one your dad scratched. The other guy got it too, right across his upper chest. So Jerry sent me into the kitchen with him to fix him up. When I was wiping alcohol on him, I noticed the tattoo on the left side of his chest, up near the shoulder."

"What was it?" I asked, leaning farther forward.

"Looked like a couple of sticks. Kind of dark and complicated. Lots of heavy ink lines. Pretty ugly, I thought. Nothing I'd like to have on my chest."

"Just two sticks?"

"That's right. Sticks, maybe with a couple of vines twisting around them, like on the back of a dime. Except his sticks were leaning a little to the side, not straight up and down. About yea big," he said, showing me about two inches with his fingers.

"What about my father? Did he leave right away?"

"The guy he came with hustled him out while I was in the kitchen. Man, I never seen white boys mix it up like that, not at the Faculty Club, anyway."

"Who else saw what happened?"

"Everybody in the place," said the kid. "We don't get big crowds on Friday afternoons, but there was probably ten profs in there."

"Do you know who the other two men were?"

"Naw. I only remembered your old man's name, Stone, 'cause I see him around here from time to time."

"How did it end?"

"The guy with the tattoo left, said he didn't want to cause no trouble for nobody."

"Why couldn't you tell me this inside?"

He chuckled. "Niggers ain't supposed to talk to the diners," he said, then flicked his cigarette high in the air. It fell several yards beyond the edge of the loading dock. He opened the door behind him and disappeared inside.

CHAPTER TEN

Gualtieri Bruchner was the enigma of Columbia's Italian Department. He had arrived in New York only six months before and was no social animal. Miss Little told me he had left for the day, so I questioned anyone who would stand still about him.

"Quiet," said Miss Little. "Keeps to himself."

"A misanthrope," pronounced Chalmers. "On the rare occasions when he shows up at a function, he's always the first to leave. Doesn't talk to anybody, except about the driest scholarly topics."

Ironic that Victor Chalmers was accusing anyone of boring behavior. This was the man who delivered a five-minute monologue in Latin on the occasion of his daughter Ruth's Confirmation. Dad had related the incident to my brother and me that evening at the dinner table.

"The strutting ass stood up, cretin's grin smeared over his face, and explained that he was going to toast the grand occasion with a parable of his own invention. Then he started in with *Olim puella erat* (There once was a girl), or some such nonsense. It was embarrassing, I tell you. Only the priest and I understood what he was saying! And he droned on for five minutes, laughing at his own wit."

"Is Dad exaggerating again?" Elijah asked Mother.

Ever kinder than my father, Mom searched for the delicate answer to Elijah's question. But in the end, she gave a quick shake of her head and said, "No, your father's account is accurate."

"Poor little Ruth," said Dad. "She was more embarrassed than anyone. None of the other parents felt compelled to humiliate their children." He shook his head in disgust and turned his attention back to his dinner.

And I turned mine back to Gualtieri Bruchner.

Bernie Sanger said: "He's creepy. Reminds me of Dracula. Like he never goes outside in the daylight."

Roger Purdy, after some coaxing, contributed: "Professor Bruchner is a fine scholar, though not much of a conversationalist."

I phoned Franco Saettano to get his opinion. He had none, claiming he'd only spoken to Bruchner a few times, and that his memory was not so sharp that he could recall the slightest impression the visiting professor had made on him.

I opened my father's office with the brass key Miss Little had provided me. After browsing through some drawers and files, I pulled out my Leica. Inside, the exposed film of the sleeping Gigi was still there, beckoning me silently. I rewound the roll, placed it carefully in a metal canister, and slipped it into my coat pocket. I loaded a new roll and opened the portfolio of my father's drawings. I was bent on preserving the collection, if only on celluloid.

Sean McDunnough was sitting on an aluminum chair next to my father's bed, reading the *Racing Form*. His pose was oddly graceful: the huge man with chicken legs, crossed daintily at the knee.

"How is he?" I asked.

McDunnough shrugged. "The doctor was here about an hour ago. Said he was no worse."

"Any visitors?"

He shook his head. "I'll be back at ten," he said, folding the *Racing Form* and clamping it against his side beneath his bearish right arm.

I settled into the chair to sit vigil. It was four thirty, and I had forgotten to buy a paper. No crossword.

Hours spent bedside in a hospital rarely figure among the happiest of your life. If the patient is unconscious, time can drag your spirit to the basement, bouncing you down each step on the way. All you can do is watch. Nothing to say, no way to help; your sense of usefulness runs out like dirty bathwater swirling down a drain. My father looked hollow. He looked dead. The only signs of life were artificially generated, compliments of Saint Vincent's Hospital: the pumping of the ventilator and the tiny beeps of a heart monitor wired to his chest.

I fell asleep and dreamt of a siren, who beguiled me with her song from across a wide, stormy river. Remotely indifferent to the dangers, I pushed my skiff toward the sweet sound of her singing, ever closer to the rocky shore and crashing waves. The siren lay languid on the highest of the half-submerged rocks, her breast heaving with each beckoning note. Her skin glistened in the spray and moonlight as if the river had licked her from head to toe. I steered closer, squinting through the mist to see the emerald-gold sheen in her hair, until a streak of lightning blazed across the sky, illuminating the hideous gnarl of her lip and hump on her back. Her hair was the green of eel retchings, and her stench was so potent it cut upwind. I dunked my oar in the river, straining against the surge of the tide, to pull back from the onrushing rocks. But it was too late. My fragile vessel rode the river's swell and crashed against a crag. The skiff splintered, and I pitched over the bow into the black water. My thrashing summoned no one, and the cold river closed over my head. I cursed her for her perfidy just as a nudge on my shoulder roused me.

"It's after ten, miss," said Sean McDunnough. "Come on, give us a seat."

I shook the nightmare from my eyes, happy to see a dry, ruddy face, and stood to stretch my back.

"Sorry if I startled you," said McDunnough, unfolding a paperback copy of *Ulysses*—of all things—as he assumed his position on the chair. "See you in the morning."

I headed straight for 26 Fifth Avenue and a warm bed. My back hurt and my head ached, perhaps due to the weather, or maybe the dream of cold water and treachery.

"A young lady dropped by to see you earlier, Miss Eleonora," said Rodney as we rode up the lift. "Left this number for you." He handed a slip of paper to me. "Said her name was Ruth. She wants you to phone her tomorrow."

"I see." Then, I absently muttered aloud that I thought it might have been Miss Jaspers. I figured I was due a visit from her.

"Oh, no," said Rodney. "I haven't seen Miss Jaspers in more than a week."

FRIDAY, JANUARY 29, 1960

The following morning, I lay in my father's bed, thinking about Ruth Chalmers. I had first met her at a Columbia family picnic sixteen or seventeen years earlier. She was a precocious girl of six—a year younger than I—with light-brown hair pulled into two brain-tugging pigtails behind her ears. She wrestled with her blue chiffon party dress, trying to disengage some of the hooks to free herself to roughhouse with the boys at the party. Her mother, Helen, slapped her hard on the cheek to stop her. It was a sharp crack that startled everyone within earshot. Silence descended upon the gathering, as everyone turned in horror to watch. But Ruthie didn't cry. She pinched her reddening face together, brave in her pain, as she teetered on the brink of tears. I thought she was a remarkable child, even then, when I was no more than seven. In subsequent years, Ruth and I often ran into each other at university functions. Then, when I was a sophomore at Riverdale Country School, a precocious freshman named Ruth Chalmers enrolled and became the toast of the English and Art Departments. Ruth was a poetess and painter; quite a good one, if the faculty of Riverdale was to be believed. She edited the *Riverdale Philomathean* that year, and later on, so I heard, founded an alternative review that published students' poetry and art work. From Riverdale, Ruth shipped out to Wellesley, where she graduated in May 1959. I understood she had published some poems in several literary journals whose names I didn't recognize. I didn't know what she was up to now.

After a shower and a cup of coffee, I called the Chalmers residence and asked for Ruth.

"Who's calling?" asked a male voice—Billy, I presumed.

"This is Ellie Stone. Is that Billy?"

"Yeah," he said. "Hi." He was an odd one.

"Hi, Billy. Is Ruth in?"

He put down the phone, and a few moments later I heard another extension pick up.

"Hello, Ellie," came the clean, measured voice from the other end. "Thank you for calling."

"How've you been?" I asked. "You seemed a little under the weather the other night."

She spoke slowly and deliberately—she always had—as if every word were precious to her.

"It was so horrible. I was very upset by the whole thing, and after what happened to your father . . . How is he?"

"The doctors don't know yet."

"I'm sorry," she said. "Then I suppose you wouldn't be interested in meeting me this afternoon. I need to talk to someone."

I wondered why she didn't speak to her family, but then I remembered her insufferable parents and strange brother.

"Sure, I'd love to meet," I said. "I'd like to talk to someone, too. Just say where and when."

"Your place," she said abruptly. "Let's make it five thirty. Good-bye, Ellie." And she hung up.

I held the phone in the crick of my neck for another few seconds as I jotted down the appointment. As the moments passed, I realized there was no new dial tone. I listened a few moments longer, waiting for it. Ten, fifteen seconds, then a quiet click from the other end of the line, and a fresh dial tone.

Miss Little informed me by phone that Professor Bruchner had called to say he would not be in the office this day. I asked for his telephone number and address.

"He lives in midtown, in one of those big apartment houses. Let me check his card." A rustling of papers. "Here it is: 145 East Thirty-Eighth, apartment 2210. MUrray Hill-6-2391. Any other numbers you need, Miss Stone?"

"As a matter of fact, yes. Bernie Sanger's, Hildy Jaspers's, and Roger Purdy's. And do you still have Professor Petronella's number?"

She waited a moment, as if she expected me to ask for someone else. "Why, no. When he left Columbia he moved from his address on the Upper East Side. I think he's living somewhere in the Bronx, but he didn't give us a new address."

She dictated Bernie Sanger's address: 110th Street, near campus; Purdy lived on East Eighty-Second, just off the park. Hildy lived in Chelsea on Nineteenth Street.

"Anyone else? she asked, her voice loaded with suggestion. "Oh, but you must already have Mr. Lucchesi's telephone number."

"Thanks, I've interviewed him already," I said, ears burning from the censure.

I rang off and dialed Bruchner's number. No answer. I buttoned a cardigan sweater over my white blouse, wriggled into my tweed overcoat, and grabbed my purse and camera. Then I made for the elevator.

When I was a girl, I used to gaze in awe at the lions guarding the entrance of the New York Public Library. I still give them a smile when I climb the stairs. They sit serenely, with majestic bearing, their proud heads raised, giant paws posed so tidily before them. I had spent many afternoons in the cavernous reading room, digesting the first volumes of the education that stretched out before me. The public library had been for me a kind of cathedral—like Yankee Stadium—different only by virtue of its custodial responsibility for Knowledge. Lined up like bricks in some colossal wall, millions of volumes waited for the next pair of hands to pluck them from their shelves and open their wisdom to the light.

The library also has an impressive collection of telephone directories. I wasn't looking for anything exotic, like Bombay or Peking; just the Bronx.

I located an Anthony Petronella on Garrison Avenue in Hunts Point, the Bronx. Fishing for a dime, I sat down in a phone booth and tried the number. An elderly Italian woman answered, and after some word wrangling, I established that Anthony Petronella was her son.

I asked if he was in, speaking deliberately, as if she had suffered some horrible aphasia.

"No, Antonio, he teach now. *È a scuola a quest'ora.* At school."

"Which school?" I asked, sure it was but the first of many attempts to get the name.

"*Che?*"

"*Scuola? Quale?*" I said, dredging up the little Italian I had picked up along the way; one of the benefits of having spent a summer in Florence with my father.

"PS *Cinquantadue,*" she said finally.

I thanked *Signora* Petronella, hung up, then reached for my notepad to write down the information. It wasn't in my purse, however, and I remembered having left it near the phone in my father's apartment. I tore a corner of a page out of the phonebook instead and jotted down a note.

I dropped another dime into the phone, intending to try Bruchner's number, but I again remembered it was in the pad I'd left at my father's place. I hung up and grabbed the bulging phonebook underneath the Bronx, and opened to the *B*s. Bruchner, G., 1306 East Sixteenth Street, ESsex 3-5861.

I shook my head: 1306 East Sixteenth Street? I couldn't remember the address Miss Little had given me, but I knew it was in Murray

Hill, and Sixteenth Street was not. Besides, there was no 1300 block of any east–west street in Manhattan. I flipped the book closed, my hand marking the page, to see if the book was current. 1958–59, *BROOKLYN*, New York.

If "G.," by some chance, belonged to a Gualtieri Bruchner, this was an unexpected development. Either the rarest of coincidences, or the visiting professor from Padua was an odder fellow than people suspected. I am, by nature, curious, and saw no reason to change my spots now. I tried the Brooklyn number but got no answer. Jingling the subway tokens in my change purse, I wrote down the address and phone number, calculating in my head which train I would need to take and where I would have to transfer.

✺

East Sixteenth Street in Brooklyn runs southeast from Prospect Park to Brighton Beach, flanked by the stilted legs of the elevated train line. I got off at Avenue M and climbed down to Sixteenth Street, where the rumbling of the trains above seemed to shake the very earth. I found 1306 East Sixteenth: a five-story tenement, indistinguishable from its neighbors on either side of the El track. A black fire escape zigzagged down its dull, brown-bricked face, and another passing train rattled the metal as I watched. I climbed the steps to the entrance, searched the mailboxes for Bruchner's name. No luck. I thought I'd made a long, dreary trip for nothing, but rang the super just to be sure.

"Bruchner?" asked the fat lady in a green housedress. "He's in the walk-down, just outside to the right. Got his own mailbox."

I followed the woman's directions to a dark, narrow stairway leading down half a flight below the sidewalk. The passage smelled of urine, and there was loose trash in front of the door. The name on the dented, black mailbox read *Gualtieri Bruchner*.

CHAPTER ELEVEN

That there could be two men named Gualtieri in New York was possible, but two Gualtieri Bruchners? I had found only four Bruchners in the entire Brooklyn phone directory. How was it possible, then, that a visiting professor, in the country for no more than six or seven months, could have found the time to rent a walk-down in Brooklyn? Or, indeed, why? Professor Bruchner seemed a refined man to me. He kept an apartment on East Thirty-Eighth Street in Murray Hill, dressed well, and never strayed outside the lines of proper, albeit stony, behavior.

The bricks and mortar of the stairwell shook as another train passed overhead. No one answered the door when I knocked, so I returned to the super's apartment on the ground floor.

"Do you know when I might find Mr. Bruchner at home?" I asked.

The lady eyed me suspiciously, looking me up and down. "Who wants to know?"

"My name is Ellie Stone," I said. "He works with my father, and I wanted to have a word with him."

"Your father works in the subway?" she asked, screwing up her face. "You don't look like a transit worker's girl. A little too fancy for that."

"Pardon me?"

"You sure you got the right guy?" she asked. "Little, mole of a man, he is. Quiet, never says a word. Just comes home and goes to work."

So far the description she had given could fit Bruchner, but the subway?

"Maybe I am mistaken," I said. "How old is Mr. Bruchner?"

"Well, he looks a lot older than he is. I know for a fact he's just a little over fifty. Been here since '48; you learn things about a tenant in twelve years."

"Since '48?" I asked, subtracting in my head December 1908 (the date in Bruchner's file at the department) from 1960: fifty-one or fifty-two.

"Where does Mr. Bruchner come from?" I asked.

The woman shook her head in woe. "A sad story. He doesn't talk about it, but he was one of them deported Jews in the war. Was in Auschwitz."

"But where was he from originally?"

"You'd never guess it by the name, but he's from Italy." (She pronounced it *It-ly*.)

"What does he do in the subway?" I asked, interrupting her musings.

"He's a motorman. Drives the F-Train."

※

The dispatcher at the Stillwell station on Coney Island told me Gualtieri Bruchner was indeed driving the F-Train.

"Karen knocks off at three," he said.

"Karen?" I asked through the glass. "Is that a woman? I thought his name was Gualtieri."

"Could be," said the dispatcher. "I suppose he'd have to have a real name, but nobody around here calls him that. It's been Karen for as long as I've been here, and that's nine years."

"Why do you call him Karen?"

The man shrugged. "I call him that because that's what everyone's always called him."

I looked at my watch: five past noon. "Which train is he driving?" I asked. "I've got to go back into Manhattan anyway; I might as well take his train."

The dispatcher flipped through some papers. "The 1502," he said finally. "But if you ride his train, girlie, don't you go talking to him. It's against regulations."

Forty-five minutes later the 1502 finally rolled into the station, probably for Karen Bruchner's last run. I boarded the front car and stood by the porthole that looked out on the tracks before the train. When we pulled to a stop in the Avenue U station, I knocked on the motorman's booth.

"What?" came a muffled voice from inside.

"Open up, Karen," I said. "I got a message from the dispatcher."

The door popped open, and I peered into the dark room. A gaunt, little jerboa of a man sat at the controls of the big train, looking to me expectantly.

"Are you Mr. Bruchner?" I asked him.

He nodded. "Who are you?" He had a foreign accent, but I couldn't exactly place it. His voice sounded barely stronger to my face than when it had been muted behind the door.

"I'm not from the dispatcher," I said. "My name is Ellie Stone."

He squinted at me. "What do you want? I'm working."

"I thought I knew you," I said. "You're Gualtieri Bruchner, is that right?"

"Yes," he said. "What do you want?"

"I've got to ask you about your past."

The little man gaped at me, silent for half a minute. "What are you talking about?" he asked finally.

"I'm asking because I know another man here in New York named Bruchner. Gualtieri Bruchner."

He seemed unnerved.

"He's fifty-one years old."

The gray man said nothing. He just stared at me.

"And he was born in Merano, in the Alto Adige," I said.

"*Non è proprio possibile*," mumbled Bruchner, staring down the tracks into the dark tunnel.

The radio in the motorman's cabin rasped at the driver: "Hey, Karen, when we gonna get moving?"

Bruchner came back to life, picked up the mike and said, "I'm going, Ralphie."

He turned to me as the doors to the platform slid shut. "Don't go away," he said. "We'll talk at three. I'm off duty then."

He closed the door to his cabin, and the train eased out of the station, then picked up speed as it rumbled down the tracks. I stood at the front window, watching the railroad ties disappear beneath the train. Station after station appeared as a small light at the end of the dark tunnel, looming ahead, then rushing forward to meet us. The hole was an eerie place; I'd never ridden in the first car before, never shared the motorman's view. We streaked past endless columns of huge support beams that held the city on their shoulders. We rolled over trash, we switched tracks, and slowed for signal lights. We were in the belly of the city, traveling through a netherworld of soot and foul air, illuminated only occasionally by the blue flash of some nub of metal scraping the electrified rail. Outside the shell of the subway car, the subterranean landscape was a black and desolate highway, punctuated every so often by rank, decaying orifices, known as stations, which spat the itinerant souls back up onto the streets to the light of day. I watched without realizing the passing time.

An hour later, we turned around in the 179th Street station in Jamaica, Queens, and ran the same route in reverse: Kew Gardens, Forest Hills, Woodside, into Manhattan, down the West Side, back east again into Brooklyn, under Prospect Park, and out of the hole onto the El to Coney Island. Terminus.

It was 3:20 when Bruchner emerged from a door marked *Personnel*. The top of his ratty tweed cap barely reached my chin, and I thought him better suited for riding horses at Aqueduct than jockeying trains beneath the streets of New York's three largest boroughs. He looked up at me, trying to read my soul through my eyes.

"What is this, Miss Stone?" His accent was clearer now, similar to Bruchner's, a little heavier perhaps.

"I'm as confused as you," I said. "I found your name by accident in the phonebook this morning, and I couldn't believe there were two Gualtieri Bruchners in New York."

"But why are you looking for Gualtieri Bruchner?"

We began walking down the platform toward an exit. "My father was attacked in his home last Friday night and has been in a coma ever since," I said. "Earlier that afternoon, he'd argued with this Bruchner fellow. I wanted to ask him what had caused the disagreement."

The little man seemed to darken as I explained the details and outlined the coincidences between him and the visiting professor from Padua.

"I don't know what this is about," he said, "but I am Gualtieri Bruchner. I was born December 21, 1908, in Merano, Alto Adige. Not this other man. I have naturalization and citizenship papers."

"What about an old Italian passport?" I asked.

He shook his head and clicked his tongue. "No, I never had an Italian passport."

"Then how did you get into the United States?"

His eyes trembled in their sockets. "Come to my home; I don't like to talk of it outside."

Bruchner's one-room apartment was stark, nearly bare. The place was clean enough and ordered—how much clutter can two folding chairs, a table, and a bed make? It was ponderously depressing. No light from the street could cut through the grime that covered the two barred windows in the front. In the back of the room, Bruchner had long since covered the only window with yellowed newspapers. I couldn't fathom a guess.

"When did you come here?" I asked, offering him a cigarette. He shook his head wearily.

"In 1948," he said.

"War refugee?"

He cast his eyes down, then spoke softly. "I was a proud man, Miss Stone. Second engineer on the Venice–Trentino line at the age of twenty-four. The *podestà* decorated me for service during the winter of 1942. I was too small for the army, but I knew the trains. I drove through snow, damaged tracks, and under bombs from British and American planes. Then, after Mussolini was executed, the Germans took northern Italy." He swallowed hard, and I could almost see his temples throb in the dim light. "On December 30, 1943, the SS took me from my train and put me in a camp. Three weeks later they locked me inside a closed cattle car with a hundred others." He paused, his face as rigid as a dike holding back the sea. "They said they were sending us to a new home, a place where we can be with others like us. Men, women, children, babies, all jammed together like . . . animals. *Sono un uomo, io!*" His last outburst released the tears he'd been holding in, but the cathartic effect returned him to calm in short order.

"The shame was heavy, and the conditions were hard," he said, resuming his story. "Three days we traveled, through freezing cold, locked inside with the filth, *la merda, la piscia, la morte.* Twenty-five of us died in that hell."

Karen Bruchner crossed the room and meekly held out a broad, coarse hand. I looked at him, unsure at first what he wanted. Then realizing he'd changed his mind about the cigarette, I passed him one. He turned around again and retook his distance from me. He lit the cigarette with a wooden kitchen match.

"Thank you," he said softly, barely more audibly than his deep inhale of the cigarette. He closed his eyes and savored the smoke's burn in his lungs, then let it out slowly, his nostrils fuming like an idle locomotive for the next minute. "I don't smoke much no more," he said. "Too much bad air in the hole. I spent most my life in trains. The smoke is very strong. Now, I drive an electric train," he laughed and took another drag. "But the air is more worse down there. That's why I don't smoke no more."

"Where did they send you?" I asked. "The Germans."

He looked at me. "Auschwitz."

Then he did something I almost wished he hadn't. He approached me again. Again, he held out his hand. But this time, he pulled back the worn sleeve on his left arm to expose his wrist. The dark skin was rope-tight, stringy muscles underneath. Then he turned his arm over, and I saw the two-inch line of blue numbers on the outer side of his wrist.

"They give me this tattoo when I arrived," he said, rubbing the deep mark hard with his right thumb. "It don't come off. They branded me like a cow, then worked me like a dog."

"How did you survive?" I asked.

Bruchner pushed his sleeve back down to his wrist and took another deep drag of his cigarette. "I did what I done all my life," he said. "I drove the train."

"The train?"

"The Germans took the mines in the Silesia, and we were slave laborers for the Nazis. When we arrived, they asked us our professions. I said railroad engineer. They said I was lucky; they hanged the engineer that morning for stealing coal from the locomotive. So, they put me on the train in the mines. *Beato me.*" He forced an ironic smile.

"Did you ever go back to Italy?" I asked.

"No. After the war I tried, but I had no papers. So they put me in another camp: displaced persons. Displaced? I knew where to go, but the Russians said no. Finally, they sent me to the British Sector in Berlin. I told them I want to go to Italy or Palestine, but the English, they stopped the Jews from going to Israel. So, they give me to the Americans. I still want to go to Italy or Palestine, but they tell me I can go to America. I said, 'OK, take me to America, far from trains and sulfur.'" Again the ironic smile. "Look at me now. Still working in the mines, driving a train."

"Do you have any idea who might want to assume your identity?" I asked. "Did you have any enemies back in Merano? Someone, maybe, who thought you were dead?"

He shook his head. "I had no enemies."

"Would you be willing to meet Gualtieri Bruchner?"

⁂

Ruth Chalmers approached 26 Fifth Avenue on foot as I watched from the window of the Rose Café restaurant next door. She was wearing a green wool coat, open despite the chill January air, navy skirt and stockings, and dark glasses. Her shoulder-length hair bobbed in the breeze to the rhythm of her unhurried pace. She was a pretty girl, gentle and lovely, but she inspired none of the beguiling lust of a Hildy Jaspers. She looked sad.

I scooted out the door to meet her before she went into my father's building.

"Hello, Ellie," she said, the hint of a smile peeking through the gloom. "I'm glad you could meet me today."

"Me, too. Would you like to go have a coffee? Someplace on Bleecker, maybe?"

She nodded her indifference. "Sure, why not?"

We walked down Fifth Avenue, through Washington Square, and down MacDougal Street. At the corner of Bleecker we ducked into the Figaro and sat next to a table of Bohemians. They were talking about an experimental film they wanted to make. Something about no lights, no characters, just some kind of moaning off camera for an hour and a half. We moved to another table.

"What's wrong, Ruth?" I asked, staring at the ruby on her left middle finger.

"It's all this violence," she said, sighing, her eyes sparkling beneath unshed tears. She glanced around the room absently.

"You hardly know my father," I said. "He's barely an acquaintance, let alone a friend."

She shrugged. "It's upsetting. And I've always liked him."

"And Ercolano?"

She twisted the ring on her finger. "The same."

A bearded young man arrived to take our order. We asked for two coffees.

"That's a pretty ring." I said. "Where did you get it?"

"It's a keepsake of someone I knew. Just a girlish romance that ended. You'd be bored."

I watched her as she spoke. The clear green of her irises shone in the low light, and the skin of her cheeks was a soft matte. There was more she wasn't telling me.

"You're right," I said, shifting in my chair. "This whole thing is upsetting. I was in Ercolano's apartment the other night." She didn't move. "The police took me there."

"Why? You didn't know him, did you?"

I shook my head. "But it appears that Ercolano's death and the attack on my father are related."

Now her eyes narrowed. "What?"

The waiter interrupted to drop our coffees on the table, then withdrew.

"The police suspect Ercolano was the burglar who tried to kill my father and stole his manuscript," I said.

She struggled to understand. "That's impossible," she said calmly. "Ercolano was a good scholar, Ellie. He wasn't stupid enough to steal a noted professor's latest book and try to call it his own. And he was a nineteenth-century scholar, besides."

"I said the police suspect him. I don't."

"What makes them think he had anything to do with the attack on your father?"

"We checked his mailbox and found a return receipt from the post office for a package sent to Princeton. When we retrieved the package, my father's manuscript was inside, with Ercolano's name on the title page."

"It's absurd," she said.

"Maybe. But we did find my father's gold pens and strongbox in his desk."

"Then someone planted them," she blurted out. "Ruggero was an honest man. And he respected your father. He liked him very much."

Before Ruth and I parted company, I managed to find out that she had gone on a date Wednesday, and had seen *Suddenly Last Summer* by herself on Friday night.

"Alone?" I asked.

She shrugged. "It's better than spending time with my family. I'd already seen it, but I had nothing else to do."

I sipped my coffee and decided not to mention that it was my mother's ruby she was wearing on her left hand.

I walked her to the West Fourth Street station then headed back through the park and up Fifth Avenue. The phone rang a few minutes after I'd walked in the door of my father's apartment.

"McKeever here. I'm calling about Tiffany's. We know who bought the tie clip for Ercolano."

"Surprise me and say it wasn't Ruth Chalmers."

Silence down the line. "Why do you bother asking me to look into things if you already know the answers?" he asked. "It took two men three hours to get that information out of a Tiffany's clerk without a warrant."

"Sorry," I said. "I just spent a couple of hours with Ruth. It was clear she was in love with Ercolano, and that she was defending him with a lover's passion."

"Just a hunch?" he asked.

"I got lucky; the ring she was wearing just happened to be one of my mother's favorites."

"What?"

"Mom wore that ring until the day she died. I had assumed it was buried with her."

"I thought no jewelry was missing from your father's apartment."

"You tell me," I said. "I asked if any had been taken, and the police said it appeared not."

"So, what do you figure?" he asked.

"I think Ruth was Ercolano's young girlfriend, the one his neighbor mentioned. Do you remember what the police report said about Ercolano's death?"

"I can recite it chapter and verse. What about it?"

"Who did it say found the body?"

There was a pause on the line. "Ruth Chalmers's father."

"Exactly. Victor Chalmers paid me a visit the other night to explain how he had happened to be in Ercolano's neighborhood after midnight on a Saturday. Chalmers lives across the park on the Upper East Side. He tried to have me believe Hildy Jaspers had called him from Ercolano's apartment."

"Are you sure she didn't?"

"I haven't found any of my mother's possessions on Hildy's person."

"So, you're saying that Victor Chalmers went to Ercolano's apartment to bail his daughter out of a bad situation?"

"I believe so," I said. "Ruth was there that night. And if the neighbors and super are to be believed, Ercolano died at ten thirty. Chalmers called the police at what time?"

"The call was logged in a little after one o'clock."

"Then I'd say Ruth found her boyfriend dead in the bathroom and panicked. She called her father, who came over and decided what to do and what story to tell."

"Then how did Ruth get the ring?"

"She probably found it in Ercolano's apartment before her father arrived. She wanted a keepsake of her lover and took it. She seemed to treasure it."

"Then we're back where we were with Ercolano as the most logical suspect," said McKeever.

"The ring was in his apartment," I said. "But that doesn't necessarily have anything to do with logic."

"You think she's innocent?" he asked, already convinced of his answer. "Innocent enough to sleep with a debauched professor ten years her senior? Do nice girls do that, Ellie?"

"Nice girls do a lot of things you wouldn't suspect," I said. "Ruth Chalmers was in love with Ercolano; so much in love she couldn't see how he was playing her for a fool against that other woman. All the other women."

"I'm bringing her in," announced the cop.

"Give me a couple of days," I said. "With a little luck, I'll clear this thing up."

He mulled it over. "If you're not pressing charges for theft of the ring, I suppose I can wait."

"I appreciate your hanging in there on this," I said. "I mean for not taking the easy way out and pinning this on a poor dead man."

He was quiet for a long while, and I felt he wanted to say something important to me. I thought his silence betrayed a pain, though not one I could identify. In the end, he said simply that it was his job. And then he told me the pens found in Ercolano's office, the ones I knew belonged to my father, had all been wiped clean. No prints at all.

"That doesn't exactly implicate Ercolano," I said.

"It doesn't clear him, either."

I took a few minutes to go through my father's mail, which had been accumulating on the secretary near the door in the foyer. There were some bills, a letter from Carnegie Hall, a couple of journals and glossy magazines, and various pieces of bulk mail, but little in the way of personal or professional correspondence. The only letter worth noting was an airmail envelope plastered with colorful foreign stamps and a postmark from Padua, Italy. A Professor Nardone had written the letter, and it was in Italian. I could make out the gist in only the grossest terms, relying on cognates and my sketchy memory of a summer in Italy years before. Why hadn't I, the daughter of a renowned Italianist, studied Italian? My father has often begged me to answer that one. One of the few words not needing translation was Bruchner. The letter was obviously a response to an earlier inquiry from my father about the visiting professor.

Chiarissimo Professor Stone,

La prego di scusare il ritardo di questa mia risposta alla Sua cortese lettera del 15 novembre scorso; purtroppo mi trovavo all'ospedale per un intervento non tanto grave quanto scomodo.

Le posso assicurare innanzi tutto che il Professor Bruchner, da quanto ho potuto osservare negli anni in cui era mio collega qui a Padova, si è sempre comportato da persona colta e perbene . . .

Formal Italian. The object, my father always said, is to achieve a one-sentence, multi-paragraph letter. That, of course, is impossible, but

Italians take a stab at it anyway each time they pick up a pen to write. Wading through the successive clauses, I managed to cull something of the mess: Nardone, a colleague of Bruchner's in Padua, was writing to dispute some kind of accusations my father had leveled against Bruchner. But, my Italian being what it was, I couldn't figure what the accusations entailed. I fetched an Italian–English dictionary from a shelf and looked for the word that had me stumped: *ebreo*. Nardone had insisted that Bruchner was indeed "*ebreo*." Aware of Bruchner's background in the concentration camp, I was surprised to find that the word meant Jewish or Jew. My father suspected Bruchner was not a Jew.

There was one other thing: if I understood Nardone's closing, my father had also solicited a response from Professor Arturo Marescialli, the old friend who had recommended Bruchner in the first place. Since Nardone opened his letter with an apology for his tardy response, Marescialli must have already sent his answer. Where, then, was the letter?

Nelda had cleaned up the study, swept up the bits of broken vinyl and shellac, and put the desk back in order. I slid open the lower right-hand drawer and flipped through the hanging files Nelda had returned to their rails. Near the front I found a folder tabbed *Correspondence* in my father's handwriting. Inside were two manila folders labeled *Personal* and *Professional*, respectively. I dumped the contents of *Personal* on the desk. The birthday card I'd sent him the previous August was in the mix, along with notes from colleagues, friends, and relatives. The latest postmark in the bunch was a January 10, 1960, letter from my Aunt Lena, my mother's sister, from Florida, wishing him a happy New Year. Apparently my father's concerns about Bruchner were anything but personal.

Back to the *Professional* file, this time to find my father's letters; he kept meticulous track of his own correspondence, making carbons of everything he ever wrote. The file for 1959–60 (the rest was archived somewhere else in the room) ended abruptly on October 25, 1959, except for one brief letter. It was from my father's cousin, Max Zeitler, a noted pro bono lawyer in Washington, DC. He looked forward to seeing my father on December 28 in Washington, and he outlined where my father should carry out the research he'd mentioned in his letter. In closing, he asked my father not to forget to bring the book on Southwestern Indian Art. Cousin Max had finally succumbed to the harping of his friends and agreed to take a vacation to Arizona. A train lover from his days as a child, Max wrote that he had reserved a sleeper from Washington to Phoenix on January 19. I wondered why my father considered Max Zeitler's letter professional instead of personal.

There were no other letters, received or sent, after that date. I found it hard to believe my father hadn't written a letter in three months, or that he had run out of carbon paper, which he hoarded as if speculating.

I lit a cigarette, leaned back in my father's chair to think, and watched the smoke rise to the ceiling. Some of the correspondence could be at the Italian Department, but all of it? Even his weekly letters to his cousin Max Zeitler?

The rest of the mail from the foyer was discardable altogether, except for the letter from Carnegie Hall. It had been addressed in an elegant hand, and the envelope was a fine rag-content variety: not a run-of-the-mill bulk mailing. So I opened it.

January 19, 1960

Dear Dr. Stone:

I am writing to thank you for your generous contribution to this year's fundraising drive. It is especially important to us at this time, as we fight to save our beloved hall from demolition. We will send you your complimentary tickets (under separate cover on the 20th) for Van Cliburn's recital on Sunday, January 31, at 8:00 p.m. If you do not receive them, please contact the box office immediately.

I would like to take this opportunity to invite you to a special reception with Mr. Cliburn in the Recital Hall following the concert. I look forward to seeing you there.

Sincerely,
Laszlo Vanek
Events Manager

I went back to digging through the drawers in my father's study. This time I was looking for complimentary tickets to see Van Cliburn. None. I checked the bedroom, his briefcase, and the pockets of all his suits. No tickets anywhere.

I relieved McDunnough bedside at eight o'clock for the night watch. The burly Irishman said he'd return at seven the following morning. I settled in for a long night of beeps and pumping bellows; my father's heartbeat had strengthened, according to Nurse Tielman, and his blood pressure was higher. Reason for hope, although the improving signs said nothing of possible brain damage.

I tried Bruchner's number without success every hour on the hour, from the public phone outside the ICU. Among other questions, I wanted to ask him the name of the man who had arrived with my father the previous Friday afternoon at the Faculty Club; what my father had meant by demanding to see his "other" tattoo; and how Bruchner could share a name, birthplace, birthday, and history with a man living in a walk-down tenement in Millwood, Brooklyn.

As I sat vigil bedside, I struggled to make sense of the two attacks. An endless procession of scenarios marched through my head, including Victor Chalmers's story of Hildy and Ercolano. I was sure it had been Ruth in the dead man's apartment that night, but maybe a playboy like Ercolano shuffled girls in and out like a hustler dealing three-card monte on the street. Maybe Hildy had been there that night. And what about my father? The elevator man at 26 Fifth Avenue knew Hildy's name and said she'd recently visited the apartment. I didn't even want to think about the possible implications of that piece of information.

CHAPTER TWELVE

SATURDAY, JANUARY 30, 1960

When Sean McDunnough showed up Saturday morning at seven, I headed straight to Murray Hill and the tower on Thirty-Eighth between Lexington and Third. The concierge stopped me, asking which apartment I wanted to visit. I had anticipated just such an eventuality, so he didn't catch me off guard.

"My name is Joanna Morgan, from the firm of McKim, Mead & White," I said, thinking of the Morgan Library which I'd passed a few minutes earlier on Thirty-Sixth Street, and the architects who'd designed it. "I'm here to serve Mr. Bruchner a summons. Would you be so kind to call up?"

The man frowned. "Isn't it a bit early to be serving papers? And on a Saturday?"

"I've made every effort to contact Mr. Bruchner during normal business hours," I said. "But people do their best to avoid us."

"Yeah, wonder why," he sneered at me as he picked up the house phone. After consulting a list of tenants, he dialed a three-digit number, and listened. "No answer," he said finally.

"Could you accompany me up to his apartment?" I asked. "My office requires that I make a physical knock on the door before reporting that the servee is not in." (What a crock.)

The concierge looked around. "Look, it's 7:20 on a Saturday morning. I got one guy on the door and an engineer in the basement; do you think I'm going to leave my desk just so you can knock on the guy's door?"

"If you wouldn't mind." I didn't want to be the one to suggest I go up unaccompanied. Somehow people are less suspicious when they're the ones who actually suggest bending the rules.

Again the look around the lobby. "Oh, go on up," he said finally. "But if he asks, don't say I let you in."

I thanked him humbly, still offering to let him escort me up and down, but he just waved me by.

"It's 2210," he said as the elevator doors closed me inside.

The car whooshed up to the twenty-second floor, stopping only at the twelfth floor where a confused woman with a Chinese pug had pushed the *up* button instead of the *down*.

"Can't you let us go down first?" she asked. "Little Leon, here, has to do his business."

I explained that the elevator wouldn't change directions just for little Leon, even if I relinquished my right of way. She seemed distrustful, and I shrugged my shoulders apologetically as the doors closed once more.

When the car stopped again, I stepped out onto the twenty-second floor, face-to-face with 2210, bang opposite the elevator. I buzzed, waited a few seconds, then buzzed again. Glancing to either side, I reached down for the knob to give it a twist; you never know. Just then, however, the door swung open, and a man in a long silk robe and pajamas stood before me. I nearly fell into his arms. It was Professor Gualtieri Bruchner.

"What are you doing here, Miss Stone?" he asked, his gray eyes even darker than usual with early-morning rings.

I consider myself reasonably unflappable, but I confess the sudden appearance of the grim Bruchner set my heart to racing like a piston. In truth, I hadn't expected him to be at home or, at least, not to answer. Now, as he stood there glaring at me with his spooky eyes, I groped for something to say.

"Good morning, Professor Bruchner," I said, righting myself. "I've been trying to contact you for a couple of days now."

His right eyebrow climbed his forehead. "Indeed?"

"Yes. Sorry to intrude at this hour. I didn't think you would be in."

"Then why are you here?"

A good question. I probably would have tried to break in, though I wasn't about to tell Boris Karloff that.

"I was going to leave you a message to call me."

"Why didn't you leave a message with the concierge?"

He had me there. I was letting him dictate the proceedings. We had been talking for at least a minute, and he had asked all the questions. I struck back.

"Look, I know you're avoiding me, but I really need to ask you some questions. I've been phoning you for two days, and there's never an answer."

"I was out. You should call when I'm in."

At least I had regained control. "All night long? Five minutes ago?" I asked. "I called from the lobby before coming up here."

"Tell me, please, why I must endure this in my own home on a Saturday morning," he said, trying to reverse the tide himself.

But I had my trump to play. "Because you had lunch at the Columbia Faculty Club last Friday afternoon, and plenty of people saw what happened."

Bruchner stiffened, thought of answering, then gave up. "Perhaps we have started poorly this morning, Miss Stone. Would you like to come in for a coffee?"

Gualtieri Bruchner's apartment was a modest one-bedroom facing north. A spectacular view of the Chrysler Building made the northern exposure more palatable. The furniture was functional—rented, I figured—just a sofa, two stuffed chairs, and a small dinette set. The walls were bare, except for a framed Chagall poster from the Museum of Modern Art and a pair of prints by Klimt.

"About this misunderstanding," said Bruchner, pouring me a cup of black coffee.

"My understanding is that you had an altercation with my father at the Faculty Club last Friday," I said, cutting him off.

"It was more a *contretemps*. Your father is an excitable man."

I wasn't about to contradict him. "Why didn't you mention it to me the other day?" I asked. "You said you'd had lunch with him; that wasn't exactly true."

"I didn't think it necessary to tell you; it was a misunderstanding on your father's part."

"Can you tell me what it was about?"

He fidgeted. "I'd rather not discuss it," he said. "It has to do with the camps; I try to forget it."

"Were you in a concentration camp?" I asked.

He nodded. "Auschwitz. But I told your father this. For some reason he believed that I had manufactured the story of my deportation, but I can prove it."

He disappeared into the bedroom, rummaged through some drawers, then strode back to the dining table where I was sitting. He said nothing at first; he simply thrust a fading yellow Star of David under my nose. The edges were frayed, threads dangling from all sides, and in the center the word *Jude* was stitched in black.

"They made us all wear this star on our clothes before we arrived in the camp. And then there is this," and he produced a tattered gray card, printed with heavy black German characters.

I tried to read it, but couldn't make out much; only that it was an identification card of some kind from a work camp.

"Do you see my name here?" he asked, indicating a preprinted line with *Bruchner, Gualt.* in handwritten script. I nodded, and he took back the papers. "What else can I show you? I have the papers and the yellow star. And finally there's this," he said, voice trembling as he rolled up his left sleeve to show me the blue ink numbers tattooed into his wrist. They looked identical to ones I'd seen on Karen Bruchner's arm. "This, they gave us to mark us forever, even if we escaped.

"Why did my father think you were lying about your experience at Auschwitz? And why should he care?"

Bruchner took a seat at the table before his coffee. "I don't know," he sighed. "It began one day last October when we met at the gymnasium. He had just finished his swim, and I was in the sauna. Your father joined me, and we chatted for a while. Then, after my shower, I saw him again. He looked at me strangely, and since then he has been unfriendly to me."

"Did he ever explain why?"

"No, but I learned from colleagues that he was making inquiries into my past. You can imagine my alarm. My reputation, questioned before people whose respect is essential if I am to continue in this field: the only field I have, Miss Stone. Surely you understand my distress."

"Absolutely," I said. "I'm impressed by your restraint. From what you're telling me, I would expect you to bear him a bitter grudge."

Bruchner slammed a hand down on the table. "Are you implying that I hit him on the head? That I stole his possessions? Because of a grudge? A grudge I do not bear?"

"In your place, I would have wanted some satisfaction for the injury to my reputation."

"You and your father are of the same cloth," he said, barely containing his scorn. "He offended me, Miss Stone, but I did not wish him harm. Now you come to my home and make more accusations."

"I'd like to see your tattoo."

The professor was unnerved. "I showed you my tattoo," he stammered.

"Not the one on your wrist. I want to see the one on your chest."

"Young lady, this is preposterous!"

"Did you attack my father in his study last Friday evening?" I asked, leaning toward him.

Bruchner's panic grew. "Of course not! Do not come into my house and accuse me of such a crime."

"If you didn't try to kill him, you shouldn't be afraid to show me the tattoo."

He stood up abruptly, took a step back, and stared me in the eye. "All right, then. You want to humiliate me? I've suffered much worse at the hands of animals," and he ripped his pajama shirt open at the collar, sending mother-of-pearl buttons spraying like buckshot.

He flipped the torn fabric back over his sinewy white shoulders, thrusting out his bony chest.

I came closer to examine the two marks on his torso. They looked like bars of some kind—sticks, tattooed in dark blue.

"Are you satisfied?" he bristled.

"What are they?" I asked.

He hitched the shirt back over his shoulders, his ears burning red from embarrassment. "It is a tattoo, Miss Stone, to mask an error of my youth. I once tattooed the name of a girl into my chest. This ugly thing was the only way to cover it."

I wondered what my father could have found so scandalous about the innocuous little bars. Had I seen the tattoo in a steam bath, I never would have given it a second thought. Should I ignore it, then? I wasn't sure; my father had seen something there. Or was he wrong?

Whitlock Avenue rims the edge of the Hunts Point section of the Bronx. Rows of dreary houses on dreary streets huddled together as if for protection. The smell of industry and automobile exhaust thickened the morning air, and I remember being thankful I didn't have to live there. Gangs of jackhammers and backhoes were working nearby, even on a Saturday morning, making way for the future Bruckner Expressway. A pack of construction workers whistled at me and made lewd propositions as I passed. One lone wolf followed me for a block entreating me to reconsider. I was frightened. Finally he gave up when the foreman called him back and read him the riot act.

"Is Anthony Petronella in?" I asked the little old woman standing behind the chained door.

"He no here," she said. "What you want?"

"I need to find him. *Io voglio trovare Anthony. È molto importante.*" I hated speaking Italian.

"*Non c'è. È in città. Va sempre in città* the weekend."

"I'm a friend from school," I said. "I work with your son at PS 52. PS *Cinquantadue*," I added, feeling like an idiot.

This seemed to please her, and she was about to invite me in. I declined, explaining that I needed to contact Anthony about a teachers' strike. She didn't understand. I changed my lie.

"Anthony asked me to bring him this," I said, reaching for the only thing in my purse worth offering: a ten dollar bill.

Her eyes sparkled. "*Un minuto*," and she returned with a slip of paper. Now, she threw the door open wide and handed it to me. It was a phone number: PArkview 4-1919.

I found a pay phone on the subway platform in the Grand Concourse Station and dialed the number Petronella's mother had given me. I had rehearsed what I wanted to say, but never got the chance. The voice that answered the phone dripped with the haughty arrogance I had encountered more than once in recent days. I hung up the phone without saying a word, and jumped aboard the express train that had just pulled into the station.

I returned to the public library to consult the Manhattan phonebook. If the number Mrs. Petronella had given me matched the one of the person I was looking for, the ins and outs of Columbia's Italian Department were murkier than I had thought. I slid my finger down the names, passing Pierce, Porter, Pugh, Purdy. Roger Purdy, 56 East Eighty-Second Street, PArkview 4-1919.

The brownstone was one of the quietly dignified residences that you find off the avenues of the Upper East Side. A far cry from Hunts Point. A wrought-iron gate enclosed a small garden with a ginkgo tree and dormant flower beds. Atop the stoop, I peered into the foyer, spotted Purdy's mailbox—3-A—and tried the front door. Locked. Resorting to the simplest of Indian tricks, I rang a different apartment and waited. Nothing. The second choice produced the desired result, a dull buzz, and I was inside.

"Who is it?" called a woman's voice down the stairway. "Who's there?"

"Sorry, I pressed the wrong button," I answered. "Just going to 3-A."

A middle-aged woman in a dark sweater and slacks waited until I had reached the second floor landing, watching me with a sharp nose, as if I smelled.

"Are you a friend of his?" she asked.

"Of whose?"

"That young man in 3-A. Purdy."

"No, ma'am," I said, sensing her strong disapproval for young Roger. "I'm just here to serve a summons."

"A summons?" she snorted. "What's he done? You can tell me."

"Nothing, ma'am. He's being called to give evidence in a lawsuit. He's not directly involved."

She seemed disappointed. "Well, I can tell you we don't approve of him around here."

There was some fumbling behind the door of 3-A and a long moment of waiting after I'd knocked. Finally a man called through the door, asking who I was and what I wanted.

"Meter reader," I said.

"I don't have a meter in here," answered the voice.

I thought it might work; I wasn't good at this kind of thing. "Avon calling?"

The door jerked open and Roger Purdy towered over me in a bathrobe, his hair still mussed from a late Saturday sleep-in. It was only eleven. His eyes focused on my features for several seconds before he recognized me.

"You're Stone's daughter!" he accused. "What the hell do you want?"

I smiled sheepishly. "Sorry. I thought you might not open if you knew it was me."

"You were right about that," he said, closing the door.

I managed to insert a foot between the door and the jamb before he could shut me out.

"You'd better let me in," I grunted through the pain; Purdy intended to close the door whether my foot liked it or not.

"Go away or I'll call the police," he said, throwing his full weight behind the door.

"I don't think so," I said. "I've come to speak to Anthony Petronella."

The pressure on my foot eased a touch, then Purdy released the door. He opened it slowly, staring at me with a look halfway between terror and fury.

"What do you want?"

"I want to speak to Anthony Petronella," I said. "And I suppose you might be able to help, too."

"I have nothing to say to you. And Professor Petronella is not here. He's never been here."

"Don't let's be naive," I said. "I know he's here, and if you don't want anyone else to know, you'll let me in."

Purdy stared at me for another few seconds. I could see in his eyes that he was beaten. In the end, he stood aside, though he never actually invited me in.

"What's she doing here?" asked Petronella, emerging from the bedroom in a robe that matched Purdy's exactly. His and His.

"I can't take the credit for this one," said my host. "She's come to see you, Anthony."

"How did you find me?"

"Your mother helped me out."

"I hate your father and I hate you, too," said Petronella.

"Excuse us for a moment," said Purdy, leading Petronella into the bedroom. About five minutes later they came out, dressed, hair neatly slicked down with Brylcreem.

"All right, Miss Stone," began Purdy, taking a seat opposite me. "You know that we would like nothing better than to throw you out of here on your ear. But we're also painfully aware of our own delicate situation. So, let's just get it over with. What do you want to know?"

"I'd like to ask Dr. Petronella about his tenure case," I said.

Petronella gave an ironic snicker. "What's to tell? Your father derailed my bid for tenure. He ruined my career."

"How did he do it?"

"He fought against me tooth and nail in committee. He ridiculed my scholarship, assailed my character, and exerted his influence on the others to vote me down. I'll hate him for the rest of my life."

"If not his," I added.

"What are you implying?" he asked.

"Someone's tried to kill him twice, after all."

"If you're suggesting that I had anything to do with it, you're not only as odious as your father, you're an idiot. Do you think I would sit here and tell you how much I hate your father if I had anything to do with the attack on him?"

"What makes you so sure my father convinced the others to black-ball you?"

"I have my sources."

"Could you tell me who?"

He looked at Roger, mulling it over. "Victor Chalmers," he said finally. "When he called me in to explain the department's decision, he told me how the final meeting had gone."

"And how was that?"

"Your father announced that he would fight my tenure all the way to President Kirk's office. Victor and Franco were nervous about that, since your father and Kirk had known each other for years; his wife had bought some paintings from your mother, it seems, and they met at social functions. So, they all felt compelled to buckle under to make it unanimous."

Not quite the version I'd read in Miss Little's minutes.

"What about you, Mr. Purdy?" I asked, turning to Roger.

"I have nothing nice to say about your father, because of what he did to Anthony and what he did to me."

"The B?" I asked.

He seemed surprised that I knew. "Well, yes. But only because I deserved an A. A-plus, really."

"You pursued the matter vigorously."

"As well I should have," he said. "Your father was bent on ruining my future, so I'm fighting him on it."

"It's not over yet?"

Purdy looked surprised. "Of course not. What makes you think that?"

"I just assumed that my father was unwilling to budge."

"He was. But who knows what will happen now?"

I was stunned by his question and found it difficult to believe he'd said it to me, the man's daughter. I knew my father was at times insufferable, opinionated, and harsh, with a vindictive streak to make Stalin shudder, but he was principled. To him, weakness was a blight on the human spirit. He was arrogant because he knew he was brilliant. These paradoxes had helped to drive a wedge between him and me, ever deeper since the death of my brother. My nature, too, contributed to the estrangement of affection, but before Roger Purdy, I felt the urge to defend him.

"I wish you'd remember that you're speaking to his daughter," I said.

"I am aware of the fact," said Purdy, eyes narrowing with scorn, "and I chose my words with care."

I returned to 26 Fifth Avenue for a bath and a change of clothes. Rodney was sitting on his usual stool near the elevator. He returned my hello with a nod to the sofa across the lobby. Bernie Sanger was waiting for me.

We stepped into the elevator, and Rodney whispered to me that Bernie was the young man who'd accompanied my father home the night of the attack. Bernie couldn't help but overhear. He seemed miffed but said nothing.

"Thank you, Rodney," I whispered back.

"Would you like me to wait here?" asked Rodney, once we'd reached the fifteenth floor. I told him I was fine.

"I don't think he trusts me," said Bernie, indignant, as the elevator doors rolled shut.

"He's just protective of me," I said. "Now, what's so urgent, Bernie?"

"This arrived on my doorstep this morning," he said, handing me a small package.

I looked at it: a box wrapped in kraft paper—opened—with his name scrawled across the front. No postage, no return address. The handwriting was ambiguous, and I figured it could have been written by a man or a woman.

"Go ahead," said Bernie. "Open it."

What I found inside was a photograph of Adolf Hitler, torn from a book, with a caption written in large block letters across the front: *STAY AWAY FROM HER, YOU DIRTY JEW. IF YOU SOIL HER, I'LL KILL YOU!*

After the shock had dissipated, my attention came to rest on one word, perhaps more telling than the threats and diatribe: *SOIL*. Inconsistent with the tone of the note, *SOIL* was about as home on that page as Utica Club beer in a crystal flute. But what truly gave me pause was the certainty that I had heard the word recently. Helen Chalmers had pulled the evocative term from her bag of contempt for Bernie Sanger. He had "soiled" Hildy Jaspers, and would "soil" her daughter, Ruth, if given the chance.

"Do you have any idea who might have sent this?" I asked.

"Yes," said Bernie. "I got a telephone call yesterday, threatening me to stay away from her. I think it was Billy Chalmers."

"He said to stay away from Ruth?"

"Actually, I thought he meant Hildy Jaspers."

"Really?" I asked. I had never imagined Hildy was the her. "Why would Billy Chalmers care about Hildy Jaspers?"

Bernie shrugged. "I think he's sweet on her, but why he would threaten me, I don't get. He should call Gigi Lucchesi instead."

That stung me unexpectedly. "What do you mean?" I asked.

"Just that Gigi and Hildy are the cozy ones, not Hildy and me."

I flushed red, wanted to ask him for details, but I didn't dare.

"What's wrong, Ellie?"

"Nothing," I said, still fixated on Gigi and Hildy.

"You know, now that you mention it, I was talking to Ruth the other night at the reception," he said. "Billy was there too. Maybe he did mean Ruth after all."

"What?" I hadn't been paying attention.

CHAPTER THIRTEEN

Victor Chalmers and family lived in one of the brand-new, white-brick high rises that had sprouted up along Third Avenue when the El came down about five years earlier. He had given up his Carnegie Hill apartment and moved into the battleship building docked on Third Avenue and Eighty-Fourth Street. I remember my father speculating on several occasions why Chalmers had moved to the Upper East Side. He was fond of laying the blame at Helen Chalmers's feet.

"She wanted a doorman in a green blazer to walk that ugly little lapdog of hers."

A doorman in a green blazer met me in the lobby, and I asked for the Chalmers's apartment. He called upstairs to announce me, then dispensed directions on how to get to where I was going; the building sprawled from the southwest corner of Eighty-Fourth Street halfway to Lexington Avenue. The wrong elevator bank would take you to a different postal zone.

"Ellie, please come in," said Chalmers, greeting me at the door. "Can I fix you a drink?"

Why did everyone want to feed me liquor? "Sure," I said, following him to the study.

"Scotch, right? Quite strong for a girl, isn't it?" He didn't seem to expect an answer, as he started pouring immediately. "Now, what's this all about?" he asked, handing me the glass.

I sat on a short sofa, he took an armchair. "I called you because I wanted to show you this," and I produced the package Bernie had given to me about an hour earlier.

He took one glimpse and blanched. "My God!"

"Don't you want to know who sent it?" I asked.

He looked at me guardedly. "You know who it was?"

I was waiting for more reaction, drawing out the moment as long as possible. I thought he might know. "I suspect Billy or your wife sent this."

He winced, then summoned some grit and fought back: "That's an outrageous accusation, Ellie! How can you say that? What makes you think they would stoop to such behavior?"

"Bernie Sanger received a threatening phone call yesterday morning. He recognized Billy's voice."

"Sanger? That damn . . . How? How can he prove it?"

"I suppose he can't. But he's pretty sure it was him. And at first, he thought Billy wanted him to stay away from Hildy Jaspers."

Now my host nearly choked on his alarm. "What? Billy and Hildy! Impossible!"

"That's what I thought at first. Then I realized he was referring to Ruth."

Chalmers seemed relieved, but still managed some outrage. "Billy's no anti-Semite, and neither is Helen."

"You're probably right," I concurred. "At least no more than most. But I'm used to that; I always figure it's not my problem when people are bigoted, it's theirs."

"God, I can't stand this," said Chalmers, dropping his head into his hands. There was something more. "Listen," he said, suddenly raising his head and drawing a deep breath. "Helen had nothing to do with this, I'm sure of that. She would be as horrified as I am."

"What makes you so sure she had nothing to do with the letter?"

"Helen believes in direct confrontation. She's not shy. If she had wanted to keep Sanger away from Ruth, she would have told him so to his face." He sighed. "It's Billy, I'm sure. But he's no anti-Semite. He's just confused."

"What should I do about this?" I asked.

"Please, leave it to me, Ellie. I'll straighten Billy out. This won't happen again, I promise you. He's really a good boy, you know. Just a little emotional about the family."

I felt I'd tripped over some old family bones. He thanked me for the discretion I'd shown in bringing the matter to him instead of the police. Then at the door, he returned to Hildy Jaspers.

"What you said about her and Billy," he began. "You said you were mistaken, right?"

I nodded. What was it to him?

"You gave me a fright there," he said, smiling now. "Of course I shouldn't have worried; everyone knows she and Luigi Lucchesi are an item."

I left the Chalmers's residence feeling like a chump. I was being played for a fool, and it was the first time in my life that I cared. But why should I be surprised? Hildy Jaspers was gorgeous, stunning in her tight skirts and sweaters. She was an incorrigible and intoxicating flirt, a good-time girl with a "giving nature." Why wouldn't an exquisite boy like Gigi go crazy for her? Why would he even look at me if not for some ulterior motive?

⁂

"Miss Stone," said Joan Little, opening the door of her apartment on Barrow Street. She touched the red-and-black kerchief on her head, embarrassed to be caught in house-cleaning attire. She wiped her nose with a handkerchief. "I wasn't expecting anyone, please excuse the disorder."

She stood aside to let me in. The apartment looked fine to me, with only a few books out of place and an afghan thrown nonchalantly over the couch in front of the television. On the whole, it rated very clean in my book, right down to the waxed end tables and dustless corners.

"I wasn't expecting anyone," she repeated, and I could smell the alcohol on her breath. "May I offer you something? Some tea, perhaps? I have this terrible cold, so I'm drinking tea."

Tea and gin, I thought. "No thanks," I said, and she excused herself to go to the kitchen. When she returned with a cup of tea a few minutes later, I could see the kitchen hadn't been her only stop; she'd removed the kerchief, and her blonde hair was now neatly combed. There was a trace of pink on her lips, the blush of rouge on her cheeks. She was a nice-looking woman in her late thirties, not svelte, but curvy. She smiled weakly and invited me to sit. I pushed the afghan aside and sat on the couch.

"Sorry to intrude on your weekend like this, but I was hoping you could help me. I'm trying to get a handle on the department's personalities."

"I'm not sure how I can help, Miss Stone."

"Please, call me Ellie." That seemed to please her. "Let's start with Gualtieri Bruchner."

"I've already told you everything I know about him. He's a loner."

"What about his personal history? Have you ever heard anything about his past?"

"If you mean the concentration camp, yes, of course. Poor man; that probably explains his reticence. I remember he arrived in New York last summer, right in the middle of a heat wave. We were holding a departmental meeting, and everyone was wearing short sleeves and open-collared shirts, except Professor Bruchner. He had on his usual gray suit, tie knotted tightly around his neck. Professor Chalmers finally invited him to take off his jacket. That's when I saw the horrible tattoo on his wrist. It was ghastly. I felt so sorry for him."

"I just left Victor Chalmers," I said. "I'm sure you could tell me a lot about him."

"I don't think it would be proper, Miss Stone. I mean, Ellie." She smiled.

"This isn't for my titillation," I said. "Someone has tried to kill my father twice. The same person, I believe, succeeded in killing Ruggero Ercolano. I need to understand the dynamics of the department to get to the bottom of this. That means all the information has to come to light, because I don't know what's germane and what isn't until I hear it."

"You talk like a detective, but you're just a young girl. Don't you want to find a guy and get married?"

"Don't be fooled by my age or sex," I said, ignoring her question. "I'm after the man who attacked my father and killed Ruggero Ercolano. And I'll find him. I'm quite good at this kind of thing, and I don't easily give up."

She seemed to accept that. "All right," she said. "I'll speak frankly, but I need your assurances that what I say about these people will not be attributed to me." I gave her my word. "Dr. Chalmers is a level-headed, consistent man," she began. "He was an average scholar, when he was producing scholarship."

"Would you say he is a serious man? A man of conviction and honor?"

"How do you mean?"

I thought of a tactful way to put it: "Does he fool around?"

Miss Little cocked her head. "Is that pertinent to the attack on your father?"

I shrugged. "It could be. I don't know."

"Well, it was the biggest, yet most hushed-up scandal since I've been with the department. And that's five years."

"What scandal?"

"I don't want you to think of me as a gossip; I'm just telling you what you want to know. A year and a half ago, Professor Chalmers found himself in a most embarrassing situation. He was investigated by the ombudsman on a charge of impropriety. It involved Miss Jaspers. It all began after he went to see her in that disgraceful play."

"*Our Town*?"

"Yes," she said. "Well, not that *Our Town* is disgraceful, just the version she was in. Stark naked on the stage, she was. No shame, no modesty—naked under the bright lights in a theater full of men."

I swallowed hard, thinking of Gigi watching her from the front row. But then, Gigi hadn't yet arrived in New York at that time. Of course, since then he's probably enjoyed her private performances . . .

According to Joan Little, Professor Chalmers began pressuring Hildy Jaspers for a date after he'd seen her perform. As she understood it, Miss Jaspers dodged him for about a month, then he started to follow her, wait outside her apartment, and send her flowers, all to no avail. I

184 STYX & STONE

could just picture him, making a fool of himself, chasing a girl young enough to be his daughter. His devotion grew all the same, like ringworm, and he endured her repeated refusals, hoping to breach the chasm that separated him from the reach of Hildy's ten-foot pole. When none of his efforts bore fruit, he supposedly used his authority as chairman for leverage, a kind of extortion. But he had underestimated Miss Jaspers's resolve and smarts. She marched down to the ombudsman and filed a complaint. When the dust settled a few weeks later, Dr. Chalmers was suitably apologetic, though he acknowledged no wrongdoing. He maintained that it was all a misunderstanding on Miss Jaspers's part.

"What about his daughter, Ruth?" I asked. "She withdrew from Wellesley for a semester, didn't she?"

"Yes," said Miss Little hesitantly. "But what does Ruthie's leave of absence have to do with this?"

"I don't know, unless you tell me."

"She withdrew for some personal, family reasons. Dr. Chalmers never told me why. She just came home from school."

"And did she go anywhere? Did they send her away?"

Joan Little screwed her face into frown. "No, I told you she came home. She used to come to the department at least once a week; she was helping her father with a research project. What are you implying, Ellie?"

I shook my head. "Nothing, I guess. I thought they might have pulled her out of Wellesley to send her somewhere for a while."

Her eyes began to smolder.

"All right," I said, coming clean. "I thought she might have been pregnant. You're sure she didn't go anywhere, even briefly?"

"Absolutely not! I saw her every week that semester. Ruthie is a good girl. The only one they ever sent away was Billy. And, now that you mention it, they sent him away just before Ruthie came home."

"Where did he go?"

"I'm not sure. It was some boarding school in New England."

"What about Roger Purdy? What's the dirt on him?"

Miss Little shrugged. "He's a petulant little so-and-so. Spoiled rotten. Arrogant and unpleasant."

"Nothing else about him?" I asked. "No gossip about his personal life?"

She shook her head. "He didn't have one, as far as I could tell. Someone once joked that he'd never kissed a girl."

"Petronella?"

"I didn't like him. No one really liked him," she continued. "He was the kind who tried too hard to endear himself to everyone, but he was awkward and devoid of charm. His fawning was false, and people sensed that. I'm sure he was the prissy, little tattletale when he was a child. The boy the bullies picked on. I pitied him at times, but then he'd say something ugly or condescending to remind me why misfortune dogged him. I can't say I was sorry to see him go."

"His personal life?"

"Single. I don't know how any woman could stomach him."

Unwittingly perceptive, Joan Little was a smart woman, but simple enough to mistake two queers for hapless ladies' men. It just didn't occur to her that they didn't like women.

"What about Ercolano?" I asked, shifting gears. "Can you tell me anything more about him?"

"Oh, I don't know," she said, sipping her tea. Then she wiped her nose again with the handkerchief. "What's to tell? He was a nice man, a good man. It's a tragedy what happened."

"Do you know anything about his personal life? Did he have a girl-friend? Girlfriends?"

Her mouth dropped open slightly, and I wondered if it was the question or some mind-numbing cold medication that accounted for the dull look on her face.

"What do you mean?"

"I mean, did you, or anyone else, know if he had dates?"

"No," she said crisply, then rose to refill her teacup from the liquor cabinet across the room. I watched her from behind as she poured, shoulders shaking, then shuddering. She bowed her head, and I realized she was sobbing.

The older girlfriend used to scour that place at least once a week. I saw her on all fours in the open doorway, hair tied up in a red kerchief—a red-and-black kerchief—scrubbing his floors right out to the hallway.

Awkwardly, I tried to comfort her, amazed at how ingenuous I, too, could be. She was his "angela" as in *angel*, not Angela the name. Tillie Arnsberger's words echoed in my head as Joan Little wept on my shoulder.

For the next hour, I listened to the story of Joan Little's heartbreaking fall for Ruggero Ercolano. It was the first time all week that I felt someone was telling me the truth, or at least the first-hand truth. Grief flowed from her weeping form, as she related their first meeting, their first tryst, their first fight.

Ruggero Ercolano had come to New York to interview at Columbia three times in the spring of 1958. The department was searching to fill the faculty position vacated by Petronella's dismissal, and the young scholar from Yale was the top candidate. Joan Little noticed his Latin good looks the first time he walked through the door, but the thought of romance didn't enter her mind. He was younger than she by almost five years, and the only handsome young men who pursued older women were gigolos.

Ercolano stopped to chat with her at her desk that day, then returned to New Haven to wait for a call. A month later, he was back for a second interview, and again he made time to speak to her. He complimented her on her hair and told her she was pretty. Still, she figured his flirtation was a ploy to curry favor in the department. Then he got the job, and Joan secretly reveled. When he moved to New York in August, the courtship began in earnest. Ercolano cornered Joan Little as she was leaving the office one evening.

"I don't know New York," he said with a crooked smile she found adorable. "I have no pots and pans yet. Do you know a good restaurant near here?"

"Why, yes," she answered, blushing from the attention and his irresistible charm. "There's Chez Mon Oncle, a French Bistro. Oh, but that's near where I live in the West Village."

"I have heard about Greenwich"—he pronounced it *Green Witch*—

"Village. May I invite you to dinner with me tonight? Chez Mon Oncle?"

Joan Little fell in love that night, but resisted the temptation to give in to his repeated entreaties for a nightcap *chez elle*. In the weeks that followed, Ercolano wooed her discreetly, secretly. She thought he feared that discovery by Professor Chalmers might lead to a dismissal for both of them.

"It's not that I am worried to tell people, but my life is my own business," he explained to her one October evening in 1958. She remembered it as just a couple of days after Pope Pius XII died. The pontiff's death didn't strike me as particularly romantic or germane, but Ercolano was Italian, after all.

Miss Little told me how Ercolano's persistence finally won her over, and without blushing, she recounted the time she had "yielded to him." In fact, she had done the yielding the night Pope John XXIII was elected, on the very couch where we were now sitting. It would have been insensitive to change seats at that moment, so I suffered in silence.

The affair burned with the glow of fresh love in the following months. A wink at the office, a grope in the conference room when no one was around. The clandestine nature of the relationship enhanced the romance, and Joan Little found it delicious. No more papal milestones.

But novelty eventually turns into routine and becomes stale. By March 1959, Ercolano's passion had leveled off, and Joan suspected he was dating other women. She discovered a copy of *Playboy* magazine in his apartment and confronted him. He shrugged it off, explaining that he appreciated jazz and was reading it for the music reviews. She lived with it.

Then in June, Ercolano put the relationship on ice, telling Joan he had met someone else. She was crushed, and retreated from the world for two weeks. She didn't go to work, inventing a story about a sick aunt in Pennsylvania. In reality, she was holed up on Barrow Street, yearning for the man who had shown her the dizzying joys of passion (her last chance, she figured), only to snatch them away once she had fallen. She felt discarded and cheap, and that made her want him even more. In the darkness of her closed apartment, she decided that she must hold on until he realized his error. And so she suffered the humiliation of begging for a part of him. She went to his apartment and offered herself to him on his terms, when and if he wanted her. She became the other woman in Ercolano's new ménage.

Love's tides rise and fall; they're rarely constant. And, so, in the autumn of 1959, Joan Little's tolerance paid off, at least to her mind. Ercolano grew tired of the new girlfriend, and Joan was the temporary tonic. But when one lover realizes he holds the cards in a relationship, it's hard to resist shuffling and reshuffling the deck to taste. People will take what you give them, and Joan Little had given him unchecked control. The status quo from October 1959 to Ercolano's death was Joan Little during the week and the other girl (who was, of course, Ruth Chalmers) on the weekends. Joan told me tearfully of her last night in Ruggero's arms, the Wednesday before his death. They had argued, and now he was dead.

I arrived home around seven o'clock. Raul was on duty in the elevator, and I had a few questions I was sure he'd like to answer.

"Have you seen Mrs. Farber's gentleman friend recently?" I asked.

"The guy who didn't show the other night?" he asked. "Geez, Mrs. Farber chewed me out something awful yesterday. Said that wasn't Mr. Walter I let up. Don't go getting me into trouble, Miss Stone. I've always minded my own business around here."

I let it pass.

"I can't figure it, though," he continued. "I seen that guy before," he said, referring to Chalmers. "I remember faces. Not much else for me to do around here, so I watch the people."

"That other time," I asked, "did he come with the lady and the young man like he did Tuesday night?"

"No, I never seen those two before."

"You don't suppose you saw him when he was visiting my father?" I asked.

Raul snapped his fingers. "You know, that's a possibility. I hadn't thought of that."

"He works with my father," I said by way of instruction, and let the matter drop. I promised myself never to ask Raul anything ever again.

"Ellie?" a voice called behind me in the hall as I jostled the key in the lock.

"Mrs. Farber," I said, turning to see my father's neighbor in the kimono from the day before, a drink in her hand.

Angela Farber fairly vibrated in her doorway. Her eyes gleamed, half-shut, and she teetered on her feet, slurring her words. She was gassed.

I opened the door and wished her good night, but she stepped into the hallway and followed me into my father's apartment. With the door still open, she sashayed into the parlor and dropped into the sofa.

"Are you all right, Mrs. Farber?" I asked.

"Oh, God, Ellie, you don't know what it's like to be hungry when you're still a flower, when your love is still thirsty for a companion." Then she sipped her drink and looked up at me. "You're so young, Ellie. Still young and attractive. I was young and attractive once."

"You're very attractive," I said, removing my coat and folding it on a chair.

"It's my own fault, I suppose," she said. "I like men wild and mean. They break women's hearts like cracking their knuckles. Love 'em and leave 'em, right, Elijah?"

"Ellie," I croaked, looking for an out.

"I don't want to be alone," she moaned. "There's nowhere to go to meet eligible men, if not to tacky bars for singles. The Sterling Room, The Crystal Palace, Capri Lounge . . . You know the kind: the sign with a tipped Martini glass and bubbles. Oh, it's death, Walter," she slurred.

It was the most fortuitous of circumstances that saved me from the sad narration Angela Farber had in store for me: she passed out ten minutes later. Huffing and puffing, I lugged her body from my father's apartment back into her own, I managed to drag her to a sofa where I massaged her hand and waved air into her face until she came to about two hours later. I hadn't dared leave her alone.

"Where am I?" she mumbled. "Who are you?"

"It's me, Ellie. Ellie Stone," I said to no effect. Then, blushing: "Ellie Jelly. You're home. I helped you back from my father's apartment."

She tried to sit up, but I restrained her.

"You?" she said. "What was I doing there? Was I there when you came home?"

I shook my head. "Of course not. I met you in the hall. You've just had a little too much to drink. It'll be all right."

She struggled to sit up, alarmed. "Where's your father? Did he see me?"

"Calm down, Mrs. Farber," I said. "No one saw you. We all have a little too much once in a while."

I made a pot of coffee in her kitchen and after a while she regained her composure. With time, her head cleared, and she smiled and giggled at herself.

"It wouldn't be the first time I made a fool of myself, and it won't be the last."

"It's Walter, isn't it?"

She shrugged. "He hasn't called. And after all I've done for him."

"What's he like, this Walter?" I asked.

"He's an intellectual," she answered, running an absent hand through her hair. "But I'm beginning to think he's a coward, too."

"How's that?"

She snickered. "You wouldn't understand. He's been trying to throw me over. He just doesn't have the guts to come right out and say it, so he looks for excuses. 'It's not safe for your reputation; people will talk.' You know the song. All men learn it when they're young."

I'd heard it.

"Why can't they just say no? I'll tell you why," she said. "Because when their little things get stiff, their brains take the day off."

"Why don't you call Walter?"

"I've called a hundred times. He won't answer the phone anymore. But I've taken other measures."

"Forbearance?" I asked, remembering Joan Little's strategy. "Or seduction?"

"That may be effective on a young man, but Walter is different. He's a puritan; that's why he enjoys the wickedness of sex when he gets the urge. But afterward, he hates me and he hates himself. He begins to shake when he's finished, he quivers as if he's cold, and once I saw him cry. He's ashamed of his thing, you know. I think it's because he's not circumcised," she whispered. "I've never known a man like him; it's like making love to a priest, and that makes me want him more. Sex is rather complicated for him."

(Not circumcised? Did she really have to tell me that?) "So what's your plan?"

"He got himself into a jam, and I was the only person who could help him out of it. He's indebted to me now."

"What was it?"

She shook her head. "I'm sworn to silence."

"Well, what makes you think he'll honor his obligation to you? You've already done this favor for him; what's to stop him from walking away?"

She smiled to herself. "He won't do that. He can't do that; without my help, he's up the river without a paddle."

The conversation was decidedly pessimistic, and I felt pity for her. She was a hanger-on, like Joan Little. But instead of trying to win her man with love, Angela Farber wanted to trap him. I was skeptical that she'd ever see Walter again, but she seemed confident. I wondered if he was worth trapping at all; he sounded like a creep, the kind of pervert who hates sex except when some pheromone has commandeered his wits. He considers himself the supremely evolved being, free of the base desires that erode character and rob dignity. He's repulsed by the frenzied humping and perspiration, the vulgar act of copulation—bucking, panting, and spasmodic seizures that lower him to the level of a mongrel dog mounting a bitch with cataleptic oblivion. Ironically, disgust increases his arousal, once he has given in to desire. But the pleasure he derives is not the healthy sensuality of lovemaking; it's the inflammation of genitalia, the debasement of self and the female on top of whom he performs his sin. Fun date.

"Are you well enough to be alone?" I asked.

She sat up, put herself back into her kimono, and followed me to the door. She thanked me, and I wished her goodnight. I wondered where Gigi was. I thought I knew.

CHAPTER FOURTEEN

My wanderings throughout Manhattan and the Bronx had proven enlightening, if exhausting. I resisted the urge to nap, however, figuring I could sleep all night at the hospital. I outlined in my pad the information I'd gathered that day and made a task list of people to corner the following morning. Then I called my editor, Charlie Reese, long distance to update him on my father's condition. He reassured me, telling me again not to worry about work and concentrate on my own business.

"Who's covering the high school basketball while I'm away?" I asked, teasing Charlie a bit.

"Now don't laugh," he said. "George Walsh. He's been doing his homework on basketball."

Walsh was the publisher's son-in-law and a Grade A ass with a capital *A*.

"George Walsh? He thinks Wilt Chamberlain is the British prime minister."

Charlie laughed, then lectured me on my attitude. But it was hard to take him seriously, as he was still sniggering.

I had some soup and saltines for a meager dinner, sitting at the dining table alone and staring at the building lights across Fifth Avenue. My mother had always insisted we take dinner at the table, never in front of the television or near the radio as Janey's family used to. When we got our first television set in 1948, Elijah used to beg to watch the wrestling on Dumont during supper. My father backed up my mother on the dinnertime policy, pointing out that the wrestling was fake anyway. Elijah countered that theater was staged and fake as well, and yet my parents both enjoyed that. Mom and Dad presented a united front, and in the end, Elijah and I learned to eat faster.

At a quarter past nine, the intercom buzzed, just as I was just touching up my lipstick, preparing to leave for Saint Vincent's.

"Miss Stone?" came the voice. "This is Raul, in the elevator. A Mr. Bruchner is here to see you."

I was surprised, though not disappointed, to open the door to Gualtieri "Karen" Bruchner, not the ghoulish professor I had expected.

"Please come in," I said, stepping aside to let the little man pass. He clutched his worn tweed cap in his hands and entered meekly, mumbling the perfunctory *permesso?* as he did. "What can I do for you, Mr. Bruchner?" I asked after offering him a seat in the parlor.

"I have considered your suggestion," he said, his coal black eyes fixed on mine. "I want to meet the man who has my name."

The cab ride through Union Square and up Fourth Avenue was a quiet one. (I can't bring myself to call it Park Avenue South, despite the recent official change in name. My God, that's exactly the sort of thing my father would say . . .) Karen Bruchner opened his mouth only slightly more often than the Sphinx. I did manage, however, to elicit some response.

"Why do they call you Karen?" I asked as the cab idled at a red light on Twenty-Third Street.

Bruchner looked out the window, away from my invasive stare. "I did not choose it," he said. "They give it to me. They give it to me at the camp."

"The Germans?"

He shook his head, face still in the window. "No, it was a Jew from Bremen," he explained.

"What does the name mean?"

Again he shook his head, and I could discern the reflection of a bitter smile in the window. "Karen comes from a name in Italian: *Caronte*. Americans say it wrong. Should be Karon."

I waited for elaboration.

"You know *Caronte* by his English name: Charon."

I remembered Dad's drawing: Charon, ferryman of the Styx and Acheron, who transports the damned souls from hell's vestibule across the river to Limbo. But how did that apply to Karen Bruchner?

He wiped his eyes and bowed his head. His voice trembled as he spoke: "He named me *Caronte* because I took the Jews into the camp; I was the engineer of the train, the train from the station to the camp, from the camp to the mines. I took them to their doom." A short squeal escaped his throat before he could swallow it, then he collected his anguish and packed it away. "I'm sorry," he said, almost whispering.

"You don't have to go on," I said, half wishing he wouldn't.

"It's OK," he said, shaking off my suggestion. "I have this name for sixteen years; I live with it. The man who give it to me, his name was Maschiewicz, a miner in my barracks. He was a student, about my age."

"You must have hated him," I said.

Karen Bruchner jerked his head to look at me in the dark as we passed Twenty-Eighth Street. "Oh, no. He didn't realize. That was how he lived with the death: to make jokes."

"How did the name stick? Why did you keep it when you came to America?"

He wiped the last of the tears from his eyes. "I don't know how it happened," he said. "Maybe I told someone the story, and he told others. I can't remember now, but everyone calls me Karen."

The cab turned at Thirty-Eighth Street and pulled to a stop near the corner of Lexington. I paid the driver, and Karen and I stepped out into the cold night. Professor Bruchner's high-rise building soared twenty-nine stories above us, and my companion looked at it with no small measure of trepidation.

"Are you sure you want to do this?" I asked.

He nodded.

"You know who we're going to find up there, don't you?"

Again the nod. "I think so."

I gave the concierge my real name, and not only did Bruchner answer the phone, he agreed to see me. My anticipation was running high, though I confess the situation made me nervous. I buzzed Bruchner's door, Karen standing by, looking old, desolate, and small, but determined to meet the man who had usurped his name. Just before the door opened, Karen remembered his manners and snatched the cap from his head.

"Miss Stone," said Bruchner in his stiff tones. No good evening, no how are you; just the statement: Miss Stone.

"Professor Bruchner," I answered, then waited for a reaction to the man standing next me.

"Please come in," he said, opening the door wide. I stepped inside, and Karen Bruchner followed.

"I forgot to introduce you to my friend," I said with relish. "Gualtieri Bruchner meet Gualtieri Bruchner."

The professor's jaw dropped. His eyes grew large, and I thought I saw the hair rising on his neck.

"You'll agree it's a singular coincidence," I said, perhaps a bit too blithely.

"What is this new charade, Miss Stone?"

He knew the jig was up, but the habits of fifteen years don't go without a fight.

"This man's name is Gualtieri Bruchner," I repeated.

"Then who am I?" he asked.

"Jakob Maschiewicz," I said, my heart pumping furiously.

"But Miss Stone," interrupted Karen Bruchner. "This is not the man. This is not Maschiewicz."

The professor drew strength from Karen's denial. "What is going on here?" he demanded.

I paused, considering where my logic had failed. If all had gone according to script, the professor would have been the student from Bremen. He would have taken Bruchner's name for some unknown reason, perhaps because he'd lost his own papers.

"Let's get this straight," I began tentatively. "When were you born, Professor Bruchner?"

"December 21, 1908."

"And you, Mr. Bruchner?"

"The same," he said, throat dry.

"And where?" I asked, this time giving Karen the chance to answer first.

"Merano, Italy," he proclaimed, voice stronger. "In Trentino-Alto Adige."

"Professor?"

"The same," he blushed.

"What is the number on your arm, Professor?"

He looked flustered, but he rolled up his sleeve and recited the number without looking. "194274," he said in English, then repeated it in German. "We had to memorize it. I have never forgotten. I cannot forget."

"*Dio mio,*" whispered Karen Bruchner. "*È uguale.* Mine is the same."

The two men stared at each other. Karen Bruchner's eyes peered from beneath his furrowed brow, studying the man standing before him. I couldn't tell what he was thinking, whether he recognized him or not. Then he spoke to Bruchner in Italian, and I was unable to follow their words.

"I am the real Gualtieri Bruchner," said Karen, turning to me. "You believe me, don't you?"

"This is ridiculous," answered the professor. "I have a passport, papers, any proof you could want. This man is a liar!"

"It's true, I have no passport," said Karen meekly. "Because I was a displaced person."

"You see? I can prove who I am," said the professor. "He cannot."

"*Sono Gualtieri Bruchner!*" He turned to me, his dark eyes trembling in their deep sockets. "Miss Stone, I am Gualtieri Bruchner. I have little of my own. But I have my name and I want it!"

"How is this your business?" the professor asked me. "This is between me and him," he said, pointing to Karen Bruchner.

"It became my business when someone hit my father over the head," I said. "And I intend to find out which of you is the fake."

"How can I assure you I had nothing to do with the attack on your father?"

"You can start by telling me who the other man was at lunch last Friday. You saw him, and you know who he was."

He shook his head violently. "I saw no one."

⁓

I offered to pay Karen Bruchner's carfare to Brooklyn, but he refused, opting for the subway instead.

"Why has he taken my name, Miss Stone?" he asked, poised to descend into the hole at Grand Central Station.

I shook my head. "I don't know, Mr. Bruchner."

He twisted his tweed cap in his broad hands, searching for words. "Will you . . . Can you find out for me?"

I felt overwhelmed. "I'll try."

⁓

My next stop was Saint Vincent's to relieve Sean McDunnough at my father's bedside. I arrived late and apologized, but he shrugged it off.

"Don't sweat it," he said. "I get time and a half for overtime. See you tomorrow."

"What about church?" I asked.

"I've spent three days in a hospital named Saint Vincent's," he said, securing the *Racing Form* under his right arm. "That ought to hold me till next week. Besides, Sundays I get double time."

Charleen Lionel, the nurse who'd been called away by the anonymous phone call the night my father's respirator was disconnected, gave me some encouraging news on his prognosis. His blood pressure had risen, and his pulse was stronger. He was still on the respirator, though, as he had bucked and fought hard when they tried to remove it from the tracheostoma they'd cut into his throat. His heart began to race, and they had to leave the respirator in and sedate him to calm him down. Nurse Lionel said he had even mumbled a few incoherent words that afternoon.

"Dr. Mortonson is optimistic he'll come out of the coma soon, and then we'll get him off the breathing apparatus," she said.

"Did the doctor mention anything about brain damage?"

"No," she frowned. "He still doesn't know about that.

Nurse Lionel found me two foam pillows that I stuffed between the back and seat of the chair Sean McDunnough had been breaking in all day. I kicked off my heels and put my feet up. The result was that I could now sleep poorly in a softer uncomfortable position.

Noise travels far in a hospital once the lights go out. You can hear the humming of machines, beeps and ticks, and the groans and snoring of patients. And the nurses, with their hushed conversations, should know to keep their voices down.

"He hasn't called me since," whispered one. "I knew I shouldn't have, but I couldn't help it."

"What did he say afterward?" asked the other.

"Not much. He seemed fine, nice, you know."

"Well, maybe he'll call. Maybe he's been busy."

"I don't know. I mean, I really shouldn't have."

The whispering was interrupted by a moan across the ward. One nurse investigated while the other manned the fortress. A few minutes later, the nurse returned, and the muted conversation resumed:

"Did I tell you about my mother?"

"No."

"She wants to move from Jersey to New York."

"That's a little too close for comfort."

"Too close? She wants to move in with me!"

The elevator doors opened down the hall, and an orderly pushed a gurney along the tiles. He stopped to flirt with the two nurses.

"Come on, the broom closet's safe."

"Oh, Tony, you're so bad!" Giggles. "Get out of here before Sister comes."

"She can come along too," he said, turning the gurney around, pushing it down the hallway, and back into the elevator.

"What do you think of Tony?" asked one nurse after he'd gone.

"He's funny, but he's such a pervert. Sex on the brain, all the time."

"I heard he's really big. You know, big."

"No!"

Giggles again. "Have you ever seen a really big one?"

"I'm a nurse, aren't I?"

The elevator doors slid open again, and a portly nun scooted up the hall to the nurses' station. She spoke in a stern whisper.

"Have you seen Anthony?"

"I saw him get out of the elevator a while ago."

"No-good, lazy . . . How're things going here, girls?"

"Fine."

The nun headed back to the elevator, which pinged as the car arrived on the floor, and she disappeared inside.

"Sister looks like one of those troll dolls, don't you think?" said one nurse. "The kind with the pink hair."

"Maybe she wants to see Tony's thing," said the other, and they both laughed, a little too loud for the hour.

When their whispering subsided around one o'clock, I fell asleep on my lumpy cushions.

A noise woke me from my tenuous sleep sometime later. I sat up in the chair to listen, but the only sound I heard was my back cracking. Standing up to stretch, I paced up and down the ICU in my stockings, to the nurses' station and back to my father's bed.

The white sheets of the ward bore a ghostly gray cast in the dark, painting an eerie landscape, and the hissing machinery kept time. Every now and then, a patient would emerge from a drug-induced stupor long enough to moan for a nurse or a loved one. I tried to ignore them, their thin voices and shadowy figures. Death was hovering over the ward, waiting for an opportune moment to snatch one of the vulnerable souls from this world. I felt a draft, and returned to my father's bedside.

Resting my feet on the corner of the bed, I threw back my head and tried to sleep. The pump-pump-blip-hiss in the background played a rondo, with a different machine, attached to a different patient, taking turns leading off each round. I closed my eyes and began to doze off, lulled by the humming equipment. Then a shriek tore through the night: a hellish wail of lament and suffering. I fell from my makeshift bed to the hard floor, landing on my behind. The two nurses scrambled out of their fortress across the floor like roaches surprised by light in the night. I pushed myself to my feet, rubbing my lower back, and watched the scene unfold. Another scream blared across the floor, like a foghorn at close range. It didn't sound human, and I couldn't even guess its gender.

"Get the doctor on duty!" one nurse called to the other. "Tell him we need morphine."

The other nurse sprinted away, just past my father's bed. The little nun returned, scooting (nuns don't run) through the darkness. She joined the attending nurse at the bedside of the agonizing patient.

"Hold him down!" she shouted, trying to make herself heard over the howling. "Hold him down while I strap him in!"

They struggled, two shadows wrestling with a bed, until the other nurse returned with an orderly and doctor.

"Tie him down," the doctor said to the orderly, who practically threw himself onto the thrashing sheets. Moments later the patient was secured, but the screaming whirled around the room like a wind blowing ever stronger. I covered my ears as the attendants pumped the patient full of morphine. A minute later he was quiet, but the air still vibrated with the echoes of the shrieking.

"Man, that's strong stuff," said the orderly. "Quieted him right down."

"It wasn't the morphine," said the doctor dryly. "He's dead."

I eased back into my chair and drew closer to the bed. A few minutes later, my heart had slowed to where I could at least close my eyes and swallow. Then, a noise on my left. I was startled. Opening my eyes, I looked around for someone, but there was nothing. Then the noise again, and I realized it was him, my father, speaking. I pushed out of the chair, sending it skidding back across the tiles into the wall, and pressed my ear close to his lips.

"What is it, Dad?" I said. "Speak to me. Say something. It's me!"

His eyes remained closed, but his jaw moved slightly from side to side. Then his dry tongue peeked out of his mouth to moisten his lips.

"Say something, Dad! It's me. I'm here with you now."

He swallowed gingerly, then in a raspy whisper, called: "Elijah . . ."

※

SUNDAY, JANUARY 31, 1960

At seven the following morning, Sunday, I was shuffling through the light snow on Twelfth Street, in no hurry to get back to my father's place. All I could think of was Elijah's room: that empty chamber. Even from beyond the grave, he was closer to Dad than I, who sat holding his hand at his bedside. Our sorry relationship had crumbled to where he would rather reach through the ages to a ghost than throw me a bone of his affection. I cursed him, and I cursed Elijah as I stopped for a cup of coffee at a diner on Twelfth and Sixth. I stared out the window, huddled over my coffee, and watched the early morning traffic. The faithful on their way to church, the faithless returning home from a late night of revelry, and the irresolute on some unknown errand at this early hour. All marched purposefully toward their destinations.

I descended into gloom, still crushed by my father's cry for Elijah, his rejection of me. But what could I expect? I hadn't even phoned him on his last birthday and let him spend Thanksgiving alone while I did the same in New Holland. I didn't know him anymore, what he did with his days, his nights, or how he was managing since Mom had died. We had become strangers with the same last name and—somehow— the same eyes. Spiritually dead, each toward the other, these were the shambles we had made. How sad my mother and brother would have been. It was hopeless, even if he recovered.

When he recovered, I thought. When he recovered, he would probably name his attacker. (I figured he had seen who hit him, which prompted the second attempt on his life.) Then he'd ask me how I'd spent my week in New York.

"Well, Dad," I'd say, "I've been trying to find out who clubbed you on the head."

"And how did you proceed, Ellie?" he'd ask, as if in an oral exam.

"Well, I screwed one of your junior colleagues, Gigi Lucchesi."

"That's fine, Ellie! You give new meaning to the investigative term 'poking around.'"

Damn it! Where had Gigi disappeared to the past few days? Somewhere with Hildy Jaspers, no doubt. I hadn't heard a word from him since first thing Thursday morning. I tossed a quarter onto the counter and pushed through the door to the street. Striding over Twelfth Street and down Fifth Avenue, I reached my father's apartment building with sweat beading beneath the wet snow on my brow. The revolving doors spat me into the lobby, where I found Jimmo McKeever waiting on the sofa. Elbows resting on his knees, he dangled his rain-soaked hat between his legs. When he saw me come in, he dropped the hat and jumped to his feet.

"Hello, Ellie. I wanted to speak to you about Ruth Chalmers."

"I've only got about five minutes," I said.

"Well, I spoke to Miss Chalmers yesterday," he said, following me into the elevator. "About the jewelry and Mr. Ercolano."

"And?"

"And she came clean, confessed everything about the relationship. Said she found him in the tub Saturday night. She even admitted she'd taken the ring from his bureau drawer. Thought it was his."

"Well done, Jim. While you were fishing for confirmation of something you already knew, I found out who the older girlfriend was."

He looked startled. "Who?" he asked, and I realized my brusque tone was unwarranted.

"Joan Little, the secretary. The arrangement was Joan during the week, Ruth on the weekends."

The elevator stopped on fifteen, and we exited. Inside the apartment, I changed clothes in my father's bedroom while McKeever digested the new information in the study.

"Do you think Joan Little killed him?" he asked once I'd redone my face, tied my hair back, and emerged in a fresh skirt and blouse.

"No," I said. "She loved him, accepted every indignity he heaped on her, and loved him more despite it all."

"Maybe she got fed up with his other girlfriend."

"I doubt it," I said. "But why don't you go talk to her?"

McKeever looked discouraged.

"It's easy for you," he said. "You don't have to write reports and justify your opinions to your superiors. That means questioning everyone, in order, to the last man, woman, and child."

I shrugged my shoulders in empathy. "Sorry. I've got to talk to Bernie Sanger," and I headed for the door.

"What about?" he asked, trotting after me.

"My father's lunch last Friday."

We rode the elevator down to the street, and McKeever drove me over to Seventh Avenue. In the car he asked me about my father.

"You're really close to him, aren't you?" he asked.

I snickered. "Not at all."

"Well, you must have been once. I can see it. It's a special bond that a girl has with her father. He must have thought you were the most beautiful thing in the world."

I ran a finger down the steamed-up window absently, looking away from McKeever.

"Once," I said, "when I was about seven, we were reading together in the parlor. It was evening, winter, I think, and we were waiting for dinner. Just reading on the sofa, me leaning against him. We were warm. He had a drink on the end table. I still remember that smell of alcohol being consumed. Being consumed by others, I mean. It's a different smell altogether: very grown up and complicated." I paused.

"Nice story," said McKeever awkwardly after a bit, thinking I'd finished. "My old man drank gin, and it didn't smell none too good on him."

"My mother came into the room to tell us five more minutes till dinner," I resumed. "We both looked up from our books and smiled at her. Then I felt my father's hand stroke my cheek, ever so gently. I turned my eyes to him, and he gazed at me. 'You're my girl,' he said. I think that was the best moment of my life."

There was a silence as we waited at a stoplight. Had I been paying attention to McKeever, I might have noticed he was uncomfortable with my confession. But I didn't look at him so I don't know.

The squad car stopped on the northwest corner of Seventh and Thirteenth. I made no move to climb out, and the car idled patiently.

"My old man was a drunken brawler," said McKeever without preamble. "Little Man's Disease. Hated the world for making him short. Used to get in fights every Friday night to prove he was tougher than all the guys taller than him. He got thrown out of every tavern in Jamaica, then all of Queens." He chuckled softly, bitterly. "It got so bad, he had to go into Manhattan to drink in the gin mills on Third Avenue. Then he'd come home and beat up my ma."

"That's rough," I said.

He shrugged. "I had pals who had it worse than me. At least I had sports after school to keep me away from him."

"Baseball?"

He shook his head.

"Boxing?"

"No, I got smacked around enough at home. I didn't feel like getting hit for fun."

"Not basketball," I laughed. "You're too . . ." I stopped myself.

"Short? Yeah, I know. And yet I was an All-City basketball star at Andrew Jackson High."

"Really? How tall are you, Jim?"

He flushed a bit. "Five foot seven," he said and paused. "Or nearly. I started playing in the Police Athletic League when I was a kid. It didn't matter then that I was short. We all were."

"Tell me more. I love sports heroes."

"You're a card," he sneered. "In high school I was a shrimp, not even as tall as I am now. But irony of ironies, I was the best shooter in Queens. Averaged twenty-six points a game my senior year."

"Funny I never heard of you."

He mugged a sarcastic smile. "I went to City College in the fall of 1950."

I looked at him pointedly. "Did you say 1950?" He nodded solemnly. "But that was the year of the scandal . . . Did you play on that team?"

"No, that was the year before. The news broke in the middle of the next season, but I didn't get to play anyway," he sighed. "I went to try out for the team, but Coach Holman wouldn't have it. Said I was too small."

"I'm sorry."

"It's all right. I used to outshoot the players during practice to teach him a lesson."

"But I thought you didn't make the team," I said.

"I wanted to be there. After the twin championships in 1950, I just had to be part of the team, so I signed on as the equipment manager."

"And the coach never gave you another chance? After seeing you shoot at practice?"

McKeever shifted in his seat and shook his head. "No," he sniffed. "He admitted I was good, but said I was too short. My old man said the same thing, then rubbed it in good every chance he got. Just kept telling me what a chump I was."

"So you knew those guys?" I asked, wanting to get him off the subject of his father. "Ed Warner, Ed Roman, Al Roth?"

"You sure know a lot about sports," he said. "Yeah, I knew them. Ed Warner used to call me leprechaun."

"Ouch."

Jim smiled and pushed the memory aside. "It's all right," he said. "I got my degree and went on to join the force. Never would have made it without City College."

"What did your father say about that? About you becoming a cop."

"He never knew. He died. Wouldn't have liked it, though. He hated cops. Hated just about everybody. Negroes, Jews, Puerto Ricans, Protestants . . ."

"You've done OK, Jim, for a leprechaun basketball player from the mean streets."

"Thanks for the kind words, Ellie. Let me know if I can cheer you up sometime."

"You know," I said after a long pause, "despite all the pain that's happened since, I love him. I love my father for that one moment on a winter's night so long ago."

"That's not much, Ellie," he said.

I turned back from the window and smiled weakly at him. His face was troubled, and I appreciated his kindness.

"It's all I've got," I told him.

"He must love you very dearly. Some men just don't know how to show it."

"Don't you think I know that? I know he loves me," I said, returning to my foggy window. "He just doesn't like me."

"Are you going to see Joan Little?" I asked through the window after climbing out on Thirteenth.

"Gotta go by the book. Let me know how you do with Sanger."

I agreed, and McKeever sped off. I turned away from the subway, heading west along Thirteenth Street instead, hating myself every heart-pounding step as I went.

It was just a quarter past eight on a wet Sunday morning when I pressed the buzzer of 340 West Nineteenth Street, a four-story brownstone between Eighth and Ninth Avenues. The intercom was out of order, according to a sign taped above the buzzer, and the door was open. I checked the mailboxes for the apartment number, 4, and went in.

"Who is it?" a sleepy voice asked through the door marked 4.

"It's Ellie Stone," I said. "Is that you, Hildy?"

I heard her swear, and there was a frantic rustling inside.

"Just a minute," she called, and I heard a man's voice.

A cold hand crawled up my back, and I felt my eyes turn green. I'd never experienced the nauseating churning of jealousy, not with Steve Herbert, not with any old flames or passion-pit Romeos, not even with Stitch Ferguson, and I didn't like it. Hildy and Gigi, just as I had suspected? I pressed my ear to the door, listening closely, feeling like a wronged woman on the heels of her erring man.

"I'll be right there, Ellie," called Hildy amid more shuffling and hushed voices. Finally, about a minute later, she opened the door, puffy-eyed, wrapped in a terry cloth robe, her teased brunette hair looking like cotton candy.

"Not alone?" I asked, my heart thumping in my chest.

"As a matter of fact, no," she said, piqued by my intrusion. "How may I help you this early Sunday morning, Ellie?"

I slipped past her inside, looking around the disheveled studio apartment. There was a bed, rumpled sheets pulled back, but no handsome Gigi Lucchesi lying supine in postcoital glow. A straw bottle of Chianti lay on the floor, empty, as were the two tumblers—stained red—on the end table next to the bed. The sink in the kitchenette was stacked high with pots and pans, crusty with some kind of tomato sauce. The bones of an intimate dinner.

"What do you want, Ellie?"

I scanned the room again for signs of Gigi. The bathroom door was closed.

"Ellie?"

"I want to talk to you, Hildy," I said, trying to cap my rage. "And I want to talk to him."

Hildy seethed. "Look, Ellie, I'm sorry, but it's no big deal. We're both adults, we can do as we please," she said, gathering some indignation. "He's not your property, whether he's your father's favorite or not."

"What are you talking about?" I asked, a glimmer of my misunderstanding just dawning. "Who is it in there?"

She glanced to the bathroom door and back to me, words failing her. Then the door creaked open, and a hand emerged.

"Ellie," he smiled sheepishly in a T-shirt, a towel knotted around his waist.

"Bernie!" The nauseous soup in my gut fell calm, as if the high flame boiling it had been blown out.

"You won't tell your father I've been here," he said.

"Grow a spine, Bernie," ordered Hildy.

"What's this all about, Ellie?" asked Bernie.

I felt my land legs beneath me, and smiled. "I came to ask Hildy if she knew who had lunch with my father last Friday."

Bernie looked to her for an answer, and Hildy frowned. "No, I told you the other night that I saw him in the office last Friday, but not at lunchtime."

How could she have remembered that, I wondered. She was quite drunk when she told me at the reception.

"What about Friday evening?" I asked, well aware Bernie had been with my father that night.

"I told you, Ellie," she glared. "I had a date. It doesn't concern you."

"You had a date?" asked Bernie.

"Let it go," ordered Hildy.

"OK, well, what about Chalmers?" asked Bernie, the stress showing in his neck. "If he finds out about this, he'll have my head. And yours too, Hildy."

Hildy threw back her head and laughed. "You're right about that. Chalmers would pluck the hair off your head, Bernie, if he knew. But don't worry; Miss Eleonora Stone won't tell anyone. Isn't that right, Miss Eleonora?"

I didn't like the "Miss" bit, but I nodded, intent on hiding my jealousy and bother from Hildy. I forced a broad smile, as if I were enjoying Bernie's discomfort as much as she was.

"We don't know who had lunch with your father last Friday, so why don't you just shove off?" said Bernie, now clearly annoyed with the ribbing. "Go ask Roger Purdy; he told me he saw your father leave and come back from lunch that day. Or ask Gigi Lucchesi."

"Gigi Lucchesi?" I asked. "What's he got to do with this?"

"I don't know," said Bernie. "Didn't he help your father catalog his books? He spent hours with him a couple of months ago. Of course that was before the Barnard girl fell in love with him. Your father was incensed that Chalmers tried to cover it up."

"Don't be jealous, Bernie," said Hildy with a snicker. "Your boyfriend needed help, and Gigi was Johnny-on-the-spot. You were too slow off the mark. And that girl was moony over Gigi. He did nothing wrong."

"That's enough of that, Hildy," said Bernie, but I was suddenly sobbing fiercely into my hands. My lungs burned with each gasping breath. The tears poured down my cheeks unchecked. I was disconsolate, beyond humiliation; my emotions had dissolved without warning, and later I wondered if it was my anguish for my ailing father or for Gigi that had pushed me to tears. I felt a wretch, alone and unworthy of affection or even sympathy. And pathetic to have tried to surprise Hildy Jaspers on a cold Sunday morning. I didn't respect myself; why should anyone else?

"Ellie . . ." said Hildy softly, coming to my side to comfort me. "I didn't mean anything by it."

I waved her off and ran through the door and down the stairs. My jealousy was stronger than my love for my father, I feared, and I was crushed.

I wandered through Chelsea, past Seventh and Sixth Avenues, and ended up sitting on a cold bench in Madison Square Park, staring at the

Flatiron building. I wiped my nose with a handkerchief and thought of my father—he insisted on calling it the Fuller Building. He was always stuck somewhere in the past, stubbornly defending some obsolete garrison of prescriptive grammar or fighting a lost cause against the advances of Philistinism.

I drew a deep sigh and wished my life was different, not the isolated existence I had built around myself. No real friends, just boyfriends and pals. No family, just relations. It felt like a dirge was playing in my head, an insufferable lament that never stopped. How had I come to this spot? Was there anywhere else to go?

I don't know why, but I thought about my mother and her quirky, sweet nature. Despite my father's cantankerous disposition, they had never quarreled. It seemed a miracle to me, but she was patient with him, and he was tender with her. Perhaps she acted as a tonic for his hot temper, and he a stimulant for her quiet temperament. She could be prickly with him at times, but I had never heard her raise her voice to him. They fit together like pieces of a puzzle, flanges neatly accommodated by bespoke notches.

I sat on the cold bench, considering my parents' enduring love affair, and I felt distracted, if not comforted, from my misery. The interruption allowed me to breathe, relax, and the tightness in my throat eased. It allowed my mind to wander off on other tangents, focus on the mundane—a greasy black pigeon poking around at my feet—and the sublime—a carillon of church bells sounding somewhere to the east. I looked up at the gray Sunday sky and remembered I had work to do.

I pushed myself off the bench and crossed Fifth Avenue to the northwest corner of Twenty-Third Street. There, I folded myself into a phone booth and dialed Roger Purdy's number, saving myself a subway token.

"I'm on my way to church," he said after I'd identified myself. "What do you want?"

"One question, if you please," I said. "Then I'll leave you to your genuflection."

"Please, Miss Stone," he said with disdain. "I'm a Presbyterian, not a papist."

"What about Anthony Petronella? Isn't he Catholic?"

A pause grew stale down the line. "You had a question?"

"Bernie Sanger says you saw my father last Friday on his way to lunch at the Faculty Club."

"It was a supreme pleasure, yes."

"And you saw him return."

"I wondered if I was worthy."

"Who was he with?" I asked, thinking what an ass he was.

"Come on, Miss Stone," he said, the coy boy. "I'm sure an investigator as tenacious and perspicacious as you should have an educated guess."

"I do. But I need confirmation of my hunch."

"I'll show you mine if you show me yours."

He'd have to hit me over the head first. "Ruggero Ercolano."

Static down the line. Then, "That's right." He sounded disappointed.

"Thank you," I said. "I think I know who hit my father on the head, and who threw that radio into Ercolano's bathtub."

I needed a motive, something more than the vague threat my father posed to Bruchner. I needed to know exactly what he suspected the gray man had done, and how the tattoo fit into the picture. Without understanding the tattoo, I didn't know where to look for the proof. All I had were my father's suspicions. On the surface, it seemed unlikely that a Jew would be an anti-Semite. It was even more improbable that a concentration camp survivor would harbor such hatred toward his own people.

I believe in logic; people do things for reasons, whether choosing a color for a new car or deciding to murder someone. There is always a sense to an action, unless you're dealing with a defective mind. So, I dismantled the enigma in a taxi uptown and as I walked west toward Riverside Park and Professor Saettano's apartment.

My first question was, what had kicked off my father's suspicions? Bruchner himself admitted that the incident in the steam bath at the gym was the beginning. The tattoo on his chest, as innocent as it appeared, communicated a significant clue to my father. I couldn't figure what it meant to him, so I moved on to my second question.

How could Bruchner be an anti-Semite if he was Jewish? That's where Karen Bruchner came in. One of the two Bruchners was a fake, why not the professor? Maybe my father had discovered Bruchner's charade. But would such a discovery prompt such hostility? I'm sure there are lots of people using assumed names, especially war refugees; it shouldn't make my father blow his stack in a restaurant full of colleagues. There was something more to it, and I was back to the tattoo.

Three: something had convinced my father that his doubts about Bruchner were justified, or he never would have leapt at his throat in public. What was it? Perhaps a letter from Professor Arturo Marescialli had arrived that morning. I didn't know for sure that such a letter existed, but I hadn't located it among my father's files. Or did he have other sources of information? Being the compulsive cataloguer that he is, he would have filed the letter in his correspondence folder. The burglar—Bruchner, I thought—knew to look for the damning evidence, and had apparently found it.

Four: Why kill Ercolano? This was the only question I could answer. Roger Purdy had seen my father leave the office with Ercolano before lunch and return with him afterward. I figured it a safe bet that Ruggero Ercolano had been the man with my father at the Faculty Club lunch that Friday afternoon. Bruchner's motive for killing Ercolano, therefore, could have been the latter's knowledge of my father's suspicions and/or proof of Bruchner's charade. Unfortunately for my cluttered mind, this scenario presented another question.

Five: How did Bruchner get into Ercolano's apartment? No idea.

Libby opened the door tentatively.

"Please excuse the intrusion," I said. "Is the professor in?"

"It's a bit early to be calling on a Sunday," she said peevishly. "But come in. I'll let him know you're here."

Libby showed me to the study overlooking the Hudson. She brought me a tray of coffee and Danish and explained that the professor would join me shortly. A few minutes later, Franco Saettano, dressed in a paisley robe with an ascot knotted around his neck, hobbled into the room behind his cane.

"Good morning, Eleonora," he said, offering a frail hand. "You're visiting early today."

"I apologize, but it's important."

He took a seat. "How can I help you?"

"Sometimes, asking the proper question is the key to finding the right answer," I began. "I thought you might ask me the right question. So, I'd like you to listen to my scenario, and test me, question me about it."

"*Va bene, avanti.*"

"Last October, my father ran into Gualtieri Bruchner in the steam bath at the gymnasium. He noticed a strange tattoo on Bruchner's chest, and he began to suspect Bruchner wasn't who he seemed to be. My father launched an informal investigation, writing letters to colleagues in Italy to inquire about Bruchner's past. In the meantime, he may well have carried out other research here in the United States; I know, for instance, that he visited his cousin, Max Zeitler, in Washington last December."

"What did he suspect?"

"I'm not sure. But he was convinced Bruchner was a fake. It seems to have something to do with his being Jewish."

"Does this have to do with the destroyed phonograph records?"

"I think so. The importance of being Jewish is at the heart of these crimes. My brother's grave desecrated, smeared with swastikas; my father attacked, his 'Jewish' music destroyed; and in the case of Bruchner, his Jewishness is being challenged."

"Are you forgetting about Ercolano?" asked the old man. "He was not Jewish."

"You're right. That was a missing piece of the puzzle, and I couldn't link the crimes until this morning. Last Friday, my father had lunch at the Faculty Club, as did Bruchner, and there was an ugly confrontation. My father tried to strangle him."

"Yes, Victor Chalmers told me the story," said Saettano, shaking his head. "But how does that connect the attack on your father to Ruggero Ercolano's death?"

"Ercolano was the man with my father at lunch last Friday. He witnessed everything."

"Interesting," he said, ever the professor weighing his student's reasoning. "But since Ercolano cannot tell us what he heard and saw, we can only speculate. What do you think happened?"

"A busboy at the restaurant told me that my father approached Bruchner's table, exchanged angry words with him, then went for his throat, yelling in a foreign language the busboy thought was German. Ercolano helped pull them apart. I'm sure he heard everything and, therefore, as a witness, became a threat to Bruchner."

"But a threat to what, Eleonora? You have not proven anything against Gualtieri Bruchner."

"I may never be able to, but that doesn't mean he's not guilty. This isn't a court of law, Professor Saettano, nor a simple intellectual exercise. This is life and death, crime and punishment, and I intend to catch him."

"Very well," he said, as if leaving an unsatisfactory answer behind on an oral exam. "Have you any other evidence? Something, perhaps, to illuminate these suspicions of your father's? Something to compromise Gualtieri Bruchner's credibility? So far you have not convinced me."

"As a matter of fact, I do have more evidence. There is in Brooklyn a man named Gualtieri 'Caronte' Bruchner. He was born on the same day, the same year, and in the same town in Alto Adige as Professor Bruchner. I believe that Professor Bruchner stole his name and identity in the closing days of the war."

Saettano leaned forward in his seat, intrigued by the coincidences. "And you have met this man?"

I nodded.

"This name, 'Caronte,' do you know what it means?"

"I do. And he explained how he got it. He was deported in 1943 to Auschwitz, where he worked as the train engineer between the station, the camp, and the mines. He took the Jews to their deaths at Auschwitz."

"A cruel but clever sobriquet," mused Saettano, sitting back. "A ferryman of doomed souls. Is his wrist tattooed?"

I nodded again. "With the same number Professor Bruchner wears."

"You have seen them both, the tattoos? And they appear authentic?"

"To my eye, yes. They're both real tattoos, if that's what you mean; under the skin, and not since yesterday. The ink looks just faded enough, like an old sailor's tattoo."

"So, Eleonora, you have a dilemma, indeed. Which of the two men do you believe?"

"Bruchner," I answered, smiling. "Caronte Bruchner."

"But you have no proof."

"That's what I'm looking for."

"So, you have come to me."

He tapped his cane on the oak floor boards, gazing out the window at nothing in particular.

"What is your theory?" he asked. "How do you think Bruchner came to have the other man's name?"

I shrugged and shifted in my chair. "I'm not sure. I've thought that maybe he was a fellow deportee. When the Russians liberated the camp, maybe he had no papers, so he assumed Bruchner's identity."

"Your logic is flawed, Eleonora," said Saettano.

I looked at him, wondering where I had gone awry.

"Remember what you told me about the tattoos," he said.

Of course, I thought. Of course! "They have identical numbers on their wrists," I mumbled. "That means that if Professor Bruchner is the imposter, he could not have been a prisoner at Auschwitz."

"Exactly. If he had been a prisoner, he would have had his own number."

I considered my oversight and realized that my false assumption about the professor had cut off all other avenues of exploration. The idea that Bruchner had been a deportee was a brick wall; I could bang my head off it forever and come away with nothing more elucidating than a headache. Once I turned my nose away from the wall, I could see the exit. A new road opened before me, and the most plausible interpretation revealed itself to me effortlessly. The puzzle was far from complete, but I had filled in a lot more letters.

"What is it, Eleonora?" asked Saettano, shaking me from my rumination.

I smiled at him. "Thank you, Professor Saettano," I said. "I think I've got it."

"Indeed?"

"I've been in the habit of distrusting my father's wisdom for so long that I didn't even consider the ready-made analysis of what wasn't quite kosher about Bruchner."

"What was that?"

"My father knew Bruchner wasn't Jewish; his inquiries showed that. But I was looking for another explanation." I laughed, shaking my head, emotions straddling admiration for my father and relief for myself.

"Congratulations," said Saettano, though not wholeheartedly. "Eleonora, you have proven nothing about Gualtieri Bruchner. Can you demonstrate that he is not who he claims to be?"

I nodded, my smile growing ever broader.

"Have you resolved the incongruity of Anton Bruckner's presence among the Jewish composers?"

"I believe so. You see, I'm finally listening to my father."

"You speak so strangely, Eleonora. How do you mean?"

"The tattoo," I said. "The one on his chest. The one that sparked my father's suspicions."

CHAPTER FIFTEEN

Sitting in a downtown A-Train, I considered Saettano's parting counsel: "You are a bright girl, Eleonora," he said, shaking a bony finger at me. "But you must be sure that your deductions have solid foundations. Never fashion your conclusions to fit your thesis."

I jumped off the train at Thirty-Fourth Street and hurried across town on foot, arriving at Bruchner's building at a little before noon. The concierge shook his head when I asked for the professor.

"Left this morning about six," he said. "And I haven't seen him come back."

"Was he carrying luggage?" I asked, fearing he'd fled.

"No, miss. Just an overcoat, not even his briefcase. He turned down Lex, but that's all I know."

If Bruchner had flown, I had blown it. Armed with a theory that I believed would disprove his identity as Gualtieri Bruchner, I had established a clear and compelling motive for murder. But without the quarry, I could prove nothing.

I knew nothing about Bruchner's personal life. Where might he go in a pinch? Walking down Lexington in the wet flurries, I reviewed everything I'd learned about him, from visa information to the letter of support from Professor Nardone. Little there.

The wind picked up as I crossed Thirty-Sixth Street. I pulled my neck into my collar like a turtle and cut through the cold slush falling from the sky. A man crossing Thirty-Sixth heading north huddled in his brown overcoat, fedora tilted down to the wet pavement. He wasn't looking where he was going. I stopped myself just before plowing into him, and we brushed against each other.

"Excuse me," we muttered in unison, and our eyes met.

"Professor Bruchner," I said in the middle of Thirty-Sixth Street. "I was just wondering where you might be."

He squinted at me through the wind and precipitation, and a taxi blasted its horn at us as the light changed. We scooted to the north corner, out of the path of the slippery traffic, and faced each other.

"What do you want now?" he asked, hands jammed deep into his pockets.

"To talk," I said. "I've discovered something you'll find interesting."

"Interesting how?"

"About your lunch last Friday, the attack on my father, and Ruggero Ercolano's murder."

Bruchner sighed. "Let's not stand here in the wet. Come, we'll talk in my flat."

We tramped two blocks through the collecting slush to his building, and five minutes later, he was boiling a kettle of water for tea. Taking a seat near the small kitchen, I glanced at his overcoat and hat, dripping from the rack by the door. Then I looked at my own coat on the next hook: streaked with water, but not soaked. I figured he'd been out walking for some time.

"Why do you say murder?" he asked, warming his hands near the flame on the stove. "Professor Ercolano died accidentally."

"I don't think so."

He paused, looked at me, then took his hands away from the heat and rubbed them together. "What do you think happened, Miss Stone? I'm sure it ends with me throwing a radio into his bath."

His boldness surprised me. He joined me outside the kitchen, eschewing a seat, standing above me instead.

"I know Ruggero Ercolano was the man with my father at lunch last Friday."

His jaw tightened.

"His presence at that lunch creates a problem for you. You insisted you didn't know who the man was."

"I didn't," he said, flustered. "Your father jumped at me, and I never saw anyone else."

"Are you telling me you didn't see the man who pried my father's hands off your throat? A man you work with every day?"

"There was a big commotion," he said, turning away. "I didn't see anything. I was in shock."

"Not so much that you didn't realize Ruggero Ercolano represented a threat to your security. My father surely gave him the whole story about your tattoo and your false identity at lunch that day. He must have found the damning evidence he'd been looking for, probably that very morning in the mail."

"You're mad!" said Bruchner, turning to face me again. "You have no evidence, nor has your father."

"You're right; I don't have the letter. I think you found it last Friday night when you paid an unexpected visit to my father. You took the letter with you after you clubbed him on the head."

"Preposterous! *Alles erlogen! Sciocchezze!* You have no proof, not for your father or for Ruggero Ercolano. I had no reason to hurt either one, especially Ercolano, who never did me any wrong."

"But you did have a reason," I said. "My father believed he had the definitive proof of your masquerade, and when you showed up at the Faculty Club last Friday afternoon, he exploded. Ercolano was with my father, heard everything, saw everything, then left with him. Don't you think my father might have explained the situation to him, especially after he'd tried to strangle you? He may well have shown him the letter. At the very least, you had to assume Ercolano knew."

"Knew what, Miss Stone?" shouted Bruchner, veins bulging in his forehead. "What proof have you that I am not who I say? I have a passport, visa, Italian driver's license, and a tattoo on my wrist for proof!"

"And you have the tattoo on your chest."

Bruchner's anger gave way to alarm. The vein receded into his head and some of the red drained from his face. His expression begged for elucidation.

"I've already told you about that tattoo," he said guardedly.

"You said it was an error of youth, if I remember correctly."

"That's right. The name of a girl I knew: Chiara."

"I'm sure your tattoo was inspired by youthful zeal," I said, "but not over a girl. Chiara is one word, and you've got two lines covered. Please don't tell me you had her family name tattooed on your chest; it's not very romantic."

"How about *Chiara mia*?" he asked. "That's what it said before I had it covered with this hideous tattoo that obsesses your father and you."

"It never said *Chiara mia*, or any other such nonsense," I said, shaking my head. "I didn't know whether to believe you at first. You had more documentation than a double agent. You were a victim, a survivor of the Holocaust, I didn't dare suspect the worst. I was so blinded by the belief that you were Jewish that I couldn't see what my father saw in your tattoo. Then it hit me, like a bolt of lightning." His eyes grew in horror. "Or should I say, two bolts of lightning?"

He jumped, and his hand reached for the upper-left corner of his chest, just where the tattoo was branded into his skin, then he pulled it away quickly.

"What are you implying?" he asked. "That I am not a Jew? What am I if you deny me my identity?"

I stared coldly into his burning eyes. "You, Professor, are a *Schutzstaffel*. A former SS man."

"Ridiculous," he said, though not very convincingly.

"I couldn't figure it out until this morning," I said. "The tattoo on your wrist kept derailing me. But then I realized your mistake: you took Gualtieri Bruchner's number. It suddenly became clear that you had never been an inmate, or Jewish, because you didn't have a number of your own on your wrist."

"No," he turned away slowly, facing the wet, gray window.

"Then I decided my brilliant father deserved more credit than I had been giving him. He suspected the tattoo on your chest from the moment he saw it in the steam bath. He knew what was underneath."

"You are as delusional as your father, Miss Stone."

"SS men often had themselves tattooed with twin lightning bolts, isn't that right?"

He said nothing.

"What is your real name?"

Bruchner rubbed his tired eyes with the heels of his palms, drawing a deep sigh. "My name is Gualtieri Bruchner."

"Officially, yes. You have a passport, a driver's license, and a library card. I may never find out your true name, but I'm sure Immigration and the State Department will be interested just the same."

"But you have no proof!"

"Enough for an investigation, and the truth will come out. The government is particular about letting ex-Nazis into the country. With you and Caronte Bruchner claiming the same identity, they'll want to know who's who."

"Since you believe I killed Ruggero Ercolano, and tried to kill your father, aren't you afraid I will kill you too?"

"The thought crossed my mind," I said.

Bruchner sat down—collapsed into a chair was more like it. He hung his head low, chin nearly touching his chest. His thin fingers drew imaginary circles absently on the table before him. We sat silently for several minutes, as I let him think about the power I held over him. One phone call to Immigration, or even the Italian Embassy, would set the wheels in motion, and in the end, the good professor would be deported or worse.

"You may think this tattoo was once two lightning bolts, but that's not true," he said finally. "Not all SS men were tattooed, and I . . . already had a tattoo there: *viel geliebt Katia.*"

Had he just admitted he was SS?

"My name was Gustav Emmel," he said suddenly, his voice weak, eyes bone dry. "I was born in 1910 in Sillian, Austria, in the southern Tirol, just on the border with Italy. There were Italians in our town, and my mother was from Udine, in the Friuli on the Italian side. I learned Italian as a child, imperfectly, from my mother and her family. We traveled frequently to Friuli and even as far as Venice. My father, you see, was a builder. His father, and his father before, had been masons and bricklayers." He paused to wipe his brow, which had boiled up a sheen of perspiration. "My mother's family were early supporters of the

Camicie Nere, the Blackshirts, in Italy. When I was in school, Mussolini was greatly admired, revered in our home. And then . . ." Bruchner shifted in his seat, let his head fall backward over his shoulders, and he stared at the ceiling for a moment.

"The *Anschluss*?" I prompted.

He nodded slowly and continued his narration. "Had I been born Italian, I would have joined the Fascists. In Austria, it was the *Heimwehr*, and I joined a few years before the *Anschluss*. When Austria became part of Germany, I saw a greater opportunity. The country was alive, burning with excitement for the future. I wanted to be part of that future, of a pan-Germanic revolution and renaissance in Europe. I believed in the words, *Deutschland über Alles*. So, at twenty-eight years of age, I joined the *Schutzstaffel*."

Bruchner looked at me for the first time since he'd begun his statement, his expression humble, his shoulders drooping. I wondered if he wanted absolution from me, as if my forgiveness would erase the sins from his forehead.

"And the war?"

He looked away again, perhaps speechless before a Jew as he catalogued his past. "I was in Poland at the beginning, a radioman in a Panzer division. Then, because of my back, I was sent home for convalescence, where I stayed for several months. When my health improved, I was assigned to *Funkmesstechnik*—radar. But then the camps in the East were ready to become operational. For some reason, maybe because I had been in Poland, maybe because I had lost some hearing in my left ear, they decided I was not to be a radar technician, and they sent me east as a guard at Auschwitz."

"Did they brief you about what you were going to do?"

The gray man before me thought for a long moment before answering. "We understood what was to happen, but there was no option to protest. It's not like here. You don't understand that. One did as they said, or one faced death."

"How did you feel about it? Did the idea of murdering hundreds of thousands, millions, bother you?"

"Of course it did," he muttered. "I had no choice. I did not wish to be there. It was hell, I can tell you that, for us too."

"You're pushing the limits of my sympathy," I said. "Three of my cousins were gassed at Auschwitz."

"I am truly sorry, Miss Stone," he said, almost pleading. "I pitied those poor Jews, dying as they did, stripped of their clothes, possessions, and dignity. Even in death, the affront was bestial: piles of bodies, roaring crematoria, body parts used for . . . It was infernal, Miss Stone. My descriptions cannot convey the horror of walls of naked corpses, stacked with less care than if they had been firewood."

Bruchner's eyes, burning like coals, stared out the window, his breathing becoming shorter as his voice gained strength from the disgust. His mouth twisted in revulsion at his memory.

"Near the end," he continued, "as the Russians approached from the east, time became short. We stoked the ovens with the fury of Vulcan, burning flesh *ad nauseam*, literally. But the worst nightmare of all was when we had the work gangs dig up the mass graves that had been filled before the crematoria were in place. Those bodies had to be destroyed. No evidence could remain."

He paused, head still, no movement besides the rise and fall of his strained breathing.

"But you carried out your orders," I said. "It never became so inhuman that you said 'Enough, these are men.' You're here today to bear witness to the horror, theirs and yours, but they're gone, dead, exterminated like vermin."

"Yes," he said, looking at me, eyes sparkling now.

"Did you ever drop the gas in the chambers?"

He shook his head. "No, other men were assigned that duty. Always the same technicians."

"What exactly was your job at the camp?"

He shrugged. "In the beginning I was with the work gangs in the mines nearby, but a relapse of my back problems ended that. From July 1944 until the Russians liberated the camp in late January '45, I held a machine gun and drove the Jews from the train to the showers. I . . . ," he wiped an eye, "I even closed the doors and . . . bolted them shut. Oh, the screams and the wailing . . ."

I couldn't speak. My hostility had somehow vanished, supplanted by the horrible fascination of listening to an eyewitness to history. One, who, like Aeneas and Orpheus and Dante, had descended into the netherworld and come back out again. Indeed, Gualtieri Caronte Bruchner, too, had made the trip to hell and back. The professor—Emmel—continued:

"The showerheads were fakes," he said, voice hoarse and tormented. "Once, one fell out of the wall. It was a length of pipe, sealed on one end, leading nowhere. The fraud was complete, right down to the counterfeit drain in the floor and the hooks for towels they would never need. In the ceiling, at the center of the chamber, was the trap. The technician would drop a cylinder of Zyklon-B—a pesticide—through the slot, then close the opening. The crystals reacted with the air, producing a fog of deadly gas. Then the screaming began, and lasted for as long as ten, twelve minutes, until the hardiest had succumbed to the poison. We waited thirty minutes more before opening the doors to be sure they were dead. They died like cockroaches; Zyklon-B."

I swallowed back a dry mouth. "Then what?"

"We brought in the gangs to clear the bodies, to check for gold in the teeth, and then carry them to the crematoria. The bodies were still warm, their expressions still human. Men, women, and children in heaps, naked like the damned souls of hell. The incinerators' smokestacks vomited black clouds, and the smoke billowed so thickly and smelled so bitter you could taste it on your tongue. It tasted like agony and perdition."

As Emmel finished his sentence, he did the strangest thing: he reached into his breast pocket, retrieved a handkerchief, and wiped his flat tongue with it. Then he spat into it. Relief softened his rigid features after he'd expelled the taste.

"The so-called Final Solution was to be executed by the *Schutzstaffel*. With the debacle at Stalingrad in January 1943, the tide had turned, and the Jewish Question acquired more urgency, sometimes

even at the expense of the war effort. As the Red Army pushed back
our troops, we in the camps became more aware of the danger we faced.
The crimes we had witnessed," he paused to consider his words. Then he
amended his statement: "The crimes we had committed would demand
justice and punishment. We tried to destroy the evidence, even as we
hurried to gas and burn thousands per day. It was a factory; we were
specialists in extermination and disposal. We exhumed the old mass
graves and stuffed the decayed corpses into the ovens."

Again he spat into his handkerchief. I could see his eyes watering,
but I wasn't sure if he was crying or choking on the memory of human
smoke.

"Did you know Gualtieri Bruchner?" I asked.

He shook his head. "No, I never met him."

"Then how did you come to take his name?"

"As the Russians approached in January 1945, I planned my escape. I
stole a tattooing pen and ink from the registration office and hid them in
my bunk. Later, when the Kommandant quit the camp and we received
orders to destroy all evidence of our actions, we burned paper documents.
I thought my best chance for escape was a new identity, non-German.
Since I spoke Italian, I looked through the records of the Italians. Gualtieri Bruchner was the first northern Italian I found with a birth date
close to mine. It was the night of January 25, two days before the Red
Army reached the camp. I scratched Bruchner's number into my arm and
memorized his birth date. Then I destroyed his records. The next night,
I moved to the other side." He drew a deep breath, but didn't seem to
exhale. "I pulled the uniform off a prisoner who had dropped that afternoon on a work detail. His body was piled with the others, waiting for
cremation. Then I crossed the camp to the women's barracks, because I
feared the male prisoners would recognize me. I passed two sentries on
the way, but they let me pass because they knew me. Finally, I found an
isolated spot where I stripped out of my uniform, buried it under the
corner of one of the women's barracks, and dressed in the prisoner's filthy
clothes. The lice began to bite immediately, as I was fresh and alive."
Emmel scratched his side, then his leg. A vestigial memory.

"I slipped inside the barracks," he continued, "and begged the women not to turn me in to the guards. I told them the Russians were near, that the camp would be free by morning, and they hid me. The confusion was great at that time, and the only organized security was in the towers; no guards entered the barracks that night, nor the next morning. By noon, the Russians had arrived, and most of my old comrades were dead."

"How did you get out?" I asked.

Emmel shrugged his shoulders, a bewildered fatigue on his face. "I wandered out the front gate with some other prisoners. Hungarian Jews, among the last to arrive. They were strong, like me, but we couldn't communicate; I pretended not to know German. Four of us walked for three days, until a Russian patrol picked us up. They sent us south to a refugee camp. By May, when they shipped me to a displaced-persons camp in the British zone, no one would have doubted I was a deportee. I had lost twenty kilos, and I had tuberculosis, worms, and lice. The British sent me to Milan and helped me get new papers. There was never any question that I was not Gualtieri Bruchner."

"And you started a new life," I said.

He nodded and bowed his head, eyes dry again.

"But this story is not over," I added, doing my best to put aside the inexplicable pity I felt for him. "Why don't you tell me what happened the Friday night after your lunch with my father?"

Emmel looked up, perplexed, as if I had hit him in the ear with a spitball. "Tell you what?"

"You've come this far," I said. "Why not clear your conscience of the rest?"

"Are you referring to your father again?"

I nodded.

"I told you that I did not harm him," he said forcefully. "The last time I saw him, he had his hands around my throat in the Faculty Club dining room. I did not go to his apartment that night, and I did not hit him on the head. I did not leave this room that night. In fact, I did not even use the telephone!"

"Were you alone?"

"Of course I was alone," he said, rising to his feet to pace the room. "I cannot prove I was here, if that is your next question, Miss Stone. But I was here and I never left. Why do you insist it was I who did this thing? Your father surely had other enemies. Or perhaps it was a robbery like so many that you have here in America. And Ruggero Ercolano, there is no shortage of spurned women or jealous husbands who might have wanted to kill him. Even Bernard Sanger. He was envious of Ercolano's successes with Ruth Chalmers. And Luigi Lucchesi was his main rival for Hildy Jaspers's affections."

"What would you know about it?" I asked, my ears pricked by the mention of Gigi's name. "Was there talk of Hildy Jaspers and Luigi Lucchesi?"

"Of course," he said, voice calmer, pushing a hand through his oiled, silvery hair. "Academics are a gossipy lot, in case you hadn't noticed."

I had.

"And your father played the game too, in his own way. Look what he did to me. Writing letters to my colleagues, asking for investigations . . ."

"But he was right," I pointed out.

Emmel had to concur, though he didn't say so. "I could tell you of all their peccadilloes," he said. "Ruggero Ercolano and his insatiable carnal appetites, Bernard Sanger with his pandering and groveling, Hildy Jaspers and Lucchesi with their pathological flirtation . . . And Victor Chalmers and his family are the worst of all."

"How do you mean?"

He shook his head, angry and disgusted, with me and his experience at Columbia. "Victor Chalmers, a mature professional, making an ass of himself as he chased Miss Jaspers . . . He should have been chastised publicly for such indiscretion, and with a student!"

"What about the others?" I asked.

"His wife," offered Emmel. "The staggering alcoholic, who protects her daughter's virtue with the fury of a tiger. Sweet little Ruth, carrying on an affair with Ruggero Ercolano under everyone's nose. The entire department knew; I heard it from that sycophant, Roger Purdy."

"Even Joan Little?"

"No, she's a silly, naive woman. She suspected nothing about Ruth. No one told her about it because they all knew she was in love with Ercolano. It's like a bad comedy."

"Did Chalmers know about Ercolano and his daughter?"

Emmel shrugged. "That, I can't say for sure. But he did know about his son, William, *Guglielmino*, as his father calls him."

"*Guglielmino*?" I asked.

"Guglielmino is Italian for *Billy*," he said. "Surely you've heard of *Guglielmo Tell*, the opera by Rossini? You call it *William Tell* in English."

"Of course," I said. "The *Lone Ranger* Theme."

Emmel frowned, as if I had wiped my nose on his sleeve. He disapproved of my humor or breeding or both. "Guglielmino, Billy the spoiled brat, caused the biggest scandal of all, the most odious of crimes against nature and God. His rotten soul would have no compunction to kill, especially the man sleeping with his sister."

I remembered the threatening letter Billy had sent to Bernie Sanger. "What are you saying?" I asked, thinking I knew.

"Incestuous pervert, in love with his own sister!" and he spat into his handkerchief.

I was speechless.

"They tried to smother the scandal," he continued. "The story was that Guglielmino disappeared from that military school in Valley Forge and turned up at Wellesley, where Ruth was a student. He made a horrible scene of some kind, and Ruth left school."

"And they sent Billy to a boarding school in New England," I murmured, recalling Joan Little's words.

"New England?" scoffed Emmel. "They sent him to Haiti. To a Jesuit school in Port-au-Prince, of all God-forsaken places, just to keep him away from his own sister! Why don't you ask him, Miss Stone, about Ruggero Ercolano and your father? Why don't you ask Guglielmino?"

"Does anyone else call him Guglielmino?" I asked, breaking Emmel's concentration.

"Excuse me?"

"I've never heard him called Guglielmino before. I've known him casually for fifteen years, and I've never heard it. You said his father calls him that?"

"I don't know," said Emmel, defensive. "I am not close with Professor Chalmers and his wretched family. What does it matter?"

"I suppose it doesn't," I said, wondering if it did. Then returning to his tirade against the iniquity of the department: "What possible reason could Billy Chalmers have to kill my father?"

"Perhaps it was unintentional," said Emmel. "Perhaps he only wanted to steal your father's manuscript to discredit Ercolano."

"That doesn't explain the desecration of my brother's grave and the destruction of my father's Jewish music."

Emmel was perplexed. "Jewish music?"

"Gershwin, Mahler, Mendelssohn, Bruckner . . ."

Emmel chuckled. "You are a paranoiac, Miss Stone. You see conspiracy and anti-Semitism everywhere. Your theory is either an innocent fallacy or calculated sophistry; Anton Bruckner was not Jewish!"

"I know that," I said, nodding my head. "But I was interested to know if you did."

Emmel scowled at me. "I offer you this advice, Miss Stone," he said, his tone salty with antipathy. "Stop playing games about Anton Bruckner and ask yourself who, besides me, had the opportunity to kill your father and Ruggero Ercolano? When you find a link between the two men, your murderer will present himself." He paused. "Or herself."

CHAPTER SIXTEEN

I tramped through the slush onto Lexington, over Thirty-Fourth Street, and down Fifth until I arrived at my father's apartment building. I was soaked, my clothes wet to the skin, and I was cold. My meeting with Bruchner, né Gustav Emmel, had not worked out as I had hoped. Yes, he'd confessed to his phony identity—a Nazi, of all things—but I wasn't after a deportation.

I thought about Gustav Emmel as Rodney shifted the elevator into motion. He had denied any involvement in the attempt on my father and the killing of Ercolano. Yet he had admitted to what might even qualify as war crimes. He had certainly told me enough to have him shipped off to Italy on an airliner to a whole lot of explaining. Yet he denied the crimes in the Italian Department.

The elevator lurched to a stop, and Rodney opened the door. "You get yourself dried off, Miss Eleonora," he said. "You ought to carry an umbrella on days like this."

"Everyone's giving me advice today," I answered, stepping into the hall. "Why do you suppose I keep on ignoring it?"

"You do all right, Miss Eleonora. Just keep on like you're going. You'll figure it out."

I let myself into the apartment a little after three, doubting I would ever figure it out, showered, and changed into some dry clothes, a black turtleneck and stirrup pants. I heated some coffee then went to the study to review my notes. Franco Saettano and Gustav Emmel had parceled out some valuable advice to me that morning, as had my father, once I'd opened my ears to hear it. Now I needed to apply that collective wisdom in a systematic fashion. I pulled a pencil and a clean sheet of my father's stationery from his desk drawer and drew a vertical line down the center of the page. Above the columns, I wrote Abraham Stone and Ruggero Ercolano, respectively. Then I listed all the players from the Italian Department down the left-hand margin, and began noting possible motives and opportunity. I lit a cigarette by rote to help me think.

I eliminated the two victims right off the bat. My father had no reason to hurt Ercolano, and, indeed, was comatose at Saint Vincent's when Ercolano died. I believed the two attacks were linked, due to the attempt to frame Ercolano with my father's manuscript. The implications were clear: the person who mailed the book wanted to discredit Ercolano, for whatever reason, and had obviously stolen it from my father's study. The botched frame-up disqualified Ercolano from my short list of suspects.

Franco Saettano's age and frail condition, not to mention his noble standing and comportment, eliminated him from consideration.

Having crossed out the most unlikely, I proceeded to those I felt had opportunity, if not motive. Joan Little loved Ruggero Ercolano enough to humiliate herself for his sake. She had access to his apartment—a key she used when she cleaned—and I doubted he would have been shy about bathing in her presence. But she had no known dislike for my father, no reason to kill him. There was my father's key, however: the one he kept at the office, locked in Miss Little's key box. Although the box was accessible to almost anyone in the department, she, better than anyone, knew that my father kept his house keys there.

I moved on to the petulant pair: Roger Purdy and Anthony Petronella. They were bitter enough to hate my father, Roger for his B, Petronella for what he perceived was the deliberate sabotage of his career. What I couldn't see, however, was any strong antipathy for Ruggero Ercolano, or any possible scenario of how they might have gained access to the dead man's apartment. Finally, their frank avowals of hatred for my father inclined me to believe in their innocence; wouldn't they turn down the vitriol if they had tried to kill him?

Bernie Sanger was my father's protégé, the star student of an internationally renowned scholar. It would be suicide, at such an immature point in his career, for Bernie to kill off his mentor. Perhaps later in life, an academic psychopath might feel it necessary to kill the "father" in order to assume his mantle and surpass him, but Bernie Sanger hadn't even finished his dissertation. And he struck me as balanced and normal besides. As far as Ercolano was concerned, I wasn't aware of any malevolence Bernie may have felt toward him, nor could I imagine how he would have gotten inside the bachelor's lair while Ercolano was sudsing it up in the tub.

The Chalmers clan posed a quadruple threat. Victor, the patriarch and intrepid chairman of the Italian Department, had reason to begrudge Ruggero Ercolano, assuming he knew of the affair between the playboy and his daughter. He may well have resented my father's standing for chairman, but Dad had withdrawn his candidacy. I couldn't imagine an invertebrate like Victor Chalmers taking any decisive action, let alone assault with intent to kill, but he could have easily known about the key in Miss Little's not-so-secret box.

His wife, Helen, seemed capable of almost anything when it came to protecting her family. She had railed against Bernie Sanger and his kind for wanting to soil Ruth and her kind. Might her maternal instincts have pushed her to toss an electric radio into Ercolano's bath, just to settle the score? Possible, in theory. Her poorly disguised animosity toward my father may have been prompted by his aborted challenge to her husband's leadership, but I still had no explanation of how she would have gained entry to either victim's apartment.

Sweet little Ruthie, the precocious intellectual. She was polite, sophisticated, and well educated, a girl with a bright future and a dead lover. She had access to Ercolano's apartment; indeed, she was there the night he died, and, if she was to be believed, she'd let herself in, as Ercolano was already dead in the water. Her motive could have been the same as Joan Little's, and like her rival, she had no known enmity for my father. The fact that she'd alerted her own father to her lover's death made me believe she hadn't killed him.

Then there was Billy the Kid, Guglielmino (something about that name was itching the back of my brain), who'd stashed the most scandalous skeleton in the family's closet. Smitten by his own sister, Billy was guilty of God-knows-what transgressions. His twisted passions had boiled over once before, prompting his exile to purgatory in Haiti. I thought him capable of wanting Ercolano dead, but I couldn't say if he had the guts for murder. He barely knew my father, and even if Victor Chalmers grumbled at the dinner table about his colleagues, as my father did, I couldn't imagine a motive emerging between forkfuls of potatoes, peas, and Salisbury steak.

Gustav Emmel was the only person with motive to kill both men: my father for his relentless investigation, and Ercolano for having learned the details of it. What he lacked, however, was the opportunity to get at the two men in their homes. I wasn't ruling out some kind of burglary, surreptitious entry, or even a knock on the door, but for the moment I had nothing more than motive.

And Hildy Jaspers. She had visited Dad's apartment before my arrival on the scene, apparently in the role of decorator. But I had also heard rumors that, in addition to her other trophies, she had carried on with the venerable Professor Stone. In her favor, however, was my incredulity of any such behavior on my father's part. I could not say the same for Ruggero Ercolano. If the talk was to be believed, Ercolano would have humped a department store mannequin in a display window. A real-life splendor like Hildy would have pumped the hormones out through his ears.

Finally, there was Gigi Lucchesi. I had left his name for last for reasons of my own. I felt a tinge of shame at having been less than tenacious in pursuing the irregularities of his case. Why hadn't I asked him about the rumors linking him to Hildy Jaspers? And what about the Barnard undergraduate incident? Did Gigi know of my father's intentions to mar his record? And he had been in my father's apartment on more than one occasion, even before I met him. I knew why I hadn't pursued these questions: because I didn't want to hear the wrong answers. When you're aching with desire, you don't want to lose that touch of warm flesh, the delicious draw of intimacy. You'll do anything to squeeze one more moment of the delirium out of his pores. That's what I wanted. One more night in his bed, or my bed, or my father's bed, ignorant in my bliss or blissful in my ignorance. But the questions I was about to ask myself put the exquisite delight in jeopardy. I inhaled deeply on my cigarette, trying to feel the sting in my lungs. Nothing. I was too nervous to feel anything physical. I resumed the intellectual exercise.

So what if Gigi had slept with Hildy prior to having met me? That kind of thing had never troubled me in the past. My attitude toward relations between the sexes has always been libertarian. Some might say libertine. I don't believe in baring my soul to the men I know, though I strive to be honest. This politic has functioned smoothly, usually without seams, both for the men I go with and myself. In the case of Gigi Lucchesi, however, I felt the traffic begin to run in one direction only. A perception, and a false one perhaps, but I didn't cotton to falling like a ton of bricks for anyone, let alone a man just out for a joyride.

To return to the subject, I willed myself not to mind that Gigi had had an affair with Hildy, if indeed he had. Who cared what he'd done before he'd done it with me? I didn't, I swore to myself. No way.

But I did.

Then I realized that my musings had nothing to do with the matter at hand. Gigi was my problem, not my father's or Ercolano's. He had no real reason to harm either one of them, but he had harmed me, left me without a word.

I gazed at my handiwork: the worksheet of suspects from Columbia University's Italian Department. I'd only physically eliminated three people, of whom one was dead, one comatose, and one decrepit with age. The others might well have had some hidden motives, but I had no idea how to link any of them to both crimes. Of the entire group, Gustav Emmel stood out as the only one with motive and opportunity. Emmel's past was the key. He was lying to save his skin. Deportation was one thing; proving he was not Gualtieri Bruchner might prove impossible in Italy, where so many people know and respect him. But murder in New York State would mean the electric chair. Why shouldn't he lie?

Where, then, was my proof? If there was none, perhaps a burglar did break in and club my father on the head; maybe Ercolano got a little careless in the tub and paid for it with his life.

For a moment, I was confused, didn't know what to believe. Lucky for me, the intercom buzzed to announce Detective McKeever and chased away the doubts; doubts about things I knew to be right. These were not isolated, unrelated examples of peril in twentieth-century New York. The radio was tossed into the tub by the same person who'd hit my father on the head, I was sure of it.

"Hello, Jim," I said, holding the door open for him a few moments later. "Please come in. Maybe you can give me some information to break the logjam in my head."

"I might be able to help you," he said, removing his hat as he stepped inside. "Do you remember the key we found at the department?" he asked once he'd taken a seat in the study.

"I sure do," I said. "It was the key to this apartment. What about it?"

"Well, I do things by the book, as I once told you. And the book says when you find evidence like that key, you check it for fingerprints."

"I'll bet you didn't find Ercolano's prints on it."

"No," he said. "Either the key was left near his office door by chance, or to throw suspicion on him."

"So which was it?"

He frowned. "I don't know, but I doubt it matters." He fiddled with his hat. "You see, we'd come to a dead end on this case, so I asked for print samples from everyone."

"How did they take it?"

"Some good, some not so good. Miss Little was worried her prints would be on the key, even if she hadn't stolen it, since she handles all the keys. Victor Chalmers kind of liked the experience; said he was fascinated by police work. That Purdy kid refused to be printed at first, but his friend Petronella finally convinced him to give a sample."

"And Bruchner?" I asked, still unsure what I'd do about him.

"Volunteered without question. The old man, Saettano, seemed miffed, but submitted. Hildy Jaspers didn't like getting her fingers dirty, but she went along."

Now the question I dreaded. "And Luigi Lucchesi?"

"He didn't like it but he gave us a sample."

"OK, Sergeant. I don't have a snare drum; what's the verdict?"

"We isolated a partial print that seems to belong to Mr. Lucchesi. It was no contest for the others. They didn't come close."

I was floored. My temples began to throb. He'd duped me; played me like a harmonica. I had slept with him, damn it! The imaginary conversation with my father returned to my head:

"Well, Ellie, how did you proceed in your investigation?"

"By the book, Dad. First I investigated every possible suspect, except one."

"And which one was that?"

"Funny you should ask. By the purest of coincidences, it turned out—you're gonna love this—it turned out that he was the guilty party."

"Oh, my, what bad luck for you, my girl. I suppose you had no reason to suspect him. Perhaps you had little opportunity for intercourse with him."

"As a matter of fact, I had quite a bit of intercourse with him. You see, while I was chasing after the others, harassing and accusing, I was screwing him in your house!"

I fumbled for a cigarette, struck the match once, twice, three times, took one puff, then put it down.

"Have you talked to him?" I asked. "What's his explanation? What's his motive?"

McKeever lit a cigarette of his own, then shook his head. "I haven't asked him," he said. "We just got the results back an hour ago and haven't located him yet. But he had reasons. I understand that your father was pursuing an investigation of his behavior with an undergraduate from Barnard."

"That was blown out of proportion," I said, a little too earnestly. "And people don't kill for that."

"They might if it meant dismissal, shame, and return home to face mandatory military service."

"How do you know all that?"

"I want to solve this for you, Ellie," he said softly. "I've been digging around."

I wrestled my heart into submission, took a deep breath, and tried to remind myself that I didn't care. But my head was so muddled with thoughts of how little I cared about Gigi Lucchesi, that all I could think about was Gigi Lucchesi.

"I, um, I've been wondering if I could have another look at Ercolano's apartment," I muttered, just to have something to say. I was distracted beyond measure. "No, not his apartment, his, um, his things."

"His personal effects?" asked McKeever, voice strong and imposing.

"Right, his personal effects. Do you have them?"

McKeever shook his head. "Just the keys," he said, pulling a chain from his pocket. "The rest of it is locked up in the evidence room."

I took the keys from him and turned away absently. Barely glancing at them, hardly concentrating on the silver in my hands, I thought of Gigi swinging some blunt object at my father's head. Then at mine. I jingled the keys a couple of times, counted them in my palm—three, two latchkeys and one mailbox key—then handed them back to McKeever.

"What will you do now?" I asked.

"Arrest Luigi Lucchesi as soon as we find him."

I was quiet, and McKeever noticed. He gazed at me with some kind of emotion in his eyes. I wasn't sure if he wanted to comfort me or kiss me.

"Are you OK, Ellie?" he asked.

I nodded vigorously. "Everything's fine. Looks like you've got your man, Jim," I said, forcing a smile. "Congratulations."

McKeever left at four thirty. I lay down on my father's bed and stared at the ceiling for an hour, tormenting myself alternatively with the ache of having lost the divine object of my desire, then the sting of having been taken in by the devious incubus. It's never easy to admit to foolishness, but the shame compounds itself when you still hunger for the source of your humiliation, and you wonder to yourself if you'd let it happen again for one more night in his arms.

I slid off the bed, lit a cigarette, and paced the room. The nicotine rush I had wanted earlier hit me hard now, biting my lungs and dizzying my head. I had to sit until the spinning had passed, holding the burning cigarette in my left hand, resting it on my knee. Once my head stopped swirling, I took a last deep drag, then stubbed out the butt in an ashtray. Then I lit another, in defiance of Gigi Lucchesi; he would not deprive me of a good smoke.

I wandered into the study, poured myself a tall Scotch, and finished the cigarette at my father's desk. About halfway down to the bottom of the tumbler, I made my way over to the hi-fi, where the Rachmaninoff still sat on the turntable. On the middle shelf, among Mom's records, I found an old 78 of Cole Porter songs. I put it on, right over the Rachmaninoff concerto that I had used to seduce myself with Gigi. Why had he come to me that night? Perhaps he'd left some evidence behind and needed to collect it. And I'd helped him.

I dropped the needle and fell into the sofa, drink in hand, and lit yet another cigarette. The first track was "I Get a Kick out of You," and I remembered his smile and flirtations. "I've Got You under My Skin"— Gigi's lips, his eyes, his . . . Everything that tickled my desire, none of which I'd ever touch again. "Let's Do It." Birds, bees, educated fleas, and I was thinking of how I had enjoyed his company. The first notes of "Just One of Those Things" began, recalling Dorothy Parker and an anonymous boyfriend; Abélard and Héloïse; Romeo and Juliet; et al.— famous pairs who never managed to make love work. I could count myself as lucky among the group; Romeo poisoned himself beside his Juliet, while Abélard was castrated and shipped off to a monastery. But once the introduction's catalogue of unfortunate lovers was through, the song's lyrics spanked me, hitting my nail on the head:

> It was just one of those things,
> Just one of those crazy flings,
> One of those bells that now and then rings,
> Just one of those things.

I bounded to the hi-fi and yanked the needle off the disk, sending a shriek through the nearby speakers, and a gouge across the record. I flipped the disk across the room, where it collided with the bookcase. The bookcase won.

I drained the last of my Scotch into my mouth, poured another, equally as tall, then sat some more. The silence was too much. I thought of Angela Farber and wondered if she'd like to trade hard-luck stories. There was no answer when I buzzed her door. I called the elevator to ask if she'd gone out.

"Oh, yeah, Mrs. Farber left here about a half hour ago," said Rodney. "All dressed up, shiny dress, fox stole, saucy little hat . . . Looked like she was going out for dinner and the theater."

I drifted back to my father's apartment, cursing Angela Farber's improved fortunes; just a day or two before she couldn't get a date to save her life. I returned to the study where I picked up my Scotch and looked for another record. Reluctant for a second Porteresque experience among Mom's records, I delved into my father's collection. As long as I avoided Rachmaninoff, I'd be fine. My fingers tripped along the alphabetical path, starting with Albinoni. Then came the three *B*s, Chopin, Dvorak, Elgar, Franck, Grieg, Hindemith, Ives, and so on, until I found myself in Rachmaninoff's neighborhood. From A to Q, I had been unable to choose, perhaps subconsciously, so I would have to listen again to the late Romantic Sergei Rachmaninoff. No, damn it. I moved on, only to come nose to nose with Gioacchino Rossini. My eyes ran across the titles: *Il Barbiere di Seviglia, La Cenerentola, La Gazza Ladra* . . . I tugged at one album in particular, pulling it out of the tight line. It was one of the records I had found on the floor earlier in the week, one of those strewn about but not destroyed. It was *Guglielmo Tell*, and all thoughts of Gigi Lucchesi dissipated into air.

My ears tingled, and the shiver of imminent illumination tripped over my skin, from my toes to the top of my head. I placed my glass on my father's desk, never taking my eyes off the album's dust cover, which I raised in front of me at arm's length. Orchestral excerpts from *Guglielmo Tell*, by Gioacchino Rossini, performed by the NBC Orchestra under the direction of Arturo Toscanini. *Guglielmo Tell*, and I recalled two conversations with Gustav Emmel about Billy Chalmers and Guelphs. I brought the album to my lips and planted a kiss on Toscanini's bald head.

"That's for Gigi," I said, then ran to change my clothes.

CHAPTER SEVENTEEN

It was dark when the cab dropped me off outside Saettano's Riverside Drive apartment house. I had tried to call him, but the line was engaged. The slush had stopped falling from the sky, but the sidewalks and gutters were still rough sledding. I slipped once in my haste, but caught myself before falling, and pushed through the heavy brass door into the lobby.

"You again, Miss Stone?" asked Libby with a frown. "The professor is about to sit down to dinner."

"I'm sorry," I said, stepping inside before she'd invited me. "I tried to phone, but the line was busy. It's really urgent."

Libby showed me to the den overlooking the Hudson, where the old man appeared a few minutes later.

"Eleonora," he said, holding out his frail hand. "Two visits in one day. What is so urgent that makes you behave so rashly?"

"I have to ask you something," I said.

"Of course," he said, motioning to a chair as he himself sat down. "How may I help you?"

"I want to know about philology, history of language," I said. "Italian philology."

Saettano regarded me queerly. "Philology?"

"I want to know about sound change."

"I'm not a linguist, Eleonora."

"But I'm sure you'll know the answer."

"So ask me," he said.

"When a word comes into one language from another, what happens?"

Saettano pursed his lips. "This reminds me of my university exams," he said. "And that was more than sixty years ago. What kind of word are you talking about?"

"Suppose a word, or a name, came into Latin or Italian a thousand or more years ago from a Germanic dialect. Let's say the name is William or Wilhelm. Is there any rhyme or reason to how it turns out?"

"Absolutely," intoned the old man, punctuating his statement with a bounce of his cane. "Sound change is paradoxical, Eleonora: it is at the same time arbitrary and regular."

"How so?"

"Arbitrary in the sense that there is not necessarily a reason one sound moves to another. If all phonemes changed in the same fashion everywhere and for the same reasons, we would all speak the same language with the same accent." He wiped a handkerchief across his lips, then continued. "For a group of people living in the same community, speaking the same language, sound change is regular. The evolution of Latin to Italian is filled with such examples. It may sound complicated, but a philologist can explain and predict changes. The Latin for milk, *lactis*, for example, moves to *latte* in Italian. The regularity of this sound change can be seen in other examples: *fructus–frutto, factum–fatto, pectus–petto*."

"What about my example of Wilhelm?"

"The German *W* is pronounced like an English *V* of course, but in Romance languages it changes to a *G* sound. *Guillaume* in French, *Guillermo* in Spanish, and *Guglielmo* in Italian. It's completely regular."

"Regular enough for other examples?"

"Many. The pairs are common between English and Italian. English is, after all, the descendent of Saxon, a Germanic dialect. For example: *guadagno* for wage; *guardia* for ward; *guerra* for war. I'm sure there are more. Perhaps you could think of some yourself."

"I think I can."

Saettano squinted at me from his chair. "For instance?"

"*Guelph* and Welf."

"Yes," he said. "Any others?"

"*Gualtieri* and Walter," I said, and the old man nodded approvingly.

I tried to reach McKeever, but he was out. The switchboard transferred me to a sergeant who worked Homicide.

"What do you want him for?" he asked, chewing on something that sounded like dinner.

"It's the Ercolano murder case," I said.

"He don't need your help, girlie; he's already got a warrant for some Italian guy."

"It's not the Italian," I said. "Just tell him Ellie called. I need him to meet me in an hour at Carnegie Hall, box 59 in the first tier."

"Is this some kind of crank?"

"Please tell him. It's just seven thirty. Have him meet me there at eight thirty."

"What for?"

"He can listen to the music if he wants," I said. "But first I'm going to hand over his murderer."

Carnegie Hall sits on the corner of Seventh Avenue and Fifty-Seventh Street (if you were wondering how to get there). The placards at the Fifty-Seventh Street entrance announced a special, sold-out engagement: Van Cliburn.

It was no easy feat getting inside. I argued with the man at the ticket window that I was Abraham Stone's daughter, there to collect replacement tickets for the originals, which had been lost. After some grumbling on his part, and two pieces of identification on mine, he issued the tickets: seats 3 and 4, box 59 on the first tier. The seats, on the left side, were among the finest in the hall. But I was going to have to wait that night, as my wrangling with the ticket clerk had made me miss Cliburn's entrance. The door to box 59 was locked. I looked at my watch: 8:07. Intermission was at least thirty minutes away.

I paced the corridor, consulting the time every few minutes. Two red-coated ushers watched me cross-armed from the stairway, their faces expressionless. I asked if they might be induced to unlock box 59, but they shook their heads in unison. I took up my pacing again.

Strains of Schumann's "Papillons" fluttered up the stairways and through the corridors, but my mind was too busy to worry about missing a great concert. I pulled a pencil and paper from my purse and began jotting down the disjointed pieces of my reconstructed puzzle; I didn't want to forget anything. At 8:26, McKeever appeared at the top of the stairs. He showed his badge to the ushers, who looked my way, sure the flatfoot was after me. McKeever approached, looking put out.

"Gigi didn't do it," I said.

"Gigi?"

"Luigi Lucchesi didn't kill Ercolano. And he didn't attack my father."

McKeever winced, looked down, and drew a deep breath.

"This really bothers you, doesn't it?" I accused. "More work? More people to interview?"

McKeever frowned. "It's not that, Ellie."

"Then what?"

He seemed to search for words. "Look, if not Mr. Lucchesi, who did it, then?"

I turned my head toward the box behind me. "In there. I'm just waiting for intermission."

McKeever gazed past me at the door, his shoulders drooping, looking exhausted.

"Look, Ellie," he said. "I've got to talk to you."

Then a thunderous applause rose from below and carried through the halls. I stepped to one side of the door to box 59 and motioned to McKeever to do the same. He looked at me, almost desperately, then relented and moved to the side. A few moments passed, and the ovation subsided. The brass knob clicked and turned, then the door eased open. A bald man in black tie stepped out, followed by a portly, lipsticked woman in a green satin dress and a brown mink. A young couple came next, then a little man with white hair. I held my breath, waiting for the next to appear. I knew I wasn't wrong.

"Good evening, Professor," I said.

Gustav Emmel blanched, stammered something unintelligible, then threw a glance back into the box.

"Please, do invite Mrs. Farber to come out," I said. I drew out the awkward drama another moment before adding: "Walter."

Angela Farber appeared from the box, radiant from some kind of musical rapture, and didn't notice her escort's discomfort. Emmel's eyes darted back and forth between her, looking stunning in a sequined dress and fox fur, and me, in my wet hair, black overcoat, and soggy shoes. She still hadn't seen me.

"Angela," said Emmel, eyeing me. "She's here."

Mrs. Farber turned her head, euphoric smile spread over her cheeks, and almost looked through me. Then her glow dimmed.

"Good evening," I said. "Enjoying the concert?"

She suppressed whatever emotions were roiling inside of her—rage, humiliation, surprise—and floated a cracked smile.

"Ellie, I didn't expect to see you here tonight."

"No, I'm sure you didn't."

"Are you referring to your father's seats?" she asked, waving a white-gloved hand. "How embarrassing! You're probably wondering why I have his tickets."

I glanced at McKeever, who had stepped from behind the door into view. I waited for her to explain.

"He gave them to me," she said, unable to smile and lie at the same time. She'd caught sight of McKeever, and, remembering him from the initial investigation, nodded nervously in his direction. "He had planned on being out of town, you see. He said something about Washington and his cousin, like a few months ago when I looked after his plants. Well, anyway, he knows how I enjoy piano music, so he offered me the tickets. Walter and I have had this evening planned for weeks."

"According to Carnegie Hall, the tickets were only mailed on the twentieth," I said. "He would have received them on Friday the twenty-second at the earliest."

"So? That's when he gave them to me."

"That's the day he was attacked in his study. And you said you were in the bathtub when he arrived home."

Angela Farber blinked, looked to Walter, Gustav, or whatever his name was, then back at me.

"Furthermore, my father's cousin from Washington is somewhere in the Painted Desert right now. He won't be back until next week."

There was a long silence.

"Why don't we talk inside," said McKeever, motioning to the box. "I don't think we want to share this discussion with everyone."

The box was empty, except for the chairs and a couple of forgotten programs. McKeever held the door for Angela Farber, Emmel, and me, then closed us in.

"Is this going to take long?" she asked. "I don't intend to miss the second half of this program. And Walter and I have a table reserved at the Russian Tea Room later on."

"I wouldn't count on either if I were you," I said. "Mrs. Farber, I think you already know Detective-Sergeant McKeever of the NYPD. He's here to arrest you for the murder of Ruggero Ercolano and the attempted murder of my father."

Her jaw dropped, and McKeever blushed.

"Ellie," he protested. "I have no plans to arrest this lady."

"How could you think I'd do such a thing?" she gasped. "I didn't even know that Ercolano fellow."

"I realize that," I said. "Or you hardly knew him. That's why it never occurred to me that you might be the one. You had no direct ties to the Italian Department, besides living next door to my father, so I had no reason to suspect you."

"You have the wrong idea, Ellie," she said, trying to muster another smile. Her upper lip glistened with perspiration. "I had no reason to kill anyone, and no opportunity."

"You had both," I said, looking at Emmel, whose gray face had turned green. "Walter, here, was your motive."

"I had nothing to do with these crimes, Miss Stone," said Emmel.

"I know," I said. "But you were the inspiration."

"What are you talking about, Ellie?" asked Mrs. Farber, eyes smoldering.

"You're in love with Walter, aren't you?"

She fidgeted, but didn't answer. Emmel just groaned.

"You're in love with him," I continued, "and intent on keeping him by any means available. You told me yourself he was losing interest, didn't call anymore."

"So I went out and tried to kill your father? You're crazy, Ellie!"

Her voice echoed through the hall, and some patrons in nearby boxes interrupted their conversations to stare.

"No, not me, Mrs. Farber," I said, though not as mean as it sounds. "I think you were mad with love, mad with fear of losing Walter, mad with the turmoil inside your own head—the same turmoil that sent you away for all those years."

Her eyes clouded up with tears.

"You couldn't bear being alone," I continued. "You'd already lost one man: Garth. He's still in jail, isn't he? Or did he die? He was a junkie, wasn't he? When they sent him away, you broke down."

"Officer, can't you stop her?" she asked, tears streaming down her cheeks. "My poor Garth!"

McKeever stared at her, then me, gulped, but said nothing, did nothing to try to stop me.

"You fell for Walter in a big way, didn't know what you'd do if you lost him. And you were losing him. Some people accept rejection in love, swallow the pain and heartache and get on with their lives. And there are others who hang on to love for dear life, often at the expense of their self-esteem or emotional health. Most times, they lose in the end anyway. And then there are those who won't accept rejection and won't settle for less than everything. That's you, Mrs. Farber."

"I never did anything to harm Walter!" she said.

"No, but you wanted him enough to blackmail him back into your arms. It didn't matter that he didn't want to be there, you would win back his affections if only you had him. If he walked away, he'd never realize his mistake."

"First murder, now blackmail?" she asked. "How would I black-mail him? What leverage did I have?"

"His past," I said, and Emmel sat down on one of the tall chairs near the rear of the box. "You went so far as to smash some of my father's Anton Bruckner records, even though Bruckner wasn't Jewish, just to point a not-so-subtle finger at Walter."

Mrs. Farber's tears stopped, and her face betrayed the very fear I had just described: she was going to lose him. She was going to lose him to deportation or jail, just as she had lost Garth.

"Sergeant McKeever," I said, turning to the bewildered cop, "you might be interested to know that Professor Gualtieri Bruchner's real name is Gustav Emmel. He has been living a false life since the end of the war, making his way in the world with another man's name and past."

"It's not true!" screamed Mrs. Farber, falling to her knees at my feet. "Please, Ellie, no! Not Walter, please! I'll confess to everything, but don't send him back! No, Elijah, not Garth! Please!"

The violence of her collapse stunned all of us in the box. She melted on the carpet between my legs, sobbing and kissing my wet shoes, mumbling my name then Garth's then Elijah's alternately, no longer making any sense. Emmel knelt down to comfort her, stroking her head and cooing soothing platitudes into her ear for several minutes. I couldn't move, not even enough to see McKeever, who didn't peep. Emmel stared up at me with something akin to pity in his steel eyes. Mrs. Farber had gone quiet now, catatonic, I'd say, and I managed to wrench my legs from her grip.

"Can we get her out of here?" said Emmel. "Must we humiliate her when the others return?"

McKeever opened the door, and a patrolman helped carry her downstairs where a squad car met us outside the hall. As we packed her into the backseat, a cold wind whipped up Fifty-Seventh Street. The patrolman handcuffed her, though she wasn't a risk to anyone. She was silent as McKeever knelt in the doorway of the car to inform her of the charges. I watched as he dispatched his duty calmly and politely.

"You're under arrest, Mrs. Farber, for the murder of Ruggero Ercolano." She didn't react. McKeever paused, then looked up at me with an ache in his eyes. "And for the murder of Abraham Stone."

CHAPTER EIGHTEEN

MONDAY, FEBRUARY 1, 1960

Even though my father had lived as a secular Jew, I arranged his funeral according to Jewish custom. Rabbi Oshry, of Beth Hamedrash Hagadol on Norfolk Street, handled most of the planning. He didn't like the idea of cremation, but I insisted and won in the end. I was willing to take his remains to any funeral parlor to have it done, and Rabbi Oshry relented.

The service was held Monday evening, barely twenty hours after my father had passed away at Saint Vincent's. His heart, the one I had broken, had stopped late Sunday afternoon. The usual gang from Columbia showed up to mourn and pay respects, but I was finished with the lot of them, including Gigi Lucchesi, who tried endlessly to make eye contact with me. I avoided him. The doormen from my father's building were there, some friends of my mother's, vaguely familiar relatives from Long Island, and Sean McDonnough, too. I spoke to few of them, and remembered little of the conversations, preferring to dwell on thoughts of how I had failed my late father. I had selfishly put away all thoughts that he might die, allowing myself the freedom to pursue the solution to the crime. And my own appetites. Now the reality of his death hit me harder for the surprise of it. I'd had no time to prepare myself for it, no time to make amends, to heal the wounds of years with him. I had squandered all chances of righting the wrongs for so long, most recently in Gigi Lucchesi's arms. But the worst crime, the one that had riven the bonds of our love, was my teenage transgression: the one that had left me pregnant and my father gutted, our relationship shattered beyond repair. That wound had never closed.

I had failed him, ruined myself forever in his eyes when I fell. It was an NYU boy, a passing fancy at sixteen, a stupid lapse of good sense and propriety. And the consequences have dogged me like a pitiless hunter throughout the ensuing years. I had buried it deep inside, shutting it out of my consciousness for the pain it revived each time it visited my memory. I can only imagine how it ached in my father's chest.

He made the arrangements. My mother never knew. Elijah never knew. It was an infernal secret my father and I shared, and it consumed our love.

I felt sorry for myself. Not only was my father dead, but I was now utterly alone in the world, saddled with my own ponderous remorse and stinging guilt for the sorry relationship that had died with him. Death is final. No chances to repair, replay, or tweak. My grief was inflamed by anger and disgust, both for me and for my father, who'd never cared to fix things either.

I shook hands with hundreds that evening, wanting nothing more than to walk away and disappear into nothingness, never to face them again. I wanted to wash my hands.

When the service was over, and all the eulogizing had ended, we were herded into the annex for some awful buffet meal that would have revolted and angered my father, had he been subjected to it. I excused myself on the pretense of using the powder room, and walked out of the synagogue into the cold rain.

Forty minutes later I was soaking in Scotch whiskey at Jock Brady's, sitting at the bar in my wet overcoat. The bartender remembered me, as did Pat Duggan and his pal Dennis. This night they left me alone. People can sense when you're dangerous to approach.

Jimmo McKeever was different; he didn't know when to leave you alone. He appeared next to me at the bar and ordered a stout. We sat in silence for a while, him for not knowing how to start, me for not wanting to. Finally, he offered a simple, "I'm sorry for your loss."

I nodded.

"That's not how I wanted to tell you," he said softly. "I tried to find the words in the hall, but I couldn't. You were going on about Mr. Luc-chesi, and then the intermission came."

"It's all right," I said, and we fell silent for two more rounds of drinks.

Then I took Jim's hand and clutched it in mine. I didn't look at him, I just held him fast. He was warm, his palm was smooth and dry, even if I was making him nervous.

"Ellie," he began, but I kissed him before he could finish.

He let me kiss him, but returned none of the gesture. He froze in place, eyes open and staring blankly over my shoulder. I released him and returned to my drink.

"Sorry," I said.

"Ellie, don't do that to yourself. That's not what you want."

"I thought it was you who didn't want."

He shook his head slowly. "You have no idea what I want. Or how much."

Then McKeever offered me a lift home, but I shook my head. He tried to convince me to go, but I wanted to stay. Reluctantly he left, but not before asking to see me the next day to tie up some loose ends. I said sure. As he left, he looked like I'd wounded him to the core. Not my problem.

Once he'd gone, I bought a round for Pat and Dennis. They accepted warily, but soon we were old pals, celebrating the heroes of the Irish Rebellion. Two drinks later, Pat wrapped his arms around my shoulders and sang from the bottom of his heart at the top of his voice. We laughed, drank, and shouted about who had arrived first at the bar. Then we argued about the streetlight outside; I don't remember the context or the outcome. And we disagreed about the day of the week. I emptied my wallet, and they theirs. We drank to auld lang syne and Mayor Wagner, whom they seemed to like. At two o'clock, I wandered out the door. I didn't say good night. I shuffled drunk through the rain back to my father's apartment. It was mine now.

Rodney greeted me at the door, offered his condolences; I believed he'd attended the service at the Norfolk Street synagogue, but now I wasn't sure. He hobbled into the elevator and pushed fifteen, then spoke.

"That Italian boy stopped by to see you earlier. Waited for an hour. Wanted you to phone him when you got in."

I grunted to indicate message received, eyes fixed on the floor.

"And Raul said he forgot to give you this." He handed me a sealed envelope. "Someone dropped it off Thursday, but it slipped his mind."

"Thanks," I said, stuffing it into my coat pocket.

"And Miss Ruth also stopped in."

I looked up. "Ruth Chalmers?"

"That's what she said her name was, yes. She seemed very sad and wanted to see you. I told her today was a bad day for that, and she left about midnight."

We reached the fifteenth floor, and Rodney nodded solemnly as I stepped out into the corridor. I thanked him for his kind words.

"I'm so sorry, Miss Eleonora," he said, tears welling up in his eyes. "I was on duty that night. I feel responsible."

I shook my head. "Mrs. Farber lives in the building, Rodney. You didn't let her in. She has her own key."

"Just the same," he said, and the doors rolled shut, leaving me alone in the hallway.

I walked slowly to the end of the hall, pausing at 1504, and reflecting on how easily the tragedy might have been avoided. If Garth Farber hadn't been sent away; if Gualtieri Bruchner had died at Auschwitz . . . The French say that with "if" you can put Paris in a bottle. It was nothing more than an intellectual torment. I opened my father's door and let myself in. Once inside, I left the door unlocked, just to tempt fate and to torture myself, too. There would be no danger this night. I knew that. That was the punishment. My *contrapasso*.

TUESDAY, FEBRUARY 2, 1960

The following morning at nine, Raul called from the elevator to announce Detective-Sergeant McKeever. I wasn't dressed, but I was awake. Unable to sleep much, I'd moved from my father's bed to the sofa in the parlor.

"Glad to see you made it home last night," he said once I'd let him in. "Kind of late."

"What do you know about it?"

He shrugged and looked off to the side. "I waited for you to leave and . . . followed you back here in the car."

"Really?"

"Yeah, I kept a discreet distance so you wouldn't know."

"Why didn't you offer me a ride? I almost froze to death."

McKeever didn't know what to say, so I patted him on the shoulder and told him never mind. I invited him to sit and poured us some coffee.

"I wanted to speak to you about some of the details," he began. "I know this is a terrible time for you, but the sooner we wrap this up, the better . . . Well, it'll be over."

"It's all right," I said. "I don't have anywhere to be."

The cop retrieved a binder from the case he'd brought, opened it on the coffee table in the parlor, and dived in.

"First, Angela Farber made a full confession last night," he said. He looked a little awkward, swallowed hard, then continued. "She confessed to both crimes."

McKeever clearly didn't want to relate the story, and I wasn't happy about hearing it. I asked if I could read the report instead. It would be easier for both of us. He agreed.

Angela Farber's confession detailed how she'd noticed the lights dim on Friday, January 22, at about 10:15 p.m., and knew that my father had just returned home. She had been expecting him for hours. Her plan to was to wait for him to go to bed, let herself in with the key she'd had since she'd cared for his plants, and club him to death in his bed.

But everything changed when she heard voices in his apartment: my father's and Bernie Sanger's. She waited until Bernie left about twenty minutes later, then buzzed my father's door. She made up a story about a missing letter she'd been expecting, had the doorman mixed it with his mail by mistake? He checked his mail right there in the foyer, and said no, it wasn't there. They chatted a moment in the doorway, my father still holding his mail.

She noticed a letter in his hand: the one from Carnegie Hall, and mused how she really should investigate the spring program. My father, knowing what was in the envelope, opened it and proudly displayed the tickets for the January 31 concert. Mrs. Farber gushed her admiration for Van Cliburn, and my father offered to lend her an LP of Cliburn playing Tchaikovsky's Second Piano Concerto. She followed him into his apartment, stooping to grab the small, cast iron doorstop from his threshold as she went. He led the way to his study, never turning fully to look at her, prattling about how the concerto had no trombones or tuba and that the second movement consisted of the most beautiful violin solos. Then she dashed the iron against the back of his head without a word. She hit him again, then again, and I had to look away from the report.

"Where does Bruchner fit in?" I asked once I'd composed myself.

McKeever offered me a handkerchief. I turned it down; he needed it for his own eyes. I almost threw my arms around him.

"Bruchner wasn't adjusting too well at the department," he said a moment later. "She said he often complained about the politics, the intrigues, and personalities. He was scared that Friday afternoon after the lunch at the Faculty Club and phoned Angela Farber right after the incident. He told her everything, expressed his fear of deportation and jail. According to the statement he gave us last night, his idea was to leave, skip town, just disappear, before your father could take any action against him. She talked him out of it, or at least into waiting a while, and decided to settle the matter herself. Angela Farber knew as much as Emmel did about the department, its people, and their peccadilloes, including Ruggero Ercolano. Everyone knew his haunts, his weakness for female flesh. She simply waited outside his place and followed him that Saturday to one of the bars Emmel had mentioned during one of his rantings. She flirted with him, and he took her back to his apartment. She actually had … intercourse … with him before killing him, like a praying mantis or a black widow. Said she did it for love."

"Was it the Crystal Lounge?" I asked. "Just across the street from Ercolano's place."

"Yes, how did you know?"

I shrugged. "Ercolano had the matchbook, and Mrs. Farber mentioned the name to me once."

"We showed his photograph to the manager and he remembered him from that night. He said Ercolano met a lady and left with her after about an hour. He identified Angela Farber as the lady."

"Did she tell you about my father's manuscript?" I asked.

"She said she mailed the book Monday, like you said. She knew it would come back for insufficient postage and implicate Ercolano."

We sat quietly for a moment, sipping our coffee. I preferred talking about Ercolano's case to my father's. It distracted me, if only for a while.

"We don't know exactly how she got into Ercolano's office," said McKeever. "She kind of faded away after a while and stopped speaking."

"She took his office key," I said. "I'm sure of it. The police found two silver latchkeys and a mailbox key in his possession, right?"

"Right."

"Well, the keys to the Hamilton offices are brass," I said, producing my father's key, the one Joan Little had given me. "So, it made me wonder why he didn't carry an office key, and the answer was that someone—his murderer—had taken it from his chain."

McKeever nodded, then remembered something.

"I thought you'd like to know that we spoke to Mr. Lucchesi about his fingerprints on your father's key. By the way, turns out he's been waiting for you to contact him for the last several days. He said he'd left you a message, and you didn't respond. Didn't want to harass you."

"I certainly didn't get any message."

McKeever shrugged. "Anyway, he says he used the key a while ago when he was helping your father catalogue his books. Miss Little seems to think no one has used it since then."

"Well, that explains it," I said.

"You must be glad Lucchesi's not involved. I know how you feel about him."

"No, you don't, Jim," I said, staring deep into his blue eyes. We held each other's gaze for a long spell, until McKeever blinked and looked away.

"And all this happened because your father noticed Bruchner's tattoo," he said wistfully, bringing me back to the painful topic.

"It wasn't the tattoo," I announced.

"Beg your pardon."

"My father's suspicions weren't caused by the tattoo, at least not initially."

"Then what was it?"

I blushed. "It was Bruchner's penis."

"What?" McKeever had turned magenta.

"The man wasn't circumcised. That's what my father must have seen in the steam bath. It was only later on that he became suspicious of the tattoo."

"How did you figure that?"

"In one of her drunken ramblings, Angela Farber mentioned that Walter wasn't circumcised. I remembered it last night. That's how my father knew he wasn't Jewish. The tattoo must have seemed innocuous at first glance."

"Bruchner still insists that the tattoo is not a cover-up of an SS tattoo. He says it's a girl's name. Katia, I think."

"Was it Bruchner who made the call to the ICU the morning Mrs. Farber disconnected the breathing tube?"

"No," said McKeever. "She kept Bruchner out of her schemes. She paid a vagrant outside the hospital to make the call from a pay phone."

"What about Bruchner now?" I asked.

"He's leaving the country. We had a long talk with his lawyer and him about his options. We might have tried to prosecute him, but we don't believe he knew Angela Farber had done this until yesterday. She put the screws to him, threatened to go to the police about his identity.

That's why he went to the concert with her. I think he's done with the charade. He wants to go home."

"He was in a tough spot," I said. "His past was closing in on him from all sides, even from his lover. I believe people are responsible for their actions, but I still feel pity for him."

"That's pretty generous of you, given the circumstances."

I shrugged and sniffled. "I still can't believe the coincidence. Both Gualtieri Bruchners in New York. What are the odds?"

"Not so hard to believe," said McKeever. "After the war, Jewish refugees either went to Israel or they came here. And this was an attractive job for the professor. I understand a lot of Europeans are getting university jobs here. They call it 'Brain Drain.'"

"Still," I said, "you must admit it's a coincidence."

"Sure, but odds are that unlikely coincidences have to happen every so often. Ask an actuary. The real stroke of luck is that you picked up the wrong phonebook and found a Gualtieri Bruchner in Millwood."

"Just by chance," I mused. "Who knows if I ever would have connected Angela Farber to Emmel without Karen Bruchner?"

"And without that connection, she would have got away with murder. Two of them."

"What about Mrs. Farber?" I asked. "How is she? She was pretty pathetic last night."

"She's insane. The DA's going to have a couple of psychiatrists examine her before he decides which charges to file, but she's gone around the bend."

"Did you ask her about Elijah's grave?" I asked.

McKeever nodded. "Yes, but she wouldn't admit to that," he said. "We asked her several times, but she denied it. Emmel, too."

"I've come to believe it was just a random act of hooliganism," I said. "You were right, Jim. Just some local punks, not an anti-Semitic crusade against my family. Angela Farber didn't know about the confrontation at lunch until Friday night. Elijah's grave was vandalized Wednesday."

I spent the day meeting with lawyers and morticians, settling the bills and signing papers. The work was far from finished, but that was enough for one day. When I left the lawyer's office, I ducked into a movie theater and sat through *Ben-Hur*. I don't remember what it was about. That night, I arrived back at my father's place after ten. Rodney was on his usual chair, sitting up a little straighter than usual. On the sofa was a visitor.

"Hello, Ruth," I said.

Upstairs, I poured her a glass of sherry to steady her shaky determination.

"I had to see you, Ellie," she said, staring into her glass. "I want to apologize for lying to you. I wanted to tell you the other day when we met, but I couldn't do it."

"There's no need, Ruth," I said, pouring myself some of my father's whiskey and taking a seat next to her on the sofa.

"Don't stop me, please," she continued. "I want to clear my conscience. This belongs to your mother," she said, twisting the ruby ring off her finger and folding it into my hand. "When I found it in Ruggero's apartment, I thought it was his, a family ring of some kind, so I took it. The police told me it belonged to your mother. I'm so sorry, Ellie," and she sobbed, head bowed.

I took her hands and smiled sadly. We said nothing for several minutes, and all I could think of was that time, years before, at the picnic when her mother had slapped her face. Poor little Ruth, to echo my father's words. Poor little Ruth.

She looked up at me, her eyes sparkling behind tears, then fell against me. She cried for several minutes, her left hand still clutched in mine. She didn't notice the ruby on her middle finger until she'd regained her calm.

"Ellie?"

"This isn't my mother's ring," I said. "I found hers yesterday and put it in a safe deposit box today." A lie. "This must have been Ruggero's mother's ring. Now, it's yours."

EPILOGUE

SUNDAY, FEBRUARY 7, 1960

I arrived back in New Holland after eleven o'clock the following Sunday. I parked my car in its usual spot in front of my apartment on Lincoln Avenue, and, seeing the light still on in Fiorello's, stopped in to chat with Fadge. The radio was playing from a shelf behind the counter: The Fleetwoods singing "Come Softly to Me."

Fadge had already heard the news about my father; I don't know how. I didn't want to discuss it. We talked a while about nothing in particular, then I said I was calling it a day. I was about to leave when he remembered a message he was to give me:

"By the way," he said, pulling a scrap of paper from the cash register. "Aside from all the calls from your editor, some guy from New York's been calling here the past couple of days. He got the number from the paper, I think."

"Who is he?" I asked.

"He said his name was Gigi," he said, reading the note. "Had an accent. There's a number here; he wants you to call him," and he handed the slip of paper to me.

I stuffed the paper into my coat pocket, and my fingers felt the envelope Rodney had given me the night of Dad's funeral. I had forgotten it was there.

"Good night, Fadge," I said, heading for the door.

"Good night, Ellie," he called. "And I'm real sorry about your dad. If there's anything you need, let me know."

"How about a dirty magazine?"

"A little night reading?" asked Fadge, and I felt a little better.

Across the street, I climbed the stairs to my cold apartment and opened the radiator valves wide for some heat. Standing in the kitchen, still in my overcoat, I opened the envelope. It was from Gigi.

Thursday, January 28, 1960

Dear Ellie,

It's hard to reach you by phone, so I decided to drop off this short note. I wanted you to know how nice it was to see you last night. If it's not too late, I'd like to invite you for dinner Saturday at Barbetta. You deserve an evening out.

I know you're very busy these days. Please call me when you have a free moment.

Tuo Gigi

I folded the letter into its envelope and slipped it back into my coat pocket. Again my fingers came across something else, this time a small, hard object. I pulled it out and turned it over in my hand. It was a roll of film: Gigi in slumber. I pried the cap off the canister and dropped the roll into my left palm. Kodak Tri-X, twenty-four exposures. I stared at it for a long moment before gripping the tail of the film tightly between the thumb and forefinger of my right hand. Then I yanked it out of the cartridge, deliberately exposing it to the light to ruin it. I never wanted to see those pictures or Gigi again. I didn't want to be reminded of what we'd done.

I dropped into a chair at the kitchen table, desolate and miserable, then collapsed sobbing, my face buried in the crook of my arm. It was one of those desperate, howling breakdowns that exhaust you, rend your lungs raw and make your stomach ache. It was as violent as it was hopeless. Then there was a knock at my door.

I was sure it was Mrs. Giannetti come to complain; I must have been crying too loud for her taste. But when I opened the door, I found

Fadge standing sheepishly in the cold, a brown paper bag tucked under his arm.

"Hi, come on in," I said, wiping my eyes on a handkerchief. He followed me up the stairs, rumbling as he went.

"I thought you might like a cocktail," he said once we were in the warmth of my kitchen. He pulled two quarts of Schaefer beer from his parcel and placed them on the table. "And dinner," he said, producing a large bag of Wise potato chips.

I was still tingling from my spell, but trying to hide the evidence with bravado. "It's not fair," I smiled. "A girl doesn't stand a chance with a big spender like you."

He stared at me with his bulging eyes for a moment, making me think maybe I'd misjudged and gone too far with the teasing. I was wrong.

"Well, in that case, let's get you out of that sweater," he said, and I had to laugh.

After one glass of beer, I left the rest of the Schaefer's to Fadge, while I switched to White Label. We sat in my parlor for hours, listening softly to some of Elijah's jazz records. The break from the loneliness was a godsend, even if we talked about sad things.

Fadge told me how his mother had died a few years before, and his father before that. And he had lost a brother, too. Always sickly, suffering from some kind of congenital heart problem as well as polio, Ron's older brother, Robert, had passed away while still in high school. He told me it had been hard to lose everyone, but there wasn't any getting around it. That was the way it was. I appreciated the wisdom of his fatalism, the acceptance, and the resignation. I promised myself that I, too, would try the same one day, once I'd had my fill of grief.

We marveled at the coincidences in our lives, the shared pain, and I took a perverse comfort in it. It was as if I had been rotting for years in a dark prison, alone, desperate, and cold, when, suddenly, the cell door opens. A dear old friend, beaten and unconscious, is pitched inside with me, and I am overcome with joy.

"Why did you come over tonight?" I asked. "Don't tell me you were hoping to get lucky."

He shook his head. "With a skinny girl like you? Naw." He paused, thinking of something. "I just wanted to have a beer," he said finally.

I smiled gently at him as he looked away. I knew why he had come, and it almost felt like he'd saved my life. I've loved that fat guy ever since.

The next day, I spent hours developing the photographs of Dad's drawings. They were some of the nicest shots I'd ever taken. I made a couple of sets of prints, experimenting with different exposures and sizes. I intended to get a few of them enlarged, printed, and professionally framed. One photograph—Charon, ferryman on the River Acheron—I sent to an address in Brooklyn: a walk-down on Sixteenth Street, in the shadow of the El. I thought Karen Bruchner might want to keep it, the same way he'd kept that name all those years.

ACKNOWLEDGMENTS

Deepest appreciation to Dan Mayer, editorial director at Seventh Street Books.

Greatest respect and affection for *il grande* John Freccero, a dear friend and an inspirational scholar, who taught me so much about Dante and *The Divine Comedy*.

Heartfelt gratitude to my peerless agent, Bill Reiss of John Hawkins and Associates, Inc., without whom Ellie Stone would never have come to life, and *Styx & Stone* would have languished forever in a drawer.

ABOUT THE AUTHOR

A linguist by training, James W. Ziskin earned bachelor of arts and a master of arts in Romance languages and literature from the University of Pennsylvania and speaks Italian and French fluently. He worked in New York City as a photo-news producer and writer, and then as director of NYU's Casa Italiana Zerilli-Marimò. He has since spent fifteen years in the Hollywood postproduction industry, running large, international operations in the subtitling/ localization and visual-effects fields.

James lives in the Hollywood Hills with his wife, Lakshmi, and cats Bobbie and Tinker. He is represented by William Reiss of John Hawkins and Associates, Inc.